More Praise for Bruce Wagner's
The Chrysanthemum Palace

"Mr. Wagner demonstrates . . . that he can do the lyrical and tender with as much panache as the outrageous and corrosive. *The Chrysanthemum Palace* showcases the author's kinder, gentler side while attesting to his ever-wicked eye for hypocrisy and self-deception. [He] is as gifted at making us care about his characters as making us laugh at their exploits and self-delusions."

—Michiko Kakutani, *The New York Times*

"Bruce Wagner, author of the cell phone trilogy, is the bard of Los Angeles; he may have no equal. He gets the corrosive scum yet retains heart. [H]is books are an utter joy to visit. . . . Wagner is some fearless writer, mixing the real with his own imagined cosmos, caught up in the utter now but without a studied ironic cool. His characters live in a puddled emotional ruin much of their own making."

—Karen Heller, *The Philadelphia Inquirer*

"*The Chrysanthemum Palace* is *The Great Gatsby* for an *Entertainment Weekly* age."

—Jori Finkel, *The Village Voice*

"[*The Chrysanthemum Palace*] reads like a wicked satire of mainstream entertainment, a literary *L.A. Story* chock-full of industry in-jokes. Wagner gleefully captures the absurdity of popular culture . . ."

—Katie Vagnino, *Time Out New York*

"Wagner's writing is intricate and inventive . . . [his] insights into what it takes to find and hold one's humanity while in the clutches of Hollywood's mercenary machinery shine like brilliant little gems."

—Karen Campbell, *The Boston Globe*

"There's plenty of sharp, funny show-biz business here. . . . But Wagner boldly goes beyond satire in *The Chrysanthemum Palace*. He finds surprising depths to plumb, even in the land of the superficial. The question that drives the book is, can children ever escape the crushing gravitational fields of their parents? The answer, it turns out, is that sometimes even warp speed isn't fast enough."

—Lev Grossman, *TIME*

"[Wagner's] uproarious new satire . . . [is] a short, sharp book that puts a dagger right in the heart of Hollywood."

—*Publishers Weekly* (starred)

"Smart, high-gloss slur of fame, drugs and the fateful weight of family."

—*Kirkus Reviews*

"[S]omeone writes a book about Hollywood every three days, but few with the savage wit and survivor's compassion of Bruce Wagner. His latest novel, *The Chrysanthemum Palace*, is his tightest work to date, full of industry shadow-runners and the kind of midlife compromises you won't see on *E!*."

—*Blackbook*

"An affecting, even cathartic story about actors in alien prosthetics."

—*Details*

ALSO BY BRUCE WAGNER

Still Holding

I'll Let You Go

I'm Losing You

Force Majeure

The Chrysanthemum Palace

Bruce Wagner

Simon & Schuster Paperbacks

NEW YORK • LONDON • TORONTO • SYDNEY

SIMON & SCHUSTER PAPERBACKS
Rockefeller Center
1230 Avenue of the Americas
New York, NY 10020

First Simon & Schuster paperback edition 2006

SIMON & SCHUSTER PAPERBACKS and colophon are registered trademarks
of Simon & Schuster, Inc.

The author gratefully acknowledges permission to reprint the following material:
"The Infinite" from COLLECTED POEMS by Robert Lowell. Copyright © 2003
by Harriet Lowell and Sheridan Lowell. Reprinted by permission of Farrar, Straus
and Giroux, LLC. LEOPARDI, G; LEOPARDI. © 1997 Princeton University Press.
Reprinted by permission of Princeton University Press.

For information regarding special discounts for bulk purchases,
please contact Simon & Schuster Special Sales at
1-800-456-6798 or business@simonandschuster.com.

Designed by Paul Dippolito

Manufactured in the United States of America

1   3   5   7   9   10   8   6   4   2

The Library of Congress has cataloged the hardcover edition as follows:
Wagner, Bruce.
The chrysanthemum palace / Bruce Wagner.
          p.   cm.
1. Hollywood (Los Angeles, Calif.)—Fiction. 2. Triangles (Interpersonal relations)—
Fiction. 3. Motion picture industry—Fiction. I. Title.
PS3573.A369C49 2005
813'.54—dc22   2004043059
ISBN-13: 978-0-7432-4339-1
ISBN-10:   0-7432-4339-0
ISBN-13: 978-0-7432-4340-7 (Pbk)
ISBN-10:   0-7432-4340-4 (Pbk)

for Laura

THE INFINITE

That hill pushed off by itself was always dear
to me and the hedges near
it that cut away so much of the final horizon.
When I would sit there lost in deliberation,
I reasoned most on the interminable spaces
beyond all hills, on their antediluvian resignation
and silence that passes
beyond man's possibility.
Here for a little while my heart is quiet inside me;
and when the wind lifts roughing through the trees,
I set about comparing my silence to those voices,
and I think about the eternal, the dead seasons,
things here at hand and alive,
and all their reasons and choices.
It's sweet to destroy my mind
and go down
and wreck in this sea where I drown.

—GIACOMO LEOPARDI
(TRANSLATION: ROBERT LOWELL)

To a sensitive and imaginative man who lives, as I have lived for a long time, constantly feeling and imagining, the world and its objects are, in a way, double. He sees with his eyes a tower, a landscape; he hears with his ears the sound of a bell; and at the same time his imagination sees another tower, another bell, and hears another sound.

—GIACOMO LEOPARDI, *Letters*

I AM AN ACTOR.

Not long ago, and right on schedule, I had the hair-raising epiphany which inevitably occurs to most who ply my craft: Time is running out. At such a moment, tough-minded players can elect to soldier into denial, turning a cheek to the cooler side of their pillow toward pleasanter dreams of sudden, freakish, breakthrough stardom. One may file through a mental inventory of all those stage and screen personages who remained relatively untouched by fame until, say, the age of fifty, or even supertriumphed at sixty-five. If the lotto fantasia doesn't excite, a more humdrum (still serviceable) idyll might present itself: retirement to a Carmel-by-the-Sea bed-and-breakfast, purchased with a never-ending stream of residuals generated by TV commercials and radio voice-overs where one may live out his or her days in legendary local bonhomie and embroidered remembrance of roles past. On the other hand, if the actor is of weaker or even neurotic disposition, he may choose to put on a dignified face and set his nautical cap on that course dreadfully referred to as "reinvention." Meaning, he decides to try his hand at screenwriting.

There—I've said it.

Among such metamorphoses, enough unlikely success stories abound to either raise or sink our adventurers' spirits, depending on their mood. So: it was with a cultist's coltish energy that I spent nearly twenty-four months in solemn pursuit of the right story to apply my as-yet-untried skills, likewise the formula in which the whole shebang might be crammed for maximal artistic, commercial effect. The fact that I was completely convinced I'd create a blockbuster did not at all preclude, in my humble opinion, the deliverance of an authentic work of art—I would have my cake and screen it too. In service of this shamanic storyquest, I downloaded and Web-surfed, culled obscure regional newspapers, watched bad films from the thirties, shamelessly trolled for plotty treasures amid a flotsam of anecdotes wrung from friends and loved ones, and even went so far as to examine my own life, loves, and adolescent stirrings. I became a diner solitaire, a fisherman for dialogue, the better to eavesdrop on shadowy couples ensconced in contentious steakhouse booths. After much labored, almost scientific contemplation, I lit upon one scenario or another, imbuing each with the suitable grandiosity required to sustain propulsion for proper launch. My stamina was enviable—for even though my heart wasn't wholly in it (it never really was), once I committed to protagonist or theme, I behaved as if I'd found the message in a bottle that not only would make the world a profoundly more intelligent, amazing place, but as if that very message was one which only I, chosen by God Herself, could decode. I excitedly embarked on a series of false starts and even falser stops before the bottle, corkless and forlorn, its damp square of scratchy, smeary hieroglyphs outsourced, the bottle that only days before seemed to promise so much yet deliver so little, was tossed with a shrug to reloiter the sea.

After licking my wounds, I cheerily regarded each misstep as part of an elaborate, fateful hazing, a rite of passage inexorably moving me closer to my goal, eventually to become part of a legendary behind-the-scenes story of great and stubborn conquest. Like a novice Buddhist thrown from his meditative horse, I remounted with cool alacrity. In order to achieve the intended transformation from loser to Oscar winner (always pragmatically set two years in the future, a figure that encompassed completion of script, said script's discovery by dynamo agent or producer, production of said script through the offices of a major film studio or indie consortium, and subsequent arthouse-platform or 4,000-theater release), I shunned the Silverlake social circuit and even declined a few—well, very few—industry functions in which my profile as fledgling film and television actor could quite possibly have been enhanced. I kept recreational drug use (and romantic entanglements) to a minimum, employing the leash of AA meetings to keep myself in line.

I cocooned for the sake of my inchoate art. I was patient, I was disciplined, and I was proud, waiting diligently in the wings for my wings.

Now while it's true such endeavors require a different sort of perseverance than that required of an actor, the happiest screenplay alchemy can still be elusive, particularly when operating without guide or mentor, notwithstanding sundry software programs or annoying how-to-write-a-film manuals. Unfortunately, it became clear early on that I was *not* to the three acts born and whatever I conjured would be the product of erring not on the side of talent but on that of blood, sweat, and fear (fear of outright plagiarism too). By coincidence, my acting-class confederates were engaged in their own similarly secretive, feckless attempts. Looking back, we seemed like wanna-be witches and warlocks, scouring the countryside for toadstool and tongue of Charlie Kaufman without the faintest idea of what was toxic or edible, let alone a clue to which ingredients would combine to make that magical Sundance stew—in short, we were kids straddling branches for broomsticks. Sadly, the mystical blush of childhood was long gone from our fashionably stubbled, sun-damaged cheeks; one by one, sojourns into Storyland came to their anticlimactic ends, leaving only shredded three-hole punched Hammermill paper and a sour taste in the mouth.

Still, I must admit that with the failure of each effort I always felt a shrug and gladdened shiver, as if having quit a job in some dispiriting, faraway mall, grateful not to have been recognized at the register by a wayward relation or fellow delusional traveler.

That period thankfully ended, though my ambitions did not. Then one morning I awakened as if from deep sleep with the notion that the story of *all* stories had unfolded unwittingly beneath my very nose. Of course, I immediately set headlong upon "sorting it out" (as my Brit friends and budding warlock hyphenates would say), said phrase being really just a euphemism for the careful process of planning, staging, and micromanaging a royal fuckup. The faux sorting went on for several weeks; but it wasn't until a certain Thursday afternoon, sitting at the Sugar Plum Bakery on Beverly Boulevard awaiting my soy latte, that something decisive happened—I had a happier epiphany, this one imperious enough to allow no further procrastination. I was suddenly forced, as if by legal summons, to abandon the project at hand (a nasty little novel which I was actually being paid to adapt; more about this later) and march home to transcribe my tale.

To my chagrin, the words poured out not in script form but through the unskilled medium of prose (I'd "journaled" awhile some years ago but abandoned my entries as being too precious. I was always a bit stiff, and hope the reader will exercise patience as I limber up). In this case, I told myself all along that once I got it down I would be able, like a singer transposing keys, to convert the melody to whichever form was most ideal. I only knew the important thing was to capture as much of my saga as possible, *now*, at full gallop. It was lightning first and "message" second that needed to be bottled.

This slim book is the result.

As I said: I was at the bakery awaiting my latte when a young father came in, holding a babe in arms. Now we all warm to a doting, youthful man and his infant when no mother is in sight—it gives a kind of genial, beneficent balance to the world, sunnily deflating the notion men can't be nurturers too. I should add that I'm almost forty, so lately there's a twinkle in my eye when presented with such a scene, and a smug awareness that while at such an age a woman's time clock is approaching its final hours, my own mechanism is there to be polished if not wound. I've always been a magnet for babies' eyes. Whether it's self-love or something about my aura, ever since I can remember I've attracted a nearly embarrassing focus, to the puzzled amusement of parent or caretaker. As if on cue, the boy pivoted toward me, squirming in his bib. Cockily preparing myself for the usual prolonged mesmeric reaction, his stare defied experience, and instead froze at some point above my own. He began to chortle, not with the stagy too-cute laugh that humankind seems to already master only weeks out of the womb but with a beguiling, joyful, unbridled music of sheer wonder. Dad and I tried to find what it was that captivated him, to no avail—he'd left the world far behind, fixated on something transcendent and beautiful, that even now does not seem an exaggeration to say encompassed the cosmos itself.

His laughter burbled on, without ever striking a false note.

"What do you see?" said his father, tenderly attentive. "What do you see?"

The little seer smiled, monitoring the ineffable of the blueness beyond. For a moment, *I* smiled too—and saw.

That was when I gathered my things in tearful tumult and raced out the door, on a mission.

BUT I DIDN'T PROPERLY INTRODUCE myself.

My name is Bertram Valentine Krohn (Valentine being the hero of *Stranger in a Strange Land,* and Henry Miller's middle name too. Dad baptized me thus, and really showed his hand). I'm thirty-eight years old but most everyone calls me Bertie. The valentine-giving father is Perry Needham Krohn, creator-producer in perpetua of TV's longest-running syndicated space opera, *Starwatch: The Navigators.* You may have heard of him—he continues, after many years, to be a staple of *Variety,* the *Times,* the *Beverly Hills Courier* and 213—not so much for his deal-making activities but in conjunction with whatever organization happens to be paying tribute (I should say *he's* paying *them*), which seems to occur on a bimonthly basis. You see, Dad likes lending his name to good causes, attracting old/new money to new/old diseases, relishing the hubbub of silent auctions and black-tie balls—says it keeps him young. Mom hates all that, but I think vanity prevents her from attending the galas. More about her later.

I was raised, as you might have guessed, in a world of great privilege. In fact, sad as it may sound, I've always considered "Bertie Krohn: The Early Years" to be among the happiest of my life. And while this document tilts more toward reportage than memoir, the thought occurred it might be ideal to recount a few personal anecdotes from that era of my youth. As earlier alluded, it will help warm the muscles (I already feel a writer's cramp coming on), and besides, it's my opinion—and that of at least two critics, one biographer and a *New Yorker* short-story contributor, all friends of Dad's who've been obliquely interrogated by yours truly—that the closer one is to the storyteller, the likelier one is to embrace what is told.

Like most of us, I failed to escape the minor joys, major heartbreaks, and brushes with mortality that apply to any youth's rightful passage; so let me begin with Death and work my way back to Ecstasy. Remember that amazing show, *Tales from the Crypt?* It was actually a comic book before that. (Dad has a leather-bound set.) Well, allow me to flip through a few of my own illustrated panels—what Clea used to call the "not-so-funnies." They're a bit macabre but pertinent to my own tale, I assure.

I'm an only child. No one in the immediate family perished during my impressionable years (as opposed to the later, "depressionable years"—Clea, again). That said, there *was* an artistic cousin who died of non-Hodgkin's lymphoma who lived somewhere in the Midwest and would be buried too in that same region of my mind. A few miles from our house in Benedict Canyon, the baby sister of a friend was struck by a car and killed, but, owing to my never having seen much of her before the event, the wraith became more ghoulish abstraction than cautionary tale. Upon entering high school, a bookish junior became trapped in a second-floor house fire on South Roxbury Drive and got the fingers of her hand burnt off; she returned in the second semester of the next year and was treated by the student body as if she'd joined an Indian caste in the interim: a mixture of Brahman and Untouchable, a kind of Mother Teresa horror-show saint. Then there was Aaron, whose folks owned the town pharmacy. He only lasted till the sixth grade, dying of a cerebral hemorrhage one summer near Indian Wells.

But the highest reading on the Richter Mortality Scale by far was the death of Leif Farragon, the handsomest boy I'd ever known and the funniest too. He was tall, tousled and fatherless, with a dimpled chin and a gorgeous mom who taught second grade at Horace Mann. I can still summon the smell of his skin through the velour turtlenecks then in vogue, evoking the gregarious, gemütlich, goyish life force that was irresistibly, quintessentially Leif. Every kid I knew had money except for him. Instead of going to El Rodeo or Hawthorne, he attended the very school where his mother worked, the poorest, fringiest, farthest flung of the four Beverly Hills publics, yet by virtue of bawdy sarcasm, athletic grace, and generosity of spirit, the charismatic boy had literally crossed over (Wilshire Boulevard) to join the upper echelon of the district's social strata.

I remember being with him at a party on North Rodeo Drive. My girlfriend at the time—we were all of us nearing thirteen—was the aforementioned Clea Fremantle, daughter of legendary film actress Roosevelt Chandler née Delia LeMay Chaiken. I doubt that things have much changed but back then, rich kids began having serious parties at a fairly tender age, facilitated not only by the handy venue of mansions' shadowy acreage and multiple trysting zones but the inept, well-meaning agenda of absentee parents zealously contriving to watch over scions through the indulgent, lackadaisical eyes of long-time live-in help. We young royals did plenty of frenching and groping and cupping of half-breasts; I can still remember Clea's smells, less familiar than Leif's and sometimes immobilizing in mysterious ways—like a fearful hunter, time and again I froze in my tracks while hand, heart, and gland gamely soldiered on, shaky finger on hairy triggers. We commandeered various guest rooms for musky, R-rated kisses under the benign gaze of Mom, in movie poster form. While suffocating ourselves with cavorting tongues that slo-mo fenced like thick forest slugs, I occasionally opened a wandering eye to take in the epic, voluptuous Roos Chandler, she of the requisite small-town transformation to deathless American icon, she of the self-anointed film noir *nom de ciné*, she of the occasional madcap nude night swim during bashful daughter's fledgling soirée sleepovers, she of the three husbands before the age of thirty, she of the consecutive Academy Awards—Best Supporting, Best Actress, Best Actress.

Here's what happened when lanky Leif, eight months older than Clea and I, and more than a little stoned, stumbled into that borrowed love nest one warm Santa Ana–scoured night. He brought a bottle of scotch and that high-pitched, infectious laugh that would have sounded silly coming from the throat of anyone else. Startled by the intrusive bright light of the hall, Clea and I, fashionably mussed, awkwardly disengaged. Closing the door behind him, Leif passed us the amber bottle. I swigged first—it took all the macho I could muster not to vomit—then handed it off to Clea, whose face wore a rosy, newborn look on account of our aborted petting session. (At the time, I wondered why she was so introverted though now the *Family Ties* syndrome seems obvious: knowing she couldn't outwild her mother, she instinctively went the other way. That was probably what attracted me—had she been crazy like Roos, it would have been too much to handle.) Before I knew it, Leif was kissing her and somehow that was all right, though it didn't exactly *feel* all right . . . more like some casual rehearsal for future heartbreak and generic grief. Yet because I loved Leif in a way as much as I did Clea, I was forced to let it go. I knew she must have loved him too, perhaps even more for the sheer boldness I was incapable of. I'll admit at the time the subtleties were lost upon me; my immediate concerns were more primitive. I hoped and prayed the night wouldn't end with the two of them going "steadily"—these tide turnings weren't all that uncommon and in such cases, the prescient student body already knew of the cuckold's infamy when he arrived at school the next morning, head hung low. Nothing to do but wear one's scarlet letter jacket and get on with it.

At that age, friends come and go in superheated fashion. After the kiss, for reasons both simple and complex, Leif and I managed not to lay eyes on each other for almost a few months. In the end, we were friendly, though never like before. One *could* say we fell out over betrayal as much as embarrassment (it was almost as if Leif and I were the ones who'd kissed) but I think the estrangement was mostly the growing pains rhythm of how things go—or went. Anyway, Leif had lots of tribes, a whole clique on the other side of Wilshire who I'd never met and I was absolutely certain were as possessive of him as the richies. Looking back, it's probably better that fate conspired to separate us before he died a year later in an accident on PCH. (Losing a friend on that highway was a Westside rite of passage.) I can't remember who told me or where I was when I heard, and never learned the exact how of it. I avoided such knowledge—he may or may not have been in a VW van, he may or may not have been on a motorcycle, he may or may not have been on the back of a chopper or hitching or even dashing across the highway with a surfboard to the beach.

At that age, fatal details are never important.

—•—

A short time after he died, another loss occurred that didn't have the same impact but haunted me into adulthood nonetheless.

The death of Roos Chandler was announced in the media as "an adverse reaction to prescription drugs." Loyal to Clea and in my own naïveté, I was a wholehearted believer. Soon, whispers at school became cruel chatter, exposing the official version as one of those lies to be forever scribbled on and defaced, tagged, retagged and erased, sandblasted, whitewashed then painted over in a thousand hues of confederacy and martyrdom, before the cycle of slanderous graffiti reshuffled and relooped its mordant canticle. Being public property, Clea's mother's exorbitantly tumultuous life was long since archived in preparation for the entombment of popular myth—prefab obits had been updated, polished, and honed in clinical anticipation; once the offering of that ruined, voluptuous body's bleached bones were borne aloft by the collective unconscious, their passage lit by the eternal flame of tabloid tiki torches, her remains made their more worldly exit upon the ample, profiteering shoulders of agents, false friends, gossipmongers, and trademark attorneys who passed for pallbearers.

This is how I wound up being haunted: Soon after the announcement of Roos Chandler's death, I performed a vanishing act of my own, and it was twenty-five years before I spoke to my *own* flickering old flame. The news mortified me to my core and I'd run for my very life—as if death had leaped the fence like a brush fire, threatening to transform me into the gnarled, nubby-fingered girl who'd been caught in the Roxbury conflagration and returned to the flock a blackened sheep in head scarves. It wasn't long before I assiduously avoided my poor, dear, bedraggled Clea, so as not to catch what she had. At least she had the elegance not to press me on the matter, though maybe native fragilities bade her shrink from confrontation. (I wouldn't have been easy to find.)

As I one day would learn, her own haunts took precedence over mine.

— • —

It's funny what draws us to people; funny we don't often see the design of it. Sons dramatically rebel against fathers in order to expunge debts owed to the one who sheltered though did not nurture—it's hard to forge an identity while paying the metaphorical rent, even harder when that patriarch is wealthy and power-driven. But who's to say? I divorced Dad but it still wasn't enough. I knew his weaknesses, and delighted in giving the knife a further turn.

Perry Krohn wrote short stories in college, immodestly considering himself a cross between Camus and Philip K. Dick (this, according to Mother, whose name, I should already have told you, is Gita), one of which, "Starry Night," became the basis for a TV pilot that evolved into the sacred cash cow *Starwatch: The Navigators*. He grew wealthy beyond imagining yet in his darkest hours considered himself a failure and a hack. In moments of self-doubt, the money helped to assuage—as did the extramarital affairs, the weekly bridge game at the Friar's (stag), the Saturday afternoon pickup games with *The Simpsons* gang on his private basketball court, the clarinet playing in a klezmer band—a fixture on Thursday nights à la Woody Allen at Chickpea, the restaurant he owned in West Hollywood—as did the Krohn Family Foundation, established to put inner-city kids through med school in exchange for their agreement upon graduation to spread the gospel of AIDS prevention in Third World countries, as did the collection of watercolors by D. H. Lawrence and William Blake, the fifty or so dioramas of Joseph Cornell, the eight Renoirs, the four Degas and five Courbets, the Schnabels, Hirsts, Barneys, Rodins, Ruschas, and eighty-ton Serra in the front—yes, front—yard . . . as did the fifteen nonconsecutive pages of van Gogh's diary extracts, as did the so on and the so forth, each acquisition or cultural conquest acting as bulwark against the flood of Father's shamefully mediocre talents, which is how he perceived them in his privately aggrieved heart: an actual menace to Art. Yet, as if to quixotically inoculate himself against a disease he was already dying of, our stubborn, stalwart Dr. Jekyll continued to collect sculptures, paintings, people, and nonprofits like they were the families of Jews to be saved from Mr. Hyde's schlockmeister Holocaust hands, hiding them (from himself) behind secret bookcases from a crassly commercial, ratings-driven, compromised world, like blue shadows in a bejeweled underground subway, far away from the Gestapo eyes of revenue-streaming *Starwatch* storm troopers. To this day, my father remains a curious mixture of lowbrow and aesthete.

Knowing these things were a hedge he'd made against the one magnificently wrong, winning bet of his life—*Starwatch: The Navigators*—and knowing too I could never, by conscience or proclivity, safely tread water anywhere near the great, churning engines of that lucrative enterprise, I resolved to torment the man by becoming a sunken treasure myself, or at least aspiring to embody one of those elusive *objets* he always won at auction yet could never truly possess. After a year at Oxford, I transferred to Berkeley and formed a theater troupe. We did Artaud in the nude and put up a controversial all-white production of *A Raisin in the Sun*. In my third term, I wrote a one-act, raffishly presenting it as a bona fide, newfound Beckett; after ten performances, French lawyers bade us cease and desist. Perry flew up in his Bombardier on opening night, sitting in back of the cold warehouse space with smiling, covetous eyes. I still held parentage against him, hypocritically spurning his attempts to give me cash while accepting it from Gita on the sly.

I grew tired of the revolutionary life and decided to make my name as an actor in the movies. I quit the university and resettled in Venice. While fervently contemplating writing, directing, and starring in a film to be funded by my platinum Amex, I freelanced for a matchmaker (cupidsarrow.com) during the boom then apprenticed at a CGI house during the bust. I got a part on *The Days of Our Lives*, smugly resisting the call of little theater. I went to the right parties and clubs, becoming friendly with young, wild-assed agents and unshaven, supersmart promoters, nascent Brent Bolthouses. Somehow I met John Cusack and the director Miguel Arteta and took small roles in a couple of their films. I drank too much and ate too many pills, matriculating through the Twelve Steps—I drew the line at cold turkeying Wellbutrin, convinced it was helping me kick cigarettes—with the usual results: crushing depression and mood swings, white-knuckled sobriety, fruitless industry networking at Double A meetings with attendant amorous *liaisons dangereuses*. I landed a few more gigs before abandoning cinema for TV, even though I considered it Dad's turf, my crossover smacking of capitulation and loserdom.

Perry and I grew closer, but it was more his cancer scare than any mellowing of ambition on my part that affected our rapprochement. (I remembered the lesson of Roos Chandler and just didn't have it in me to run.) I saw up close and personal how excreting into a bag for a few months had a way of breaking a man and it broke me a little too. To my surprise, I actually began to consider working on Dad's show—as writer, actor, whatever. My therapist and even my friends saw the impulse as a sign of newfound health and maturity. I fought halfheartedly against my own idea until one morning I looked in the mirror and said, Get over yourself. It was the new year after September 11 and the world no longer felt like a sure thing; the time was nigh, it seemed, to exercise squatter's rights on a few, potentially very green *Starwatch* acres. Maybe in a subliminal way I was beginning to nest—terrible term!—anyhow, that's what the shrink said. Get a job, meet a girl, buy a house (and a Chinese kid if the reproductive organs weren't up to speed). Get a life, like everyone else.

Nest or no nest, in the back of my head, or maybe the front, were the first rumblings of the dream to create a classy show for cable. I didn't need more therapy to reveal an essential truth: I was too old to be kicking against pricks, be they paternal or self-generated. Still, I thought of myself as a tough customer, an independent thinker, a free spirit. Gita indulged me in my prideful little protests—I *won't* be another asshole driving his BMW on and off the lot, I'd say, *not me.* During cozy tête-à-têtes, Mother would bolster, "Just do what you want, Bertie. Whatever decision you come to will be the right one." She was so convincing I believed her every time. She was my "stick man," or whatever they call the guy in the boxer's corner who stops the bleeding between rounds, only in this case, the opponent was Me. Mom's art was in making me think I had a choice: that pauper or prince would be OK—with her, and whichever God that ruled. The truth was that she loved me so much, none of it mattered so long as I was safe, moderately comfortable and close by. (The thing she hated most was the idea of my moving away again.) Gita knew what was best, for both of us, and that I needed to be protected against my own bullheadedness. She knew I needed the security and self-worth a regular job would provide, something, say, in the family business. I fought it all the way, articulate and convincing in my arguments—at the onset of middle age, one still has the vigor to put an aggressive spin on defeat—while sweet Judas goat Mom led me to luxurious slaughter. I will never hold it against her.

So I huddled with the old man to lay it all out, and he couldn't have been happier. Convened with the show runners and they couldn't have been happier. Cruised with the casting folks and they couldn't have been happier . . . and Gita, who not so secretly had savored the years of heartburn I'd provided her husband, was, in the end, undisguisedly thrilled. I was welcomed to the fold— *street-legal*—now eligible for the backstage pass and all that went with it. Life was good. Life was shit. I was even allowed input as to what role I'd play on that ridiculous-looking floating Emerald City, the USS *Demeter*. I requested a non-prosthetic look (the makeup people couldn't have been happier) and some genius staffer came up with the idea of my playing a randy, all-American pilot on the good starship lollipop, a throwback goof on *Top Gun*. In just six weeks' time, I was hanging on the bridge with the legendary captain (who'd renegotiated his fee in a recent PR dustup) and his band of merry men. I fell into episodic rhythm like I was born to it, which I guess I was. I wiled away off-camera time writing treatments in my trailer with the sensual torpor of a geisha having her feet soaked—writing and producing an epic, auteur/non-dumbshit series was where it was at. I would use my time creatively, and get paid for it too. Oh, I was clever! I'd write my ass off, until I could get my HBO shot. In training for the big leagues.

—•—

Sorry for the digression.

I was talking about how often we're blind to the design of what draws us to others. It's a constant shock how early one's patterns are set, and one's proclivities too. In hindsight, it's easy to see the pull Clea exerted because, like me, she labored under the Promethean shadow of a parent whom she could never hope to outshine. (When we were kids, *Starwatch* was in the first few seasons of its astonishingly popular launch—so that in my proscribed world, Roos and Perry were on equal footing.) Our alliance was custom-made; like deaf children, or hearing children of the deaf, we were fluent in a shorthand that required no words. Classmates were mere embryos compared to our fully formed identities as The Children Of, and while we instinctively knew such status put us at a terrifying disadvantage in the long term, at that early age our social position was a boon, for along with blessed birthright came the aura and honors conferred upon any regal offspring. As said, we seemed darkly, precociously in possession of the secret knowledge that, like hemophiliacs, we would eventually pay an awful price, yet felt ourselves to be in a celestial grace period, a state of constant holiday. All children are attention junkies and we were titillated to be the recipients of the seigneurial perks incidental to our position: the crude currying of favor among peers, the indirect adulation of the latters' parents, even the covert acknowledgment by schoolteachers of our prominent placement in the local, generally overprominent constellatory array. We were the brightest stars that hung by the honeymoon of those halcyon years.

In such a lunar light, the chasm that I dug between myself and Clea upon her mother's death can now be seen as an all-the-more-ruthless act: I had committed the paramount sin of abandoning my own kind. As blue bloods, slightly inbred, we could only flourish in the absence of adversity—how could it have been otherwise? We had always enjoyed divine protection, and there was nothing in the rule book about those (parental) gods succumbing to Death.

I remembered, because at the time, I'd frantically—and futilely—scanned the index.

—— · ——

I didn't see her until my thirty-seventh year, when we ran into each other at an AA meeting in a Brentwood church. (Clea used to say they should just drop the A and call it Alcoholics—"There *is* no real anonymity.") She had three months of sobriety and didn't look well.

Ten years ago, around the time I returned from the Bay Area and moved to Venice, Clea began making a name for herself as an actress. Her career hadn't taken off but she'd done respectable work in small, respectable films, even winning an award at a prestigious festival in Berlin. For a while there were pictures of her in magazines—the lighting always seemed to emphasize the luminous bone structure and hooded eyes inherited from her mom—hobnobbing with pals, other groovy sons and daughters of icons, like Natasha Gregson Wagner or Charlie Sheen. I read all the interviews and saw all the movies (they screened mostly at the Sunset 5), following Clea's career with a kindly stalker's eye. She was good, sometimes *very* good. In a few films, she wasn't fully dressed. All right, I'll admit there was something slightly morbid about my attentions; maybe that's not the right word. I flirted with the idea of contacting her but never did. I think—no, I'm certain—I was putting off a reunion until I had a degree of success to call my own. I wanted *some* measure of achievement before we broke bread or wine or heroin or whatever it was she wanted to break. I was actually quite amazed this almost pathologically shy girl not only chose to become an actress but had made real headway. I was also reminded—as if by the whisper of our old shorthand—that kids like us were genetically programmed to fly straight into the flames of their flamboyant heritage. Call it one of our fatal, masochistic charms.

Her career blipped along a few years before dropping off the showbiz radar. There were bitchy murmurs of drug intake—the town had a great sense of rumor—and the usual gossipy, unimaginative "like mother, like daughter" psychologizing overheard at clubs, screenings, and premiere parties. I can remember Clea's unfocused face staring from the cover of a newsstand tabloid, feeling all noble about declining to make purchase (I leafed through instead). A few more mentions in the press—random, unjazzy catalogues of a tailspin, because by then she didn't even rate the front page—before relegation to obscurity. I went through a big Howard Stern phase and for a long time part of me listened with perverse dread for the inevitable sado-dissection riff. Thankfully, it never came.

When I saw her at the church on San Vicente, Clea's smile, lovely and bright, erased all the years—suddenly, we were twelve again. We sat beside one another and stood for the closing prayer, holding hands. After the meeting, overcome, I walked her to the courtyard and breathlessly made amends, confessing my shame and embarrassment over how I'd handled Roosevelt Chandler's death (as if that childish faux pas had been the great traumatizing event of Clea's life, surpassing even the loss of her mother). But she had no recollection of my cowardice or how I'd fled, even going so far as to say I had always been her port in the storm. "The best boyfriend I ever had—the *best*" was how she put it, with the sweetest, slinkiest wink. Upon absolution, I experienced the proverbial weight literally lift from my shoulders. With boundless affection and enormous gratitude, I tearfully asked her to dinner. Her eyes crinkled up and she hugged me, saying how sweet I was. Then, saucily: *"No more confessions."*

We went for sushi across from Dutton's. She'd been favoring her right arm—it relaxed in a silken makeshift sling—and midway through the meal I inquired what happened. She said that the last time she "used," she'd nodded out and fallen asleep on it, sustaining nerve damage. I'd heard of that sort of thing happening to addicts but it was a keen shock it had befallen my precious Clea. She said a doctor weaned her off the heroin with pills and she was doing "tons" of acupuncture and physical therapy. Yoga was also a help and she'd recovered "about 70 percent range of motion." When I asked where she was living, Clea said excitedly, "An *amazing* motel in Beverly Hills." I told her I knew the place, over on Reeves ("Bertie," she interjected, "I *so* want to write a reality show about the people who live there!")—I remembered it from rare incursions to Leif Farragon's south-of-Wilshire turf on my silver, high-handled ten-speed. As she spoke, I cruelly surveyed the parched plains of skin, flaky and blemished, and plumbed Clea's half-dead eyes. Eyes that jauntily seduced, working overtime to camouflage the damage done through the years gone by.

WE FINALLY CARRIED OUT AN affair that began with overheated second-story kisses and ended precipitately (from my side, anyway) with a loss of innocence having more to do with the death of flesh than its celebration. I was squeamish when Clea admitted beforehand to having hep C, even though I had a lot of similarly afflicted friends. I'd done my homework, learning it was difficult to contract the disease through the sex act. To be honest, I'm not so sure how I'd have behaved even on discovering the virus could be transmitted by a single kiss. You see, I believed it was my fate to sleep with this woman—our renewed intimacies could not, would not, be thwarted.

The entanglement, while brief, had that most shocking outcome: we became best of friends. It was like one of those awful sitcoms you love to hate. We behaved like girlfriends (or boyfriends, depending on mood), becoming mutual sounding boards for all manner of crises across the spiritual, emotional, and carnal divides. We AA'd three times a week, and I had the great pleasure of watching her grow physically and mentally stronger. When, after nine months, I gave Clea her one-year sobriety cake, we bawled like babes. The fact that this was the longest-running relationship of either of our lives combined with the Solomonic certitude it would be a terrible mistake to shoehorn ourselves into coupledom seemed to bless our messy union with the platonic promise of longevity a simple marriage could never confer. Clea Fremantle Chandler and Bertram Valentine Krohn truly *were* till death they do part. The unexpected wisdom of this unexpected development allowed us to walk the earth with a lighter step, divesting ourselves of those gloomy, decades-old self-portraits, the scowling ones reflecting how we'd failed our parents, ourselves, the world. *Good-bye to all that.* We time-traveled, forward and back, and there was something flat-out amazing about the two of us sitting before my fireplace on a rainy Venice night, honoring one another (and a certain dimple-chinned phantom named Leif Farragon too).

Although Clea spent money freely, living large in the way that actresses do, she consistently claimed to be broke. I never pressed for details. Assuming Roosevelt Chandler's estate had been in reasonable order (admittedly, a lot to assume), it wouldn't have surprised if Clea had blown through whatever provisions were made—if they *had* been made—a long time gone. Aside from voice-over work erratically provided by a friend with a loop group, there was no evidence she was otherwise engaged. She occasionally auditioned for those cliché gritty, comeback indie roles though nothing ever panned out; I think they brought her in mostly out of curiosity. I'm not even sure she had an agent. Once in a while Clea and her beat-up Alfa Romeo disappeared on weekends and I feared the worst. After the third or fourth vanishing, I confronted her and was relieved to learn she was off doing conventions in the heartland, meeting Roos Chandler fans and signing memorabilia for a fee.

She eventually moved to a little Craftsman not far from my cottage on Ocean Park. (When I'd suggested we become roomies, Clea demurred.) She still came over enough to leave a territorial mark: ashtrays overflowing with lipstick-smeared butts, discarded Tampax applicators in the bathroom wastebasket, the errant ripped, discarded panty hose tucked impishly under bed frame. When I brought home dates, I had a speech prepared—always ill received— about how Clea and I were "childhood friends" but nothing more.

As my ambivalence about having joined the *Starwatch* family mellowed, and my gig grew more secure, I set up an audition. Dad didn't come to the studio much anymore but cordially arranged to be there on the big day. (He remembered Clea from bygone times, and might even have met Roosevelt at some PTA thing or another.) I'd already made my big spiel so when I reintroduced them, he was on best behavior—as were the casting gals, as was Clea, as was myself—the whole world was gallant, dainty and civil, tender in its hopeful reparations.

She got the job without having to read.

Clea would now report to work in the engine room of the *Demeter*, where she'd limn the role of Genius Alien Mechanic With Dangerous Sexual Undertow: an expat from the rarely visited star cluster, Albion-12. When the makeup team materialized a diamond-encrusted appliqué that adhered to the upper skull (Clea called it "a rhinestone merkin"), branding Albionesque tribe and ancestry, she took it in playful stride. I was proud of her because with great élan, Clea had made the difficult decision to come in from the cold and humbly ply her trade. If a person was going to do some serious spring cleaning and adopt a new work ethic, this was as good a place as any—if that meant leaving her ego at the fortieth-century door of the *Demeter*, so be it. We both knew the courage it took to overthrow old dreams and slough off the seductive, gaudily dystopian lifestyle that had brought her so close to immolation.

The day she returned from her final skullcap fitting, she cried in my arms, in hope and defeat, and I felt she was truly my sister.

Now, I'm a little unsure if this is kosher from a "literary" standpoint but I need to introduce someone essential to our story whom as yet hasn't even been hinted at. (Remember, I'm new to this; maybe that's a plus.) Why not? In the actual chronological scheme of things—and I know that sounds odd—I'm about to meet him for the first time myself. But I wanted to make a preliminary sketch, so you're familiar.

(Call it part of my ten-finger exercise.)

All right, here we go:

The plucky, diminutive Thad Michelet was fifty-four years old, and while endowed with the rakish quality of an overgrown cherub, he was very much our elder. He was widely known as a gifted comic actor, with powerful dramatic skills as well; ten more years and he'd have made a fine, if physically uncharacteristic Willy Loman. He was supposed to have been marvelous in an Off-Broadway revival of Ionesco's *Rhinoceros* some years back—had I not been in the midst of a dry-drunk bender with a girl whose name I've now forgotten, I'd have certainly gone to see him. He was also (I was dimly aware, even before Clea reiterated) a published novelist, and like so many of us, the thing he found himself most passionate about was made manifest by talents the world deemed second-rate. What the *world* wanted was the incarnation of Thad Michelet it had known for the last dozen years—a lovable buffoon who graced interchangeable studio "tent poles" that never grossed less than $200 million, sometimes approaching a billion worldwide. He'd been George Jetson's hapless brother in Barry Sonnenfeld's delightful live-action feature and played Sancho Panza to Peter O'Toole's Quixote for the ebulliently uncontainable Terry Gilliam. He had guest-starred in just about every *CSI* permutation to date, and done three-episode arcs on most of TV's hottest half-hours. The remarkable thing being, Thad Michelet was as likely to do a turn for Polanski, Frears, or the

Coen brothers as he was for Spielberg, Ratner, or the Farrellys. A Renaissance man, he divided art and life between the avant-garde stage, studio films, indies, television cameos, and book writing. Among these avocations, Thad's literary efforts are by far the most pertinent (at least, in regards to my tale), in that his very *idea* of himself as a man of letters constituted the Significant Other that bound him so closely to Clea and myself—and at this point, it's probably best to come clean with the "reveal" that his father happened to be none other than that titan of our time, the singularly profane, lavishly gifted, beguilingly protean, salaciously elegant, carnivorously charming novelist who I presume was and is still known to most readers of these pages as both giant and giant-killer Jack Michelet—Michelet of the three Pulitzers and perennial Nobel short list, Michelet of the Lannan Prize, Michelet of the Neustadt and two National Book Awards, Michelet of the eight novels, countless screenplay adaptations, and three Academy Award noms, Michelet of the six books of essays and criticism, two children's fairy-tale compendia, five volumes of poetry, and countless short stories, Michelet of the outrageously trenchant, scabrous, scholarly, dashed-off feeling yet meticulously crafted op-ed pieces, Michelet of the Harold Bloom canon, Michelet the occasional translator from Czech and Celtic and old Italian, Michelet the now-and-then classically outrageous, outrageously classical rethinker, rewriter, and rearranger of Chekhov, Ibsen, and Molière, Michelet of the editorial stewardship of myriad international quality-lit anthologies, Michelet of the required college reading, Michelet the mythic lion in winter of whom biographers and journalists high and low had gleefully written did not go gentle into that good night (or whatever miserable cliché they saw fit to employ)—Black Jack Michelet who most definitely *didn't* end with a bang or a whimper but instead lingered in bodystink and agonized ill health so as to take pleasure in maiming and brutalizing whomsoever loved him, or at least had put in their time as blood or bloodied relations upon countless scarlet battlefields, the last being the Vineyard, where the sadistic, near-senile general's body finally fell.

In other words, Michelet the Genius.

But here's what I meant by Significant Other.

If we're lucky in life, one day we discover our passion; and while it's true we become in a sense married to that passion, what I seek to convey is something ultimately above and beyond trade or creative calling. Put it like this—I, Bertie Valentine Krohn, am bound to Perry Needham Krohn in the same peculiar way that Clea Fremantle was to her mother Roos, and dearest Thad to giant-killer Jack. It is impossible to ignore that the three of us diabolically chose to scale the Olympian summits of peaks already conquered, staked, claimed, and mythologized by the sacred monsters who bore us. Now, why on earth would we embark on a cause so futile and without distinction? Was it cowardice, sloth, delusion? Genes, arrogance, simple perversity? All of the above? The most pernicious of my theories was that we'd been subtly seduced and savagely suppressed by the gravity of whichever dominant, offending parental star, in the same way adult children are ensnarled, emasculated, and snuffed out in Strindberg chamber plays. (All right, I confess; I probably didn't have it all that bad.) While it isn't particularly convenient, and might even strike some readers as paranoid, let me put everything on the table with a cold, Oedipal eye—if, say, by the power of the *Starship Demeter*'s tractor beam my own father insidiously reeled me into the orbit of Planet Hollywood and its promise of moguldom and if, like a druggy automaton, Clea had played out her unlikely role as failed ingénue, soaked in a provocative *parfum* of sex and death daubed behind the ears by a platinum-haired succubus who only grew more controlling and persuasive in the afterlife . . . well, if these things *were* true, then it only made sense that Thad, eldest of these musketeers, was likewise mesmerized into believing he might actually compete at the authorial heights of his father—when in reality he was merely saloon dancing like the town

drunk, feet shot out from under by an artfully messianic, infantici-
dal gunslinger.

Jack Michelet, cold-blooded killer of the Modern Library.

However you sliced it, the burgeoning threesome provided more
than enough material to bring psychoanalysis back into vogue.

Thad's case was a bit more complicated than ours, perhaps
because he was older and had traveled further distances upon more
perilous roads, perhaps because he was more complicated himself.
It's no shame for me to admit that of the trinity, I was the dullest of
the lot. (Ultimately, my saving grace.) I always thought of Clea as
fragile, yet at her toughest—"tough" being one of the more helpful
chromosomes she'd acquired from Roos—she was tougher than me
by a long shot. While I can't really claim to have been an intimate of
Thad's, I never thought of him that way—fragile, I mean—though
he definitely possessed what one critic noted as the "tragic element."
Even on first sight, there was something of the comic desperado, a
charismatic pathos, hopeful and hopeless all at once, a kind of
wounded-animal magnetism that made a person rush to hug the
man or prop him up, fix him a sandwich or syringe: whatever it took
to calm his nerves and make the agonized world (all other worlds
were sure to follow) right again.

The reader has been patient with my exposition, and kind
enough to recall this as a virginal effort. Some of you, I sense, may be
tiring of my voice, so I'll take the bull by the horns and lunge into
that very first meeting, which took place in the cavernous, Benedic-
tine sanctuary of the Chateau Marmont lobby.

"My God," said Thad, with dumbfounded, courtly amplitude as
I approached.

Clea knew that my meeting her old lover was a momentous
occasion. (Proud, fresh-scrubbed, and beaming, she looked like an
excited bureaucrat on a day the inaugural ribbon is cut.) There
were so many glasses, dishes, books, scripts, and scarves on the
table before him that it seemed as if he'd been living on the com-

modious, tasseled sofa rather than in a suite of rooms somewhere skyward.

"He's just . . ."—he took me in a while longer, then looked to Clea for theatrical approbation—"well, I'm *shocked*. I mean, well— he's *exactly* as I imagined him!"

"Thad knows everything about you," she said, slyly.

"I don't know if that's a good or a bad thing," I said.

"It's a good thing," said Thad. "Thus spake the Vorbalid."

He smiled devilishly, as did Clea, his scampish lady-in-waiting and all-around acolyte-in-cahoots. His ambience—and fizzy, frizzy physicality—was at once raw and cultured, cultivated and kitschy, a curious commingling of scholar and clown. Thad's eyes hungrily surveyed the topography of human detail unfolding before him like a jet devouring a runway at takeoff (recall that I am a beginner; forgive the turbulence of simile), his bristly brows, courtesy of Holbein or Cranach the Elder, hovered gnomishly above balding pate. His clothing, out of style and synch in our town and time, was cut from seventies-era flannel: Pendleton and corduroy that collected thread, clusters of tiny twigs, dust-ball tumbleweeds, bread crumbs, and other couch miscellanea miniatures. Like a creature in a storybook, the most delicate boughs and tendrils of hair tended to grow within and without the cartilaginous folds of his ears, and from small hands—the backs of which sported alarming tufts of fur—sprang unlikely, attenuated finger-bouquets with effetely polished nails: snapshot of a friar in cozy recess of library or den accompanied by Scarlatti (harpsichord) in those charged yet leisurely hours before transformation to werewolf. His manner of speech was a charmed slurry of murmured hesitancy and ballsiness. I would eventually chafe at this dichotomy (blend of wolf and leprechaun, of capricious qualities both simpatico and cruel), but at this moment the feeling that prevailed was of complete and familiar, blood-close ease. In fact, I found myself exhilarated upon meeting the final element of what was to be a pivotal, self-historic ménage à trois; I don't think it too melodramatic to say that something inside me knew my life was about to change and would never again be the same.

"How long have you been in town?" I asked, stiffly. It was always like that when I met someone formidable.

"Town?" He looked curiously at our mutual friend and said, "Clea, what does he mean by 'town'? Haven't we already warped into Vorbalidian Space?"

I wrote the unscintillating reference off to jet lag and general drunkenness.

"Forgive him," said Clea. "We just got back from Cedars. He had a migraine shot."

"Wow," I said lamely, though I actually felt for him. "My mother used to get them."

"*Cluster* headaches," said Thad, with lurid emphasis. "They should call it cluster *fuck*. That should be the official medical terminology! They say in the *lit'rature* that when a *cluster fuck* gets beyond a certain point, all the Percocet in the world won't touch it. Won't do *shit*. It *knows* you're trying to find it, they've *proven* this with CAT scans, it's like fucking *Al Qaeda*. (Or being fucked by Al Qaeda.) Thing stays one step ahead of whatever you throw at it—moves to different parts of the brain. *Nomadic*. That's actually the word they use. Like a storm system. I've seen 'em *map* it, with dye—cluster fucks look like gypsy thunderstorms. Rollin' thunder!"

He rambled on, interspersing arcane physiological factoids with *Starwatch* jargon (I soon understood why). As he spoke, a stream of hipsters and admirers who were staying at the hotel—Ed Lachman, Rachel Griffiths, Philip Seymour Hoffman—either waved or dropped by to pay brief homage.

Twenty minutes in, a gregarious, attractively mousy woman named Miriam joined us. Thad baroquely introduced her as his book agent. Then another Philip, this one the actual manager of the Chateau, discreetly interrupted to officially welcome the actor-author to the premises. An agent from ICM offered praise while a preteen

German girl (from *The Jetsons* demographic, probably the daughter of some international film financier) stood gawking not too far off. Amid this friendly tumult Mr. Michelet gathered his things and broke camp, inviting everyone in earshot to "take the party upstairs."

— • —

Though he'd arrived only hours ago, the airy, legendary penthouse was redolent with the scent of his moppish, matted being, a pot-pourri of pot, herbal teas, longneck bottled Fig & Olive bath oils (courtesy of Clea), and seemingly, his very (busy) brain itself. At first, both women tried to curtail Thad's alcoholic intake, as it was contraindicated to whatever opiates the ER had seen fit to dispense. He put up his dukes, but folk wisdom, folk medicine, and feminine wiles prevailed. As Miriam and Clea changed him into a favorite soft sweatshirt, they marveled at a physical constitution that, after the travails of the afternoon, would still leave their old friend "upright." At least he was in a jovial frame of mind.

As it turned out, Thad was in L.A. to meet with the *Starwatch: The Navigators* team, who had written an episode expressly for him. It was news to me. The two-parter commenced filming in a month or so; Mr. Michelet's face needed to be fitted for prosthetic appendages, that sort of thing. I shot Clea a glance and she shrugged, indicating it had been a surprise to her as well. I was irked, without exactly knowing why. The fact was, just because I'm the son of the show's creator, I had no more an inside track of the goings-on, stunt-casting strategies, or "event episodes" being cooked up than did anyone else. As a rule, I had no interest—to care enough to be curious would have been an added humiliation—yet there I was, suddenly feeling left out. The explanation for my annoyance was actually quite simple: I was jealous, not only of Thad Michelet's bigger, messier, brillianter, more glamorous life (and that he had the profound luxury of a temporary docking aboard the loveboat *Demeter* instead of taking up slaveship residence, as I had), but of his father's loftier progenitorship as well, rendering my own, in comparison, more to that of blue collar than blue blood.

But I think what galled me most, though I never let on, even to myself, was his prior knowledge of Clea. I'd known about it, even if she had never spoken of the affair in any detail. One word she *had* used to describe their alliance stuck in my head: "volatile." Naturally, I took that as a rebuke to my genetically unvolatile ways. There I was again, absurdly, in the same triangle I'd found myself with Leif: unsexy third wheel in an adolescent psychodrama.

So, as dusk turned to evening, lounging around the vast modernist prairie of the refurbished suite, I did what any self-respecting triangulated schmuck would have done: doted on the bookish Miriam Levine as if she were the reincarnation of Roos Chandler herself, or at the very least, the only one in the room. While Clea flirtily wrangled her restless, doped-up ex, I cozied on the couch with the agent, sassily grilling her on where she lived, which town she'd been raised in, what college she attended (Brown, of course). *Oh, and—any sibs?* Parents still living? Where *did* they live and how were they faring? Now *when* did you enter the book racket, and please to name current stable of authors . . . by the way, how did you and Thad meet? My eyes bore deep into hers and I made sure she saw my nostrils subtly crease in randy inhalation when commenting on her lovely complexion (the latter, I'll admit, said out of Clea's hearing range), and so on and so on and so forth, lavishing her with the kind of attention that, falling short of a seasoned lothario's, more than fit the profile of any decent, serial monogamizing narcissist. During Clea's own ministrations—far more labored than mine—I caught the occasional sidelong glance betraying grudgey acknowledgment of my heedlessness to both her and the outsized Vorbalidian guest star, a passing irritation at my focus on Miss Miriam. I could have been wrong. My little display may have been laughably transparent.

Soon enough, Miriam spun from my orbit. We gathered around the fire of Thad, so to speak, as he declaimed *sans* translation:

> *Vaghe stelle dell'Orsa, io non credea*
> *Tornare ancor per uso a contemplarvi*
> *Sul paterno giardino scintillanti . . .*

"That's Leopardi," interjected Miriam. (She'd obviously heard his act before.) "Ah! To be an ensign fourth-class on the *Starship Demeter*!" he shouted, shuffling about in seductive, self-mocking dinner-theater mode. He'd taken the stage, disarmed and dangerous. "I cannot *tell* you how I've been looking forward to this"—he addressed himself to me—"I'm *Starwatch*'s biggest fan, *così fan tutte*! The stars! Oh, the stars!"

He cleared his throat, narrowing his eyes like a midget Barrymore.

> *Glittering stars of the Great Bear—*
> *Never thought I'd be back to see you,*
> *Shining down on my father's garden . . .*

Still poetizing, he looked each of us square in the eye like the old Wellesian ham he was, transported to the deathless realm of the one-man show. In full, hoary command, he cocked his neck toward the heavens.

"I could hear the murmur of voices float back and forth in my father's house, conjuring mysterious worlds and a future full of secret joys, knowing nothing of what might lie in store—nor yet how often times would loom where I'd gladly swap this bereft and wretched life of mine for death."

The doors of the massive terrace were shut, yet a breeze from Sunset Boulevard found its way through the cracks like a spirit and advanced to the living room where we sat, shifting the mood from cordial conviviality to melancholy foreboding. Thad suddenly grew pale and wobbly, and Clea signaled she was going to "put him down." Within moments, Miriam and I were traveling silently in the elevator then saying good-byes at the great wicker chairs that graced the garage's entrance.

YOU REACH DEATH VALLEY FROM a town called Baker, which features a motel called the Bun Boy. Thad got a predictable kick out of that, especially as the campy signage had its cartoonish, portly icon pointing at the low-slung resort with a come-hither neon arrow placed literally at Mr. Boy's pelvis. To make matters worse, or more hilarious, a couple of seedy, shirtless young boys lolled Bruce Weber–style outside one of the rooms, visible from the 76 station where we gassed up.

I finally understood where they shot those car commercials I'd been watching all my life, the ones with swooping helicopter shots of sedans and sport coupes traversing endless ribbons of road. (I'd mistaken the nearly mystical vastness for Arizona or New Mexico.) Being a native Angeleno, I've spent a fair amount of time in Palm Springs and Joshua Tree. I've driven to Telluride and Santa Fe—and Vegas, of course—but never got around to Death Valley. I guess getting stranded in 120 degree temperatures didn't have much appeal. This time of year, though, the weather was clement. Besides, we were only going to stay overnight, and I was in pleasant company. Miriam and her bare, backseat legs were really growing on me.

We didn't pass many cars along the way. There were rolling dunes, sandy ziggurats, and pristine mountains of tidy majesty. We drove through a town with an incongruous working opera house at the end of a long, one-story adobe hostel that wore ghostly bedsheets for room curtains. Just before the final turnoff came Zabriskie Point.

Thad insisted we have a look. Everyone went on about the Antonioni movie of the same name, which, being the dolt I was, I'd never
seen. (Not to be confused with another Antonioni film, *Red Desert,*
said Miriam.) We ascended the slope on foot, ahead of a busload of
German tourists.

The point overlooked a place called Badwater. At the top, a
plaque said something about Mr. Zabriskie being a mortician before
he got to working for the Borax Company, and also mentioned the
famous 49ers, stranded and rescued that very year. There was a
weird, pervasive, acoustic void, even with the hushed, parenthetical
polyglot of voices—people seemed naturally to speak more softly
when faced with the fire and brimstone of the valley spread out
before them—and timbrey drone of low wind. It made you see how
there were all different kinds of quiet, different levels, rungs, and
spaces. I can't exactly describe it but the intensity of silence had a
kind of calming, ionizing effect, sucking the human element from
the scene the way filters rid the air of dirt particles. Taking in the
panorama, I thought of those 49ers and wondered what it would
have been like in the peak of summer (one year, it reached 132°)
with no roads or wellsprings.

Like Zabriskie Point, the Furnace Creek Inn sat on a hill above
the wide, bleakly beautiful moonscape. It truly seemed a mirage. The
anomalous luxury hotel had been there for seventy-five years or so;
the dining room even had a dress code. We settled gratefully into
three large suites.

Though Clea had been denying it, the cat was now out of the
bag—they'd gotten back together. I decided to decide that was all
right. I'd never seen her happier.

—•—

"I thought you were going to ask where they caught Manson," the
front-desk clerk said.

"All right," said Clea. "Where did they?"

"Farther down the road."

The man was garrulous and sweet-faced, and Thad was thoroughly entranced, like a writer (or actor) who'd felicitously come across a wonderful character study. Miriam had all her maps out, efficiently poised with a fancy pen, like we were about to go treasure hunting.

"I'm from New York," the clerk continued. "Whenever a guest comes from the Big Apple, I say, 'Which part?' They tell me the street and I tell them where *I* lived and that's how we bond. Well, in Death Valley, it's different; took me a while to learn that. You don't *ask* a certain type where they're from. If you do, they give you a look."

In the discreet, universal language of VIP, the clerk had acknowledged Thad's celebrity status on check-in, adding he'd go out of his way to provide anything we might need. The dining room was already booked for supper but he would "make arrangements for window table seating" at the hour of our choice.

As it was already afternoon, explore time was limited. Tourist sites generally took the infernal theme: Dante's View, the Devil's Golf Course, Pitchfork Point, Coffin Canyon, and so on. (It was only in the high seventies, with a gentle breeze.) We drove out to one of the dunes where *Planet of the Apes* was shot. The Funeral Mountains reflected in the salt pools of the valley floor. As we cruised along, that eerie quietude flirted with hearts and minds, overtaking us whenever we pulled off road and shut down the motor, sauntering into craters and cinder fields.

The brochure said Badwater had the lowest elevation in the republic. Miriam bent to pick up a mineral chunk. Clea said "borax" but Miriam touched it with her tongue and said "salt." Clea was hung up on borax, calling our attention to the "borax-covered mountains" ringing the plateau. (It was actually snow. Hard to believe; the brochure said the mountains topped off at 11,000 feet.) Miriam didn't argue the point, which had the effect of eroticizing her further, in contrast to Clea, who traipsed around like a fool, looking for "pupfish." I wondered if she was stoned—my old friend looked a bit "faded," as one of my 12-Step cohort's nephews might say—I just didn't want to go there. A moody Thad wandered the farthest away, like a surveyor of unknowable, unnameable things. I followed his contemplative lead, striking off in the opposite direction.

There came the silence again: warm, lapping, sensual yet somehow indifferent. It was nice having it all to myself—we are greedy even when it comes to the whisper of the infinite. Once familiar with its alien though not unfriendly persona, the exotic, wadded qualities and texture of it, you became a believer, an initiate of the numinous, whose ears couldn't but help (at least for the rest of your stay) seek out its presence within "ordinary" quiet—that common currency of soundlessness that fell between voices, between reverbatory hush of wind and insect whir—in the end, mastering the ability to detect the silence embedded in quietude itself. It was a layered wedding cake, a dessert of stillness that imposed meditation, forcing each to cocoon within. Conversation ended as we walked and paused, testing and savoring its syrupy strangeness, startled and nurtured by mutual discovery. There was something slightly narcotic, and psychedelic too, about the blown-out hermetics of emptiness. I realized how much human beings crave it, as much perhaps as we crave wide open space, yet how rarely we're able to commune.

"I was reading an article by Primo Levi," said Thad. "Poor man! He was writing about translators—how they struggle with the Babel of voices." My bullshit detector sensed the beginning of a casually pretentious pontification; wickedly, I wondered if he was doing a cheap imitation of his dad. "Levi was obsessed with the Word— when *this* is what needs to be translated, no? This . . . *nothingness*. 'Luminous emptiness.' That's what the mystics are up to. Mystics are the *real* translators, trying to get us to understand—*this*. As if anyone has anything to say that needs to be heard! Or *read*, for that matter. That's why Levi killed himself. Went to the bathroom and had a big vowel movement"—he cackled at the pun—"then threw himself off a balcony. Translate *that*!"

—•—

Thad had circled a final destination on the brochure.

It was an hour away, and I was glad we'd taken my SUV. After consulting a passing ranger, we hiked to Racetrack Playa. It looked like a vast skating rink, its dry mud surface cracked by an interlocking honeycomb of trapezium shapes—like a lake of cobblestones flattened by the Devil's Fist. On the bed were large rocks with skid marks in tow, crude plinths and markers pushed by awesomely mischievous hands. The movement of the boulders was attributed to the silty rink's slick surface when it got rained on, and the powerful gusts of wind that "sailed" the stones across at speeds slower than the naked eye could detect. The explanation made sense but that didn't mean it wasn't spooky.

"The Lord is my Vorbalid," said Thad, "I shall not want." He picked up a branch, wielding it like Moses. "My agent maketh me lie down in *Starwatch* pastures. She leadeth me beside the FX waters. Yea, though I walk through Death Valley of the shadow of Death Valley, thy rod and thy brilliant writing staff will comfort me. Thou anointeth my head with prosthetics; my chai tea runneth over. Surely goodness, borax, and residuals shall follow me all the days of my life."

—•—

Dinner at the inn was delicious. (Clea and I had rattlesnake.) Well-off retirees discussed terrorism and luxury hybrid cars.

Our waitress recognized both actors—from the movies—and that was nice for Clea because the clerk hadn't acknowledged her fame. Thad was drinking, but Clea held back on my account, even though I was pretty sure she'd broken her sobriety. I flirted with Miriam as usual, and Clea said, "Don't worry, he's just a clit tease." It was much more crass than something she'd normally say—another indicator that she had, in AA parlance, "slipped."

When the food came, Thad asked the waitress where she lived.

"My husband and I work half the year up at Crater Lake," she said. "Do you know where that is? They close for winter, so we come down here. We get subsidized housing—a hundred dollars a month and no utilities. If you have a fifth-wheeler, you pay a couple bucks a day and get a little more mobility. Plug it in and you're good to go. All you got to do is pay utilities—with a fifth-wheeler, you have to pay. We figure if we work a year, we can earn enough for a house. It's kind of inconvenient living in a remote place. You have to do all your shopping on your day off. We go to Pahrump. If we *really* want to buy, we go to Vegas."

"Subsidized housing," Thad riffed, after she left. "They should have that at the Chateau! That's where the IRS wants to see me—in a fifth-wheeler. Whatever *that* is. But ahma gonna fool 'em, see? Got it *all planned out.* Know where I'm gonna live when they take my apartment away?"

"No one's going to take your apartment away," said Miriam, definitively.

"I'm *serious.* Know where I'm going to live when they take it all away?"

"No one's going to take your house, honey!" said Clea, laughing. "And if they *do,* you can stay with *me.*"

"No, no—I have it all planned. I'll *tell* you where I'm going to live." A pause, then: "In my *head.*" He swigged down the glass of wine. "*That's* where I'm gonna live when the IRS swoops down and takes ev'rythang *away. In my fucking head.*"

We went down the hill for a nightcap at the 49er. (Clea and I had date shakes.) Thad was drunk enough he wanted to set out for the Racetrack again, but that would have been a disaster. Miriam adroitly steered us back to the inn, with its anomalous Olympic-sized swimming pool and spectacular outdoor fireplace. By then, the guests had all gone to bed. Only a staff person stoking the flames remained. (I felt like one of the Hearsts.) The gentleman asked if we knew about the lunar eclipse; it was almost over. Before disappearing into darkness, he pointed to the small bite taken out of a coppery moon.

Thad, the Gemini, showed us Castor and Pollux. When Castor was killed in battle, the twin's grief was so great he wanted to die, but instead, Zeus made him immortal. With great tenderness, Thad said it was their fate to be separated for eternity, adding with a private smile—I didn't understand it at the time—how they were beacons of good luck for sailors. Then the same abstracted shadow that befell him at Badwater settled over us like a tent made of gossamer. The stone-girdled fire sparked and popped.

We grew quiet, cousined to the stillness that lay beyond.

"WHAT WAS HE LIKE?" asked my father.

There was something animated and slightly off-color about his query, as if wanting to be reminded of a dirty joke he already knew.

"I didn't really know him all that well," said Clea. "I knew *Thad*—from when I lived in New York. We went to his dad's place in the Vineyard a few times."

I'd finally gotten the nerve to ask Clea to dine at the family seat, deep in the canyon wilds of Benedict. The bones of the house were the same that she knew as a girl, though the bracketing properties had long ago been seized from neighbors, razed, and developed in architectural harmony with the ancestral home.

"I would have thought you'd have met while your mother was still alive," said Perry, the glint evacuating his eye. "Seems they would have crossed paths—or swords."

The glint came back. Most of the time, when Dad thought he was being suave, he wasn't.

"Not to my knowledge," said Clea, good-naturedly. "I'm pretty sure Jack was a fan but I don't think they ever had an encounter. Though anything's possible."

"How is it," I asked, "that a *Starwatch* episode was developed exclusively for Michelet Junior? Did you have a hand in that?"

"Absolutely. I was in New York some years ago and saw *Rhinoceros*," he said, in the even tones of an egotist on Charlie Rose.

"You're kidding. You actually *saw* that?"

"I'm not the Philistine you think I am, Bert." He used "Bert" when he wanted to bring me down a peg. "I'm in New York three times a year, for the auctions and the theater—*primarily*, the theater. I thought the play quite remarkable. Thad was *wonderful*. Saw it again, with Nathan Lane, but Thad was better. I had *some* awareness of his work in film at the time, but not much. I'm not a big movie-goer. The *Playbill* said he was the son of Jack Michelet and that got my attention." He turned to Clea. "I have all Jack's first editions, signed—he doesn't sign many, believe me—some watercolors too. Have you seen them? Pretty racy! I've wanted to adapt one of his books for the longest time. *Chrysanthemum*. Do you know it?"

"Yes," said Clea, affably indifferent.

"I've renewed the option ten years running."

"Then you've met him," she said, opening the anecdotal door. She had more than a touch of geisha in her and knew it was probably a story our host would like to tell.

"Only once. Briefly. I don't think he was all that well."

My father clasped his hands, pursed his lips and grew uncharacteristically still, as if to humbly convey that what he was about to impart—the surprising lack of any personal relationship between these two cultural totems—redounded not to him but rather to the quirks, genetic meanness, dipsomania, lunacy, or legendarily demented psychopathology of that towering figure of American letters, Black Jack Michelet. The unspoken implication was that something ugly must have happened to cause Perry to retreat after initial introductions—some horrific scene, for Dad was no piker. In short, he was game. He'd long ago bagged Mailer, Updike, Vonnegut, Styron, Roth and Bellow, with framed letters and carefully mounted correspondence to prove it. In his defense, I'll admit that as he spoke he took the high road, deferring to Genius, withholding the spiteful remark or characteristic caustic quasi-witticism, choosing to reside in a state of benevolent patronlike neutrality. At the end of the day, I think he was superstitious about speaking ill of the elder Michelet, fearing he might jinx whatever hopes he had of making *Chrysanthemum* into an Oscar-winning film.

Mother arrived à table via wheelchair to wish Clea well. (After depositing her, Carmen—Gita's favorite nurse—hung back on the living room couch and flipped through the *Star.*) Parkinson's had wreaked havoc with Mom's body, leaving spirit untouched; the greeting to my childhood love was predictably incandescent. I could tell she'd done her Internet homework, as per custom, thoughtfully counterbalancing the sometimes jarring effect her frail physicality could have upon guests, particularly those who knew the elegant woman in her prime, with details and carefully nuanced trivia from their own lives—a congenial parlor trick as likely to be employed with visitors she'd been briefed on yet never met. Gita was very First Lady that way. She nimbly conjured persons, places, and things from that long-ago time, and Clea, thrown off guard, searched her mind to recall. The very act of mental inventory distracted and leveled the playing field. Mom had been busy on IMDB as well, boning up on movie credits. It was terribly dear, and I knew Clea thought so too. It touched the heart.

We adjourned to the library where my father showed us the aforementioned watercolors—splashy, pornographic studies, all—and the hastily inscribed novel Perry had not yet managed to bring to the screen.

—·—

After supper, Clea wanted to stroll the grounds and smoke.

We took the sloping path toward the pool (its flaky, unrefurbished bottom painted years ago by David Salle), talking of tribal gatherings and make-out sessions that once took place on the hormonal, hallowed ground underfoot. "I remember this tree!" she'd shout, or, "This part is *so different*"—a faraway look in her eyes. Then, moving on, a reinvigorated, convivial affirmation: *"This* part's *exactly* the same!" Like a necromancer, she doused for mood and memory, a naked-hearted empath invoking spirit of place, aching to be reinfected by the magical virus of childhood.

"Leif *loved* that pool," said Clea as we got closer. She pointed to the darkness of the adjacent property. "What is *that*?"

"Dad bought the Freiberg house then knocked it down. I don't even know if he's ever going to build. Right now, it's a garden they let grow wild."

"Whoa! *Amazing*."

"It's not 'wild' wild—it's made to look that way. It was designed by this famous woman, Katrina Trotter."

"That is *so* your father! Perry's a trip."

"Hey . . . remember the time upstairs at your mom's?"

"I remember *lots* of times."

"I was feeling you up and Leif came in?" She actually giggled. "He didn't knock."

"God forbid!"

"He was drunk. He grabbed you and kissed you—"

"You're kidding!" said Clea, with a flush of prudery.

"You don't remember him doing that?"

She shook her head, in Victorian outrage.

"Well, actually . . . he asked me first."

"He asked permission? How kinky! What did I do? Slapped him, I hope. I should have slapped *you*."

That she had no recollection should have been comical but instead I felt sad and hollow, disconnected from the world.

"How did you meet Thad?"

"We were doing *The Master Builder,* in New York."

"How long ago?"

"Oh shit—I guess I was what, twenty-eight? That was ten years ago."

"How long did the affair last?"

She smiled at my formality. "Three years? I already *told* you this, Bertie."

To my chagrin, I took that as a cue to kiss her full on the mouth. The grope was like one of those clumsy couplings in a Julia Roberts movie where the ex comes back in her life just when she's engaged to be married. He can't help himself, lurching at her territorially, the aftermath leaving them awkward and winded—a clear case of Act Two premature infatuation. (They *do* get together in the end, but only in the movies.) Remember, we'd only "done it" a few times, unspectacularly, more than a year and a half ago, and, as Clea liked to put it, been "nonconsenting adults" ever since. The worst part was that my motivations were nefariously vain and in the end, appallingly halfhearted. I was instantly embarrassed even though Clea was gracious enough to hold the kiss a beat or two—when it was over, we broke into laughter, mercifully at the same moment. She shook her head, and said with a smile, "Can we go back in now?"

We didn't speak as we cut through the *other* adjacent lot, the one now sporting an enormous extension to the original house.

"It's not going to last between Thad and me," she finally said, as we passed through a gate on our way to the street. I knew what was coming. "Bertie, you know I love you. But—"

"If you want to get a restraining order, I'll understand."

"I think maybe Caltrans community service will do. You can put one of those orange vests on and pick up trash on the side of the freeway."

"I guess I'm just worried," I said, disingenuously diverting focus,

still stung by my ineptly amatory mini-move. "The guy gets so
loaded. . . ."

"Oh please!"

"I'm serious, Clea."

"I can totally handle that, OK?"

"Are you going over to see him now?"

She nodded. "He's leaving in the morning."

"For where?"

"Canyon Ranch. To lose some weight before the shoot."

"Stay away from his migraine medicine, OK?"

"Yes, Daddy."

"Good girl."

"You know, you kiss pretty good, Daddy."

"I'll bet you say that to all the boys."

"Just the ones who violate their positions of trust. You know—
priests, shrinks, childhood sweethearts."

She kissed my forehead and jumped into the Alfa.

—— • ——

I was restless after Clea left.

I went to say good-bye to Mom but Carmen said she'd already
retired. I chose not to disturb. Dad was on the elliptical catching Larry
King interviewing some over-the-hill sexpot, an after-dinner ritual.

I drove to Book Soup and loitered in fiction, idly skimming
through Henry Miller's *Sexus* before backtracking to the pristine
spine of Michelet's oeuvres, recently reissued in stylishly alluring,
flat-textured covers. There was nothing of his son's. Someone at the
information desk looked Thad up on the computer—his four novels
were out of print. She said I should try Alibris or eBay.

As I was leaving, I saw Nick Nolte peruse the stacks of new
releases opposite the front register. He looked restless himself. He
wore crazy yellow pants and delicate, amazingly expensive-looking
eyeglasses, with two fussy male assistants in his wake. Kind of fabu-

lous. Old Nick was on a book-buying spree (I imagined him flying off the next morning to an exotic film locale) and it was funny to watch the eccentric star alight on this or that tome while his amanuenses informally disgorged pithy, thumbnail précis, to which the master responded with a literal thumbs-up/thumbs-down. For a moment, I thought of Nolte as Jack Michelet—not a bad choice to portray him—attended by his fractured progeny: King Zeus and the Castor/Pollux Kidz. After our trip to Death Valley, Clea told me about Thad's twin, drowned at age ten. She said Thad wrote about the tragedy in *The Soft Sea Horse* (the short novel I'd been looking for on the shelf), a portrayal which apparently caused a major rift between father and son. Jack, at his blackest, had announced publicly that the thinly disguised roman à clef was no better than a tabloid tell-all, a ghoulishly unforgivable game of one-upmanship; his "spawn" had laid cowardly literary claim to that watery grave, knowing the death in Capri was something Michelet could never bring himself to write of, for it was *Jeremy* whom Jack loved inconceivably and inconsolably, *Jeremy* who was the bright, same-spirited, unbroken reflection in his golden eye. The needy survivor's outrageously meager gifts had been used in the grotesque service of ego— shameful! unholy!—and Clea said the giant-killer had not one but two huge bonfires on the Vineyard: the day the book was blasted in the *New York Times*, and the day it was remaindered.

I was mulling all these things when Miriam Levine turned the corner with an armful of high-end art books. We nearly collided.

"Bertie! I was just thinking of you."

"Something inappropriate, I hope."

"I wanted to get you something of Thad's but they didn't have any."

My mind worked with neurotic acuity, suddenly consumed by the logarithms of romance: it seemed odd that Miriam wanted to buy me one of Thad's novels, and odder still she wouldn't be aware they were unavailable, at least in a place like Book Soup, that didn't sell "used." So her comment seemed, on the surface, suspect. On the other hand, it may have been the first thing to occur to her after blurting out I'd been on her mind. Maybe I *had* been, but if that were true I was reasonably certain it couldn't have had much to do with the elusive, unheralded fiction of her client. It seemed more plausible—not to put too fine a point on it—that she'd merely given voice to the kind of subliminal consideration we sometimes lend to someone we've recently met whom we're attracted to, physically, chemically, or whatnot. (I know it sounds cocky, but allow me to indulge.) Suddenly and unexpectedly seeing said person face-to-face might provoke a genuine feeling one *was* thinking of them, even if not strictly the case. Still, I had to admit this East Coast girl was fast on her feet. Smugly finding my anthropological legerdemain to be basically sound, I used the sum of the root equation, now adroitly transferred back to the column marked Animal Instinct, as an opportunity to ask Miriam if she wanted to have a drink.

Here's what then happened:

She suggested the lobby of the Marmont. I said we might run into Thad and Clea, implying I didn't have the energy for another group encounter. She waited two seconds before saying we could have drinks in her room. (That *was* a surprise.) I followed her car, smiling and trembling to something unknown for cello on KCRW. We were stripped and ecstatically entangled within minutes of entering her small, back-of-hotel suite. It'd been months since I had taken anyone to bed and maybe years since a seduction was effected with such little effort. The expedience of it worked absolute wonders for my spirit. I felt as if in my early twenties again—we did all the nasty, glorious things new lovers do. (Another surprise.) We were ravenous, leaving no patch of flesh unturned, then starved for food, drink, and sleep . . . automatically stirring at the hour of the wolf to couple with that edge of violent, sorrowful passion befitting 3:00 A.M. When morning came, we sat in capacious white robes munching muesli and eggs on burnt toast, washing everything down with great gulps of juice like it was our first and last meal on this insanely beautiful blue-green Earth.

I was on the toilet when the phone rang.

I heard her gasp, then came back to the room and listened.

Jack Michelet was dead.

THE FUNERAL WAS AT MARTHA's Vineyard. Thad begged Clea to come and she, in turn, begged me. She needn't have: I knew Miriam would be going and I was *very* sexed up. To be perfectly frank. Besides, life had become a dull shuttle between AA meetings, the gym, *Starwatch* tapings, and reluctant dinner dates—I looked forward to a geographical break in routine, especially one promising to be historically memorable. (OK, half that is bullshit. What I wanted was more Miriam, and the sooner the better.) When Dad found out I was going, he was actually jealous.

The burial took place on Saturday,[1] amid bright sun and nipping cold while the salty seawater, ever near, rhythmically murmured *the Lord giveth . . . the Lord taketh away*. Thad was supposed to have arranged a car but it never showed so we cabbed it to a charming B&B where, remarkably, our rooms were still being held. (The island was completely booked.) Michelet's death was an international event and the presence of journalists and paparazzi permeated the Vineyard, lending a cockeyed, festive, Dia de los Muertos vibe. Thad's

---

[1] I'd only been to one funeral in my life, which at my age was below quota. It was Brandon Tartikoff's, a friend of my father's. The Forest Lawn chapel was SRO—I remember seeing a yarmalke'd Rob Reiner in the distance, arguing with someone over not being let in—with hundreds of folding chairs set out so the crowd could watch the services on some kind of JumboTron screen. I'll never forget the moment I looked down to see the wooden legs of my seat, and those around it, resting upon humble granite graves.

mother hired a cadre of Secret Service types to fend off media vultures already circling the cemetery's entrance. They wore earpieces and sharp Brioni suits.

As a novice drawn to the "set piece," I was sorely tempted to begin this diary with the great man's interment (remember *The Bad and the Beautiful?*), though am happy now to have throttled the impulse, being fairly sure I'd have botched it—a pastiche of eulogies would have been a regrettable launch for these modest pages. Comments from the makeshift podium seemed par for the posthumous course: from the heart, the head, the ego, the groin. Hardly anyone was sober and the ones who were, for all the cringeworthiness of their remarks, may as well have been stoned to the gills. It does seem fairly harmless, though, to list a small roster of mourners: ancient mariners Styron, Mailer, Vonnegut and Vidal, with Hitchens, Auster, Wallace and Lethem representing the new. A half-dozen unlikely showbiz types paid homage as well: Sumner Redstone, Ron and Ellen Perelman, Steve Martin (Joyce Carol Oates on his arm!), Jim Belushi, Daryl Hannah and Carly Simon (I assumed the last three were neighbors). And last, but not least, Nicole Kidman, willowy, alabastrine, and regal red. Supposedly she had optioned Michelet's penultimate book.

I became separated from my group and stood sheepishly on the fringe, bending an ear to discern the minister's words as the wind kicked up, with that nagging outsider feeling—wondering why I'd come.

—•—

The Michelet compound bore a sandy, legendary rusticity, still soaked, so to speak, in the cologne of its erstwhile emperor.

I actually recognized it from an *Architectural Digest* feature some years ago. The amicable gathering of houses, barns, and famously rock-bound, stand-alone study—the latter studiously avoided by downcast minions while they circulated, as if Jack Michelet might still be inside, hard at work—achieved an astonishingly poignant feng shui in its placement on the promontory. The smoky remnant of day, with memorial winds blowing warm enough from sea to bluff that brought to mind my own cherished Santa Anas, gave me goose-flesh. A splendiferous, production-designed dusk made everything reassuringly golden and as evening fell the overall mood lightened; meaning, the crowd openly brandished whatever preferred weapons of choice had gotten them through a collective thirty-five centuries of lusty, wigged-out, existential nights and jaundiced, penitential, hungover days. Miriam and I found a torchère-lit corner to have our first kiss since the Chateau idyll. That neither Clea nor Thad knew about it made postmortem intimacies all the sweeter.

Alone again, I looked suspiciously out of place. Whenever I got the nascent evil eye (on tap for potential media gate crashers), I very publicly touched base with Clea or Miriam to make myself official. Once the security boys pegged me as kosher, I was free to roam the house, dipping into this room or that, or zipping to the patio bar—I was chaining Diet Cokes—stooping beneath a tree to light up, hands cupped à la James Dean while little gusts flared to put out my flame. The cliché is true: there's nothing like a funeral to make one feel alive.

In wood-paneled rooms were portraits of the old dead king in sundry luxe-framed inaugurations. For the last four decades, he had that luxuriously photogenic shock of white hair befitting a Russian or Bolivian billionaire—I thought first of Derrida, then Gianni Agnelli, then finally, most perfectly, of Burt Lancaster. (Perhaps because I'd read somewhere that in his prime, Lancaster was the nastiest, toughest, most feared son of a bitch in Hollywood.) There were pictures of Jack and Morgana on yachts with society types, of black-tied Jack receiving this or that award of national or foreign commendation, of white-tied giant-killer with Jack 'n' Jackie O— he'd written the first of his Pulitzer Prize–winning novels at just thirty years of age—a congery, a menagerie, an agglomerated panoply of silvery and kodachrome portraits: Jack with Hall of Fame rockers, world- and working-class saints and sinners, caretakers, -givers and corporate raiders, icons, poets and acolytes—*Jack be nimble, Jack be quick*—fools and royals and unwashed unknowns. While there were no recent images of the patriarch with his surviving son, I *did* manage to scope a shot of BJM posed, a tad uncomfortably it seemed, with the very young Thad (future third-rate novelist, classily idiosyncratic staple of big-screen blockbusters, and now our very own soon-to-be Starship ensign) aboard a rather grand little boat with *The Soft Sea Horse* written in elegant cursive on its prow, and I knew it predated the drowning. I wondered how the photo had lived; perhaps Morgana snatched it from one of the legendary bonfires.

I moved on, gamely attempting to unravel the riddle of a bronze plaque propped up against a soapstone Buddha. Why it had been memorialized, I would never know:

> "Americans *define* Time as the space within which one succeeds or fails."
> —JACK MICHELET, *JONAS AND THE WHALE*

Fair enough.

And that was when I heard a ruckus.

I hurried to the hallway where Thad and his mom were tussling. He dogged her, disheveled and disgruntled, hissing as she retreated, drink sloshing in his glass like a cartoon of tiny breakers, full fingers five, vodka blown hither and thither by unseen tempests. Even at her age, Morgana had the upper hand physically, and emotionally too—it was no shrinking violet who'd managed to outjoust and outlive Mr. Giant-Killer. She continued to upbraid her son even as he remained on sodden attack though I couldn't make out their time-worn, warm-spittled maledictions. Then Miriam appeared and scrimmaged between, allowing his mother, and a reconnoitering Brioni, an awkward exeunt.

The Kabuki-faced Morgana turned for a fierce parting shot.

"Your father could get away with it but *you can't*. Miriam, you have *got* to help," she implored. "Otherwise, I *will* have him removed. And *boy*, will they *do* it!" (The Brioni thugs.) "Oh, they'd *love* to."

Once she vanished, Miriam and Thad were suddenly, unhappily aware of my presence. I scuttled to the kitchen where the widow, as if making a tardy stage entrance, breathlessly declaimed to those present (a few noshing, malingering guests plus two caterers): *"The air was thin, the sky a scalding blue. The ambidextrous wind wisped clouds around like morphine—or venom—invading the blood."* She dutifully attributed the words to her late husband, addending whichever novel or poem as if it was scripture.

I doubled back to the hall, like a spectator in one of those outré middlebrow dramas where you follow the actors from room to room. I proceeded to the library, where Miriam and Thad were now seated; my return seemed to embolden him, as fresh bodies in the pantry had his mum.

"She wanted to know if I would contribute to the funeral expenses!" he spewed, a wet, fulsome, apoplectic cast to lower lip and jaw. "Can you believe it, Miriam? 'Security is costing more than I expected.' *We're over budget*"—he italicized his mother's words with spasmodic fury—"and since I was making plenty of 'Hollywood money,' I should help defray the cost!"

"She's a bit overwhelmed," said Miriam, diplomatically.

"Don't you defend her, Miriam, not *you*."

When he shook his fist in her face, I aggressively stepped from the door frame, to remind that a price would be paid should he dare cross the line. Though he scowled at my Canadian Mountie shtick, it was evident Miriam drew comfort from my efforts, which pleased me to no end.

"Defray the cost! She's a pathological *miser*, why doesn't anyone *confront* that? Is everyone so fucking *terrified* of her? Do you *know* what she's worth, Miriam? I tell people this and they think I'm *delusional*. Her daddy left her ten million—that was *1950. 1950!*—and she's kept *every cent* of it. Not to *mention* my father's fortune, not to even get *into* that. And she *knows* the IRS has a lien against my apartment in New York, the woman *knows* it! She makes Bill Saroyan look like fucking *Shirley Temple*." He fixed me with a conspiratorial eye. "If *my mother* is forced to spend *fifty dollars* of her *own money*—that is considered a pornographic catastrophe!"

Miriam threw me an "I'll handle this" look, and I sneered before leaving—as if to show Mr. Michelet I had better things to do than attend the hot air ravings of a troglodytic has-been.

Morgana was in the living room surrounded by admirers. I'd arrived at the tail end of a condolence call from Vaclav Havel. She hung up and turned to Walter Cronkite. "Do you know who was a fan of Jack's? Ronnie Reagan. Oh, that *really* pissed Jack off. Jack *hated* Ray-Gun—that's what he called him, just like the Yippies. Jack used to joke that U.S. presidents only read 'The' books: *'The Firm,' 'The Stand,' 'The Whatever.'* Jack said one day he was going to write a book called *'The The'* and it'd be his biggest seller yet! I said, Don't forget the sequels! Oh yes—after *'The The,'* Jack said he'd write *'The This'* and *'The That,'* and they'd go *straight* to the top of the list!"

Everyone roared.

I glanced "off camera" and couldn't believe what was outside the window: Thad, creeping along at petty pace, alternately flanked by Miriam and Clea—attendant and geisha. Like a child, I suddenly panicked, as if the trio were cakewalking to Gatsby's cosmic roadster with full intent of leaving me behind while lifting off for galaxies unknown. I rushed from the room to join the dysfunctional starbound caravan.

The melancholy troll, deep in his cups, moved like molasses toward a break in the wind-smacked hedge that marked a path to the sea.

"My favorite of Dad's is *Chrysanthemum*," I heard him say as I caught up—out of thin air, the comment seemed surreal. "You've read that, haven't you, Miriam? I know *Clea* has." (The latter said with vitriol.) "*Chrysanthemum* always reminded me of Mishima." He caught my eye as he began the précis, old to them, new to me. "It's about a murderous gardener who returns to the scene of the crime. He's never caught. Goes back, day after day, year after year, and eventually comes to the exquisitely mundane realization—that . . . he— *just didn't do it*. That's why *I* keep coming back—*here*, to the fucking Vineyard—and why I'll probably visit again, day after day, year after year. In my head, anyway. I'll *keep coming back*—like they say in AA!—until I can see that I just didn't do it!"

Words and gaze trailed off, almost too wistfully.

"There he is!" came a high, reedy voice. "Sammy Jetson!"

A lean, nasty-looking boy jumped into our space, bursting the bubble. Thad grimaced reflexively, as he probably did ten times a day upon being recognized on the street. A trim, avuncular fellow in his sixties with salt-and-pepper beard materialized as well, and stuck out his hand. "Mordecai Klotcher. Old friend of your dad's—and Morgana as well." Thad pumped it, as if by sheer gusto he might cause both man and man-child to dervishly disappear. "We may actually have met when you were quite younger," he said. "I've followed your career and think you're a marvelous—you bring a *wonderful* presence to your films."

"It's a dirty job," said Thad, employing a favorite all-purpose retort. "But someone has to do it."

Klotcher laughed. "You're *better* than your films," he added, with the sudden gravitas of a watchdog essayist and all-around culture critic.

"Are they making a *Jetsons* sequel?" asked the boy.

He was a bug that needed to be squashed. Thad ignored him, instead turning to Clea with a wicked smile. "He's a dirty john, but someone has to do him. Said the whore." Klotcher appeared unperturbed by the blue remark uttered within earshot of his profoundly annoying great-nephew. In fact, he was delighted. "You get that from Jack! He was *marvelous* at wordplay." The producer screwed up his face, as they used to say, and remarked, "You wrote a novel some time back, didn't you?"

"He's written four," said Miriam.

"Number five's in the works," said Thad, oddly assertive.

"He's not a *writer*," said the boy, caricature of a sitcom brat. *"He's Sammy Jetson."*

"Number five!" exclaimed Klotcher, like his horse had come in. "All still in print?"

"Covers and everything."

"Can you send them to me? To my office?"

"We abso*lute*ly can," said Miriam, extending her hand. "I'm Miriam Levine, Thad's book agent."

Klotcher twitched, as if startled to discover someone else had been standing there all along. A burst of shop talk ensued, with glib references to mutual acquaintances; the ever-obliging Ms. Levine, on showbiz autopilot, seemed merrily distraught. To me, anyway.

"The books . . . they're adaptable?" said Klotcher, like a tourist who'd learned just enough of the local language to ask the natives for basics. "To film? I'm always hunting for properties, always on the prowl. In fact, I'd like to see the galleys of the new one. That's where we make most of our acquisitions—galleys." He turned his attention back to Thad. "You know, I did one of your father's books years ago, with Julie Christie. *Hearts and Vagabonds.*"

"Yes," said Miriam, piping in. "I *loved* it." At the moment, she was the only one in our group who seemed capable of speech. "I'll send you *The Soft Sea Horse.*"

"*That's* the one I'd heard of," said Klotcher, a reptilian glimmer of recognition lighting up precataract eyes. He fumbled with the title, as if soliciting her help to make the deposit in his memory bank: "*The Salton Sea*—"

"*The Soft Sea Horse,*" she corrected.

"Marvelous title! Come to California!" he exhorted. "Will you, Thad? We'll have a lunch or a dinner." He swiveled toward Miriam, as if she were the royal food taster—or gastroenterologist. "Can he have a dinner?"

"He'll be there all next month," she said.

"I'm doing *Krapp's Last Tape* in La Jolla," said Thad, jolting to synthetic life. Klotcher looked at him blankly. Miriam's adding the word "Beckett" did nothing to clear the producer's confusion.

"*And* a two-parter on *Starwatch: The Navigators,*" said the agent. (As if that were the plummest of plum actor things.)

"A *marvelous* show," said Klotcher, on cue. "Now *there's* a phenomenon."

"*Yup.* A real *Phnom Penh.*" Egregiously bored and egregiously drunk, Thad winced at his own wordplay idiocies. "The Cambodians *love* it. It *killed.*"

"There you go again!" said Klotcher giddily. "Your father was marvelous with the pun. And polylingual, too—like Nabokov! Now *there's* someone who rivaled your dad. Ol' Black Jack didn't even want to hear his *name.* He always thought Nabokov was the one who'd snatch the Nobel from his hands. But neither of 'em got it, did they? Big on butterflies, Nabokov. I knew his wife. *And* his kid. We tried to option one of his books. *Ada,* I think it was called. Never worked out."

To my surprise, Thad segued to a toast (he still had drink in hand)—to me, Bertram Krohn, "putative son" of the *Starwatch* creator. Klotcher pivoted, duly impressed.

"*Starwatch* is *cool,*" said the great-nephew, taking me in. "I want to do a walk-on!"

"Walk on this," said Thad.

"They've asked him to do a game show too," said Miriam, nervously unstoppable. "One of these postmodern George Schlatter things, with a floating guest spot. Sort of a permanent cameo—like

Whoopi did in *Hollywood Squares*. Merv Griffin and Ryan Seacrest are producing. They've offered a *ton* of money; they'll be lucky to have him. But Thad's got so many other projects . . ."

She looked winsomely toward her old friend but he blew her off.

"The Michelet name's hot right now," said Klotcher, hoisting an imaginary glass of his own. The crusty old pro frowned and recanted. "Sorry—didn't mean that to sound disrespectful." He delicately lifted the glass again, bowing to everyone present. "To continuing the legacy! Salud!"

As soon as they left, Thad's mood darkened. (I was amazed by his relative civility during the encounter.) He scolded his agent, cruelly mocking her postmodern floating-guest-spot riff. He called her "the unstinkable Molly Brown-Noser" and, when Clea rushed to her defense, grew venomous. There was always a mysterious—I should say sadomasochistic—undertow between those two, a tacit agreement that Clea literally bow her head in penance as the blows rained down. After a blunt screed that cut her to the quick, he strode through the sandy gap in the brush and headed for the pounding waves. Clea took her shoes off and followed, sprinting as he sped up. I leaped in pursuit until I felt Miriam's hand upon my arm, holding me back. We already possessed the physical shorthand of lovers; both touch and look assured that Clea was in no imminent danger. Time and again she'd seen the couple play out this scene and knew best not to interfere.

We went back to the main house to decompress. Miriam drank wine and I guzzled Diet Coke as we numbly mingled among guests before saying our good-byes to Morgana. For the first time, she stood back and sized me up. There was real kindness in his mother's eyes as she thanked me for having come all the way from Los Angeles "to be with the family, such as it is." Morgana knew that my father was a honcho—she was good at retaining details, however hastily imparted, particularly when they applied to money or status—and tenderly asked if I'd "look after" her boy when he did his *Starwatch* "thing." She was full of shit but I liked her nonetheless.

She turned to Miriam and stage-whispered, "There's a plot for him beside Jeremy's. When he saw that today, it made him *furious*. I know it sounds gothic, but it's . . . it's, well it's just *right* that he should be buried there. I *understand* Thaddeus having resentments. His father did *not* do well by him—not by *anyone*—it wasn't the best family but it's the only one we've got. The only one *he's* got—that's what I told him. My *God,* Thaddeus, no one fed you dog shit or Seconal! Nanny didn't masturbate you—far as I *know.* Maybe that would have been a *good* thing. By contemporary standards, we were the *von Trapps.* But Miriam, won't you *please* talk to him? About Jeremy? I mean, where else is there for him to *go?* His brother's been there over forty years. Forty years! And now Jack—" Tears welled up; she loved an audience. "And I shall be there, long before Thad. Though sometimes," she amended, "I'm not so sure. The way he *treats* himself . . ."

She took a fashionably loose cigarette from the pocket of her shirt; Klotcher appeared en passant to deftly light it before discreetly disappearing. Morgana inhaled, blowing smoke like a dragon.

"Did you know I made *every* effort? To breast-feed. But he *wouldn't take it.*" She waved a hand in the air, as if shooing a fly. "The doctors said something in the milk made him allergic. Now, how can that be? His brother gnawed that tittie till he was *five—ruined* it. Did you know Jeremy used to tear into a hamburger, then wash it down with a suck?" She smiled before returning to the matter at hand. "He *cannot,* it makes no *sense* for Thaddeus to continue . . . this—*vendetta* against his twin. So will you talk to him, Miriam? Because I know he listens to you. I know he does."

She walked us to the door.

"I don't know what's going on between those two," said Morgana, rather hush-hush. "But it *cannot* be wonderful. You *know* that, Miriam. She's not *good* for him. She's not *welcome—I won't* have her here again in this house! Why on earth did I allow it? I suppose it's because I'm getting so damn old. The old guard let her ol' guard down."

The face softened to a smile again. As we walked out, she said cryptically, "I *militated* for that boy's happiness. Absolutely militated."

— • —

I wanted to make love in the worst way but Miriam needed food in her stomach; the day had taken its toll and she was wobbly. As we waited outside for one of the drivers provided to ferry guests into town, we scanned the grounds—immensely, guiltily relieved that Clea and Thad were nowhere in sight.

Back in the village, we had burgers (*sans* milk) and Miriam drank more wine—I came dangerously close to sharing a glass— while romantically snuggling in a booth. My mood cycled again, shedding the skin of gloom, doom, and ill tidings it acquired at Michelet Manor. I felt reborn: suddenly, I couldn't have been happier being on the other side of the country, frisky, depleted, flirting with insobriety, my own migraines of the soul on storm watch. As Miriam's appetite abated, along with nausea and *nausée,* she grew hungry for something else,[2] running her hand under the table. Picturing us in various XXX-rated poses, I frantically signaled the waiter for our bill. As we loped past the registration office to Miriam's cabin, I leaned into her in erotic play, low-growling and hot-breathing while she giggled, a wolf and his well-read Riding Hood. Then suddenly, a break in continuity: eyes and ears perked: officiously, she nodded toward a taxi pulling up to the cottage adjacent mine. Out stumbled Clea. I sighed. Miriam shrugged, quickly kissing my neck before departure.

I rushed to help my poor, dear sister, who stood fumbling in her purse for a room key. When she saw me, her eyes welled with tears.

"Please . . ."

She nearly collapsed in my arms. I half-carried her to my door and, as we staggered, turned to find Miriam—already gone.

---

[2] Forgive the lapse into pulp. A writer needs to try a bit of everything.

Clea was in a state. She smelled rankly of booze, pathetically informing that her boyfriend had thrown a drink on her blouse (still wanting me to believe). She fell directly into bed, letting me strip off her clothes. The moment I lay down beside her, she seized me with agonized, asexual fury; each time the grip became too painful, I relocated those tiny starfish hands. Clea cried and cried, in contorted, schoolgirl plaint—"But *why?* Why! I'm his *friend*." "I *told* him I was sorry! I didn't mean it to *happen*, but nothing really *did*, Bertie, nothing really *did*." "He doesn't *care*, it doesn't *matter*, there's nothing I can *do*."—while I used my free fingertips to carefully blot away the tears.

I unfurled a reluctant fist with its clutchful of pills. She confessed to having swiped them from Morgana's medicine cabinet. I was touched because even though she was in terrible pain, Clea knew I'd be proud of her for not having swallowed them. She broke my heart.

I left the bed long enough to flush them down.

When I climbed back in she was fast asleep. Why was that snorish sonata of breath so poignant? I lay on my back, spooning her into me. I put her hands on my chest but they kept slipping off like penguins from an ice shelf.

Then I too slept, and was grateful for it.

CLEA STAYED ON AT THE Vineyard, or thereabouts.

The days passed in a flurry of artistic endeavor. As already mentioned, I was intent on developing a spec series for HBO. I thought the time was ripe for a literate drama about the movie industry (though others before me had tried and failed), and was busy circling an idea I'd christened with the Aaron Spelling–like title *Holmby Hills*. I didn't have much more than that—OK, I'll admit I had casually referred to it among friends as a cross between *The Sopranos* and *Entourage*—and while it sounds strange, I *did* own up to a special feeling about my unwritten saga. Dad always said "the gut" should never be discounted. I met with Dan Fauci, an old-school friend of my father's who used to run Paramount Television. Dan suggested I get to work on what he called a bible, the guidebook for any projected series. (A perfect word for it: I really *had* got religion.) Still, it was harder than I thought to let go of the writer/director fantasy. It was one thing to strive toward an Emmy but quite another to envision oneself on the red carpet at Cannes jostling elbows with Lars von Trier. Among activities outside my duties on the *Demeter*, I'd continued to stockpile ideas in the hope of eventually shoehorning them into script form. The punctilious archives, composed mostly of newspaper and magazine articles, went back years, even including a series of pieces about a traveler who somehow lost his citizenship while in transit and had been forced to live at an airport, improbably marooned without passport or country. I remember the day I read in *Variety* that Spielberg was going to direct Tom Hanks in that very saga; a movie that's already come and gone. It was moments like that when, salving my wounds, I shouted from the bridge the reliable, "Warp nine!"—a kinky confirmation that, if nothing else, I had a producer's instinct for good material.

Predictably, Miriam and I had a phone sex affair though it wasn't easy keeping up the pace. Pretty soon I was faking orgasm and I suspect she was too. We settled into a comfortable, R-rated hotmail exchange: flirty, dirty, unpressured—anything else seemed like too much work. (Besides, we were time zone challenged.) I dated around, nothing serious. I tried to avoid anyone from production or AA, which pretty much limited me to the gym. The pickings were surprisingly slim. Funny, but if I so much as kissed a girl, it felt like cheating. I kind of hated that.

It was almost a week since Clea and I had spoken (she had time off because she wasn't in the current *Starwatch* episode) and I was just starting to worry when without warning she appeared on my doorstep as I left for work. She looked lovely and rejuvenated; all was apparently idyllic with our happy, happily manic-depressive couple. There was a bit of softshoe damage control about the death of Jack Michelet as the Big Event, the tacit implication being that her once and future beau's abominable wake-side behavior was somehow justified. She was willing to guarantee that while Thad "blew it all out" and had shown the worst of himself, this was the absolute end of it. He was born again, eager to enter the genteel, chivalrous phase expected of him. I didn't buy a word of it. I wasn't sure whether to feel sorry for her or admire Clea's brave-heart tenacity, so wound up doing a bit of both.

Call me codependent (you wouldn't be the first) but I got nervous whenever Ms. Fremantle had too much time on her hands. One didn't need to go to Death Valley to find the devil's playground. Her current *Starwatch* persona, the polymorphously perverse grease monkey from Albion-12, hadn't made an appearance in the last few shows and I was concerned the writers were phasing her out. So it was with a mixture of relief and misgivings when, over ritual Sunday morning scrambled eggs and tofu at Hugo's, she told me the mechanic's role *had* been cut, in the service of a greater good—she would soon debut as Ambassador Trothex, the formidable Vorbalidian diplomat featured in none other than "Prodigal Son (Episode 21-417A)," Thad's upcoming two-part extravaganza. It was a meaty role but one I thought exclusive to that particular story; I had trouble seeing how it would recur. Anyhow, we didn't get into that. The new makeup, she said, was different enough that audiences wouldn't recognize her from her previous incarnation. (I wondered how they were going to deal with the complete change of character from a PR standpoint; but again, not my "wheel house.") I was genuinely happy for her. I saw the hand of Thad Michelet—perhaps even my father's divine intervention—in her promotion, and was intrigued the three of us would be working together on a more level playing field than I'd anticipated.

COMMANDER WILL KARP HAILED FROM KANSAS City, Missouri (according to the writers, who themselves hailed from Harvard and Yale). A highly decorated gunner, he was a veteran of the Nardian Wars. Ladies man and marginal wit, he retained the chauvinistic whiff and wink of old Star Legion glory days.

Some "bible" backstory: Karp—uh, that would be me—was the son of a legendary warrior who, after a disfiguring battle wound, became the academy professor and beloved mentor of Frederick Ulysses Laughton, current fifty-something African-American captain of the distinctively ellipsoid, overmerchandized *Starwatch* mothership USS *Demeter*. Along with Laughton, I joined Lieutenant Commander Iltriko Shazuki (relatively new to the show, she'd been a minor player on *Will and Grace* and recently staged a satirical one-woman show at a theater on Cahuenga, playing nearly twenty characters); Major Glaston Cabott 7, the captain's all-purpose android-de-camp (a storied second-generation player in Chicago's Steppenwolf group, and of H-P mascot fame); and Dr. Phineas Chaldorer a.k.a. X-Ray, the *Demeter*'s handlebar-mustachioed Sultan of Sickbay (having made a fortune as the Prius pitchman, he was rumored to own a microbrewery *and* a vineyard in the Malibu Hills). I was already friendly with our congenial ensemble—most were in AA—but will maintain character names throughout, to avoid confusion.

The morning we did our usual preshoot read through, sitting around a table while the writers fine-tuned dialogue, Mr. Michelet was in subdued, if friendly, spirits. Not wishing to broadcast their relationship, Thad and Clea were careful about hanging out. They fraternized in a cordially standoffish way, as if to throw us off the scent. I found it silly because I didn't think anyone gave a shit but since I'd concealed my own affair with Miriam, I tried withholding judgment. I was that big a person.

Michelet was a hit with cast and crew. Getting him on the show was considered a coup that raised everyone's stock. The fact that he was a Renaissance man with a long, prestigious résumé was a balm to the large part of our troupe who felt they'd sold out, or at least lost sight of one-time lofty goals and aspirations. The gang lit up whenever he walked in the room. Even if, deep down, they knew life on the bridge was as good as it would ever get, all were warmed by his fire and its inherent promise of escape from the golden wormhole of artistically stagnant sci-fi syndication. Besides, the man had made real money out there. The actors were well versed in Black Jack's harsh legend and recent passing, and when comfortable enough to give voice (it only took a few days), the complicatedly bereaved son found himself touched by their concise, carefully chosen words of sympathy. It was a gift of Thad's that he could relate to the most pretentious of cast and roughest of Teamsters, snaking his way into hearts with the ease of, well, the microbial parasite that took the genial shape of a traveling circus clown in "The Ringmaster Cometh (Episode 14-321D)." Our close-knit soundstage family was ready to kill for him before filming even began.

On the first day of the shoot, I hovered at the bridge near my marks while actors took places for camera rehearsal. Clea coyly whispered to the A.D. something about Thad being "delayed" in the makeup trailer—a detail the man no doubt was aware of. (With all her caginess, I thought it oddly reckless.) The grapevine had it that our beloved guest star was of a mind he looked asinine in his facial prosthetic, and the makeup department, Emmyless for fourteen seasons running, was in an agitated funk. A couple of coproducers were dispatched to mollify Mr. M; after an hour or so, the director called "Action!" anyway.

We got as far as Thad's entrance and were about to block the rest of the scene with a camera double when he finally appeared, stepping from the shadows in a drab ensign's uniform, his countenance a macabre yet somehow tender dodecahedron of glinting latex planes—grand variation of Clea's lower-caste Vorbalid mug. The utilitarian outfit, deliberately duller than those of the workaday crew (a brilliant stroke, I thought) made the physiognomy fabulously theatrical; like a peacock in a Pep Boys jumpsuit, we saw only the clipped tragedy of aborted phosphorescence. A hush fell over the stage.

"Ecce Vorbalid," Thad proclaimed, with Lear-like abandon, beaming gregariously through the geometry of applied flesh. Not many knew what those words meant but everyone sensed that at last he was pleased. The ice was broken, and the majesty of his creation acknowledged with a burst of applause. The makeup folks, pardoned by the king, lifted their collective heads from the guillotine.

—·—

We were surrounded by windows. Not windows, really, but their facsimiles—cutouts from which one peered at "star curtains," the crude, perennial backdrops that provided the illusion of deep space.

For those who aren't fans of the genre,[3] let me shorten and summarize: I was poised behind Lieutenant Commander Shazuki, peering over her shoulder while the harried communicator tried to make sense of a hash of data on the plasma screen. Waiting for camera to roll, I focused on the sexy, cyclonic hair swirls on the actor's neck and my mind went off on a jag—youngish people in the news who of late

[3] You may be legion.

were dying of sudden, unexplained aneurysms; the catching up I had to do with TiVo (*Venom ER* and *SeaLab 2021* were auto-deleting right and left); the spam calls I was getting on my cell phone from "pharmacies" wanting to sell me Oxycodone—when suddenly Shazuki began talking about some weird "energy ingot" which had appeared out of nowhere. She was referring to a photon probe (I couldn't believe the writers were still using *that* one) that gauged the so-called ingot to be just a meter wide, "an impossibility according to all known laws of physics." Reflexively, I told Shazuki to keep an eye on it—it was probably just expansion gas. (I always got expansion gas after a good photon probe.) At this point, Android Cabott 7, the butt, if I may, of most of my heavy-metal humor, *whooshed* through the central door of the bridge.[4]

"I've been monitoring your concerns from my quarters, Lieutenant Commander," said the droid. "Status report."

"It seems almost . . . *sentient*," said Shazuki, eyes glued to the screen.

"I can hear . . . *words*. Almost like great populated *cities*—"

The captain and ship's doctor *whooshed* in. The ingot was discussed. Everyone was pissed at the idea of anything fucking up our long-planned R&R on the pleasure colony Darius 9. In an unmotivated segue, the captain wondered out loud where the hell the new ensign was; the doc said Rattweil had motion sickness. I made a crack about how Legion recruiters were scraping the bottom of the barrel and the captain told me to stow it. Someone else made a disparaging jibe and the captain said, "I *will* not tolerate gossip or the species-ism it dresses up in. Ensign Rattweil is a Vorbalid—one of the very few, I may add, to have migrated outside that closed, repressive system. I'll remind you such a journey is punishable by death, and *not* for the faint

---

[4] The door was actually pulled open on ropes by hidden grips, with the whoosh added in post. Everything you always wanted to know about space opera but were afraid to ask.

of heart. He will be afforded the respect presumed—*demanded*—by each and every member of the starship crew. Understood?"

Our penitent eyes were still cast downward as Thad *whooshed* in, cued by a second A.D.

The captain looked him over. "Feeling better, Mister?"

Thad stood in comically rigid attention. "Yes sir!"

"I hope you found our infirmary . . . adequate." The captain's mood turned lighthearted, suddenly curious about the curious new man.

"Dr. Chaldorer gave me something for my nerves."

"A motion sickness suppository coupled with a jigger of old malt whiskey did the trick," said X-Ray.

"I think," said Thad, "the culprit may well have been the commissary bouillabaisse."

"We have the finest chef in all the Legion," the captain remonstrated. "The bouillabaisse is native to his undersea world and considered an exquisite delicacy."

"The Vorbalidian stomach," Thad said dryly, "is bicameral." The crew suppressed a collective titter. "I was merely faulting my own physiolo—"

Suddenly, a jolt.[5] Alarms blared as we braced ourselves against the curvaceous sides of the bridge. Lights flickered, and things went generally bat shit. The starscreen that hung above grew blank then staticky. We lurched to our posts as the ship stabilized.

"Lieutenant Commander!" shouted the captain. "What's going on?"

"The energy ingot, sir! It's—pulling us in!"

"Commander!" barked the captain, jarring me from an erotic reverie that had ranged, in milliseconds, from my darling Miriam to

---

[5] Again, for the cognoscente: whenever the *Demeter* came under assault, an A.D. would instruct the actors to "shake"—but only the cameras moved. Also, I implore the readers to forgive excerpted "Prodigal" dialogue, for it is not my own.

a newbie at AA to the young Judi Dench, whom I'd just seen in a seventies film on TNN. "Engage! Warp five!"

"Captain," I shouted. "The instruments are frozen!"

"Then *unfreeze* them. *Do* it, Commander!"

"Aye, sir!—"

"Red alert! Engine room, damage report!"

"Still checking, Captain!" said the script supervisor, tucked behind a camera. (Her voice would eventually be looped.)

"Warp plasma inducers?"

"Intact. We have full power, but we're 'locked in.' I've never seen a tractor beam of this magnitude, sir—"

"Bypass?"

"There's no way," said Cabott. "If we continue the attempt to free ourselves, we risk implosion."

The captain leaned into the subwoofer-thingie to bark the patented bridge-to-engine-room "Realign the power grid!" (always a crowd-pleaser) before asking Cabott how much time we had. The android nanocalculated point-two-seven hours, at the outset.

"Will," said Laughton, with (patentedly) urgent, almost seductive intimacy—it was the writers' idea that whenever the shit hit the fan, crew members were to be addressed by first names—"*Get us out of here.*"

I tried the instruments again but they wouldn't budge. I shouted that we were being sucked into a vortex (at that moment, hating myself as both actor and man). The captain puzzled over what— *who*—was pulling us—while Thad stepped forward to stare gravely at the starscreen.

"I believe," he said, "we are being appropriated by the Vorbalidian System."

"Appropriated? What's the meaning of it, Ensign?"

"It's obvious they feel that a hostile incursion on their sacred Dome is imminent."

"But, that's . . . madness!" the captain opined, a bit over the top.

It was one of those days where it seemed like he was doing an impression of himself.

"If I am to read the situation correctly," said Thad, "their behavior can have only one meaning." The bridge grew quiet as the camera dollied in on the rubbery, fetal face of the tyro ensign, his sweaty gaze pitched upward toward blue screen. A slow-zoom intercut would later reveal the lame-ass ingot in all its hoary, kandy-kolored tangerine-flaked digital glory. "It is a declaration of war."

Before cutting, the director bade us stare a few extra beats in varying degrees of freaked-outedness at the screen, which in postproduction would project the twisted, Alfred E. Newmanesque visage of the badasssssssss Prince Morloch, his psychotic smile glaring down at us from the garish, faux-marbleized sanctuary of the Vorbalidian Dome.

THAT DAY, MIRIAM FLEW IN.

Ostensibly, she was here on business—to see Thad do his bit on the *Starwatch* set. Naturally, my secret hope was that she'd arranged her visit for the sole purpose of our getting, ahem, reacquainted. With a jealous twinge, I wondered if she'd been on any dates herself and if I'd popped into her head as she had into mine. The agent was ensconced a few floors below her client, who'd sensibly downgraded (with Miriam's prodding) from the penthouse to an Art Deco apartment replete with piano, sixties-style kitchen, and long stone terrace. The girlie part of me thought it would have been fun if she'd rebooked our first-fling digs; maybe she wasn't the nostalgic type. Still, there was a brave new boudoir to explore and I looked forward to beginning the courtship afresh.

The four of us planned a late supper. Mr. Michelet wrapped at

3:00 P.M. (the sudden onset of a headache being coincidental to his early release) and went back to the Chateau to lie down. Clea and I finished "chores" a few hours later. We drove to my gym on Sepulveda. I liked spending an hour on the treadmill, watching the latest dumb and dumber CNN horrors while Clea went through her paces in a cardio class of bitch-slapping, *Showgirls*-style aerobics. By the time we shook, showered, and protein-shaked, it was nearly eight.

Walking down the darkened hall of the Chateau, I could see the door to Thad's suite was ajar. A muted Miriam greeted us with warm hugs, whispering how Thad's migraine had become full-blown and they had to give him a shot. Indeed, the doctor was injecting him as we entered. The off-duty ensign wore a threadbare LAUGH FACTORY T-shirt; there was something sadly sweet sad about the grimy ring of Pan-Cake foundation still clinging to his neck. Clea rushed to the couch and kissed his cheek. He smiled adorably and said, "Call me Olga" (which only occurred to me later was an allusion to Chekhov's headache-plagued schoolmarm). He gave me a wink.

"Bertram," he said. "Darling, *darling* Bertram . . ."

I didn't feel I'd yet earned such affections and was wary of his making fun. Such sensitivities betrayed my depths of feeling for the man.

"What are you giving him?" asked Clea of the doctor as she held Thad's hand.

"A suppository and a shot of old malt whiskey," said Thad, gamely.

The medico was in his late forties, with closely cropped white hair.

"A migraine cocktail," he said. "Demerol and Vistaril."

Clea cooed her tiresome *When Harry Met Sally* "I'll have what *he's* having" number—sleazy and overobvious. I was never a fan of the exhibitionist side of her that thought it hip to advertise addictions; to me, it vulgarly telegraphed relapse.

"V is for Vistaril," Thad uttered, on the way to feeling no pain. "V is for vomit. V is for Vorbalid."

"Will he sleep?" asked Miriam, conversationally. I imagined she'd been through this before.

"Like a patient eulogized upon a table," said Thad, droopy-lidded. It was somehow reassuring that even in his current state he still liked a pun.

"He'll sleep," said the doctor. "We like to say the medicine won't necessarily make the headache go away—it just won't bother him anymore."

"Wait," said Thad, suddenly queasy. White-faced, he shakily stood. Clea braced him, as did Miriam from the other side.

"Do you want to go to the bathroom?"

He winced, his face relaxing as the vertigo receded. He took a deep breath before settling back on a pillow.

"That fucking starship bouillabaisse . . ."

"If you need to throw up, go right ahead," said the doctor, folksily.

"Don't be facile," said Thad, soft targets refocusing.

"A *horrible* patient," said Miriam, apologetically.

"Oh, he's not so bad. But I should wait a while. He may need another shot."

"You'd like that, wouldn't you? What are they? Two hundred a pop?"

"Thad!" scolded Clea. "Give the man a break. He came all the way at rush hour."

"Dr. Chaldorer would never be so venal."

"Is that your regular physician?" said the doc, affably.

"Not just *my* physician," Thad rejoined. "He's responsible for the entire *crew.*"

"The film crew?"

"He's a character in our show," informed Clea, with a slight roll of the eyes.

"You're an actor," said the doc. He was a little square—I mean, not only could you see Thad's Pan-Cake, but here we were at the Chateau. *Hello.*

"He's doing *Starwatch: The Navigators*," Miriam offered.

I thought it strange the otherwise savvy, intuitive Miriam could grow situationally clunky, cheaply broadcasting the most negligible details of Thad's identity or career—like an old-fashioned flack, she didn't seem to have a clue about when to withhold or divulge. (I flashed on her painful chatter with Klotcher on the Vineyard.) At such moments, she seemed perversely inspired to blurt out whatever insipid, useless thing was most likely to wound or set him off.

"Now you *do* look familiar," said the doc, warming to his subject. "Were you in that Don Quixote movie?"

"Yes, he was," said the proud Miriam.

"I saw it on a plane. It was great!" Everything fell into place. "Your father's the writer?" No one responded. "Jack Michelet? The novelist?"

Shockingly enough, Miriam skillfully aborted exploration of the topic by thanking him for his services.

Turning to Thad, he said, "I want you to try the Zomig." The doctor gathered his things. "If he feels a headache coming on, he's to take a pill. They're two and a half milligrams. He can have up to four, but no more than ten milligrams—total—per day. That, plus the Vicodin. If the headache's still there, I want you to call."

"Careful with those Darian showgirls, Doc," said Thad, good humor briefly returning. "Remember: alien 'pelvics' can be a bit pesky. Better to triple-glove."

"Will he be able to work tomorrow?" asked Miriam.

That was another annoying trait—her tendency to ask a mindless question for which she already knew the answer. But why was I subjecting the girl to such brittle scrutiny? Simple: too much time had elapsed since we'd shagged.

"I don't see why not. He might be a little unsteady on his feet, but he's an old hand. The show must go on, no?" He gave Miriam his card. "Call my office or pager. And I can always be reached through the hotel."

"Do you make housecalls? I mean set calls?" asked Thad, in earnest.

"It's been known to happen. Yes. That can be arranged."

— • —

"Do you feel it yet?" asked Miriam of the drugs.

"Hasn't quite kicked in."

"Oh bullshit," said Clea, our resident expert. "It's been at least half an hour."

"I'm a woman on the verge—the mere knowledge the stoned Pony Express is galloping through the bloodstream with those leathery ol' *saddlebags* of painkiller molecules brings me exorbitant comfort."

"Are you really going to feel like eating?" said Miriam.

"It's probably not a great idea to load up on food," I said, supportively.

Clea came and sat beside him. "Why don't you let me put you to bed?"

"Because I want a shrimp cocktail, OK?" said Thad, imperious. "Don't worry—I won't aspirate. And french *fries* and a fucking *cheeseburger. Everyone* has to order, is that understood? Mister Karp? Call room service immediately or I'll kick you where the six Darian suns don't shine! As acting captain of the good starship Demerol, I command you!"

— • —

Thad's stamina was pretty amazing. We played half-assed duets on the piano, messily eating our food while Clea and Miriam sat on the terrace, smoking and murmuring girl-things. I knew it was neurotic but ever since we met I'd worried he thought of me as just another inane, rich lummox from Clea's childhood, or—far worse—that I was boring. Sitting side by side on the lacquered bench of the Kawai, I began to loosen up and be myself; maybe it was a contact high. I fantasized we could really be friends. The truth was, I *did* feel boring next to this man—I didn't necessarily want to feel his pain but coveted his cadence and complexity. I understood why Clea was so drawn. I actually wanted to please him, and decided that was all right. So we laughed and pounded the keys and I did those impressions I used to haul out at parties years and years ago. At some point, I coined the phrase "endorsement rush" (what athletes feel when they sign a big product deal) and Thad laughed so hard the girls wandered in to see about the commotion.

The three of us had early-morning set calls. Miriam and I left, so Clea could tuck him in. (To our relief, she was staying over.) I walked her downstairs just before midnight and, happily, she asked me in. My curiosity piqued because whatever Miriam had in mind wasn't amorous; she'd made that clear enough by saying she had "overdosed" (tonight's theme) on Motrin, due to "Godzilla cramping." Too bad—if she thought I was going to reject her polite invitation, the hint fell on hard-on ears.

Because the rules of engagement (or against it) were already set, the lovely suite took on a kind of formal, faintly clinical cast. For one of the few times in my life, I regretted following my dick—suddenly it felt like we were in the sitting room of a mortuary. Miriam poured herself a drink, fetched me a Diet Coke from the perfectly restored fifties fridge, then plunked herself down on the floor with great cross-legged intent. There was something she needed my advice about.

Thad was in trouble with the IRS. He had a lifelong gambling problem and Morgana perennially bailed him out—but no more. (I was shocked his mum had done as much.) The government forced a lien against his Manhattan apartment and he was struggling to make payments that with penalties and interest approached $35,000 a month. Miriam said he was drinking and drugging more than usual since Jack's death, and enduring extreme writer's block with the new book as well; whenever he was really bad off, he phoned at all hours to go on about Dostoevsky's gaming woes. The end result of these agonies was frequent headaches that necessitated "the ingestion of analgesics." Ironically, the pills caused a rebound effect (actual medical term), which began the vicious cycle of migraines all over again. It was excruciating for her to watch him self-destruct because she held the guy in such high esteem and truly cared so much. She wanted him in good shape for "all the wonderful things coming his way." "This is his time," said Miriam—and she really meant it. She had planned a meeting with Mordecai Klotcher because it was her opinion there was a good chance the producer would option one of Thad's books. Aside from that, she was keen on pursuing the potential game-show franchise William Morris was pushing. She wanted a flurry of meetings and auditions, not just with indie folk but high-power directors who also happened to be long-term fans (Joel Schumacher, Cameron Crowe, and Tim Burton came to mind). Most of all, she wanted Thad Michelet, whose life had been filled with torment, to be *happy*. In that regard, she was of the tenuous, desperate, wistful opinion that Clea Fremantle was a short-term, stabilizing influence, even though the two "had some history."

I sat down on the floor opposite her. "You said you needed my advice."

She was a little drunk. I was tired, my attention still held by the unlikely prospect of sex.

"Well—it's something I did. I did something, Bertie . . . and it's just that now I'm not so sure it was such a great idea. The thing is, I'm not so sure *William Morris* is the place for him to be. I mean, *now*. At this juncture. They haven't gotten him anything for a while—any *features*, I mean. And that's his bread and butter! I think they're a little disorganized. I still do *lots* of business there so don't get me wrong. They want him to do commercials. And that's OK. But he loves doing *movies*. I mean, if he has to *act*—which most of the time he'd rather not!—he'd rather be writing but that doesn't pay the bills. And you *know* how he likes the obscure theater stuff, but—they're not exactly lining up around the block to finance a two-act adaptation of I. B. Singer's short story 'The Slaughterer'! And the really *good* indie stuff doesn't come along that often . . . and if you wind up doing a little movie and it sucks, it *sucks*. You know? Suddenly, you're the person in the little thing that sucked. Whatever. The person who tried to do the hip indie thing and failed failed *failed*. Not that failing's a *bad* thing. But I just don't think our little guy needs any more practice *at this point in time*. But in the right *feature*—a *studio* feature—oh, Bertie, that's where he *shines*. The La Jolla thing was canceled—you knew?—the Beckett. The money fell out. Which wasn't shocking—to *me*. And it's OK because it gives him . . . he likes to do a *big movie* because he's *in* and *out*—Bertie, he can do four a year and make a *serious* chunk o' change! Which is what he *really needs—now*. Boy, does he need it! *Then* he can go write. Or *try* to. Or do *whatever*. He can check into Canyon Ranch—that's what he likes—and write and lose weight and hike. Pilates and all that good stuff. Fact is, he got *this* job cause of your dad. Your father *loved* Jack Michelet, loves his work. And that's *fine*. But you knew that. *Everybody* loves Jack Michelet. Isn't that always how it is? They love the monster? Well, they don't know Jack. Didn't. *'You don't know Jack.'* Isn't that how that goes? I mean the name, there's a game called that? Perry thought it'd be *fun*, God love 'im—I mean, *he* loves Thad *too*, in his way, and that's *fine*— fun to have him on the show. Which it would be. Which it *is*. Right? Class it up. What else is new. Thad's used to that. The 'class clown.' Clown with Class. And that's *OK*. As long as he's getting his *goodies*. You know, William Morris wasn't even *involved*. I mean, they made a nice *deal* for him, *with my help*. But . . . they would have fucked it up. They would have fucked it up if I—"

"Miriam," I said impatiently. "What was it you—"

"Bertie, Thad is *completely on his ass*." She was getting drunker. I began to kiss her neck but she warded me off with a smile and a coy twist of the head. "I mean, *financially*." I put a hand on the inside of her thigh and she let me; easier now to pay attention to her tangled speech. "So I had this amazing *idea*. I called your *dad* and talked to him."

"You called my father?"

Now I was intrigued.

"Bertie, I *know* this is going to sound *completely insane*. I called your dad and told him—of course I introduced myself and we talked about *Jack* and how Perry's a big *collector* and he told me how he optioned one of Jack's *books*, yadda yadda—I told you and I had met but I swear I didn't use your name *in vain*," she said, with a sexy lift of her brow. "And I asked if he knew Thad was a novelist too. He had no idea! Or maybe he *did*, but forgot—whatever. But I think he was actually kind of *tripped out* when I told him. Anyway, I said I was at Barnes and Noble and saw the *Starwatch* books—the series, right? *Starwatch: The Navigators*. You know about that, right? There's like, *sixty* of 'em. Sixty episodes novelized from however many seasons. And I wanted to know if Perry might be interested—I haven't even talked to *Thad*, and I was *very* clear about that when I spoke to your dad—I asked if he thought anyone—meaning *Perry*—*hel-lo!*—might be interested in *Thad* potentially adapting the episode he was currently shooting. 'Prodigal Son.' I mean, into a novel. For the book series. It's a no-brainer, right? It's genius! Because maybe that might be *fun*. And this was a bit of a shot in the dark, OK? Because his *agents* aren't thinking about him in those terms. His *agents* aren't thinking about him in *any* terms except, like, doing a Verizon voice-over. I mean, nobody knows what kind of *trouble* the man's in, Bertie! *Nobody knows the trouble he's seen!*'—she sang the latter in old negro basso, making me hornier—"and even if they *did*, nobody even fucking *cares*. So I called your daddy, OK? Because I *love* Thad and *someone has to help him*. And I know they probably don't pay all that much but it could be one of those 'event' things. We could turn it into that. A little harmless spin. I mean, Thad's getting *top dollar* for 'Prodigal Son' and I'm sure I could get him a nice paycheck for adapting it as some stupid fucking paperback they're probably going to adapt *anyway*. But that's not even really the point . . . I thought if I could at least get him *writing* again, for *money*, even if it's not some *fortune*, at least if someone'd *pay* him to *write*, which he does better than like *ninety-eight percent of anyone out there*, then maybe the creative juices would start flowing, OK? Right? For his new book. You know? No? Does that not make sense, Bertie, or does that not make sense. Anyway—there ya have it. So I guess what I wanted to know is, well . . . what do you think? Did I fuck up or did I fuck up?"

— • —

The next few days of shooting went well.

Thad was footloose and headache-free. The meds, whether contraband or prescribed, didn't interfere with his work. He was a pro as always, bringing wildly interesting touches to his work when he might easily have slipped into rote. Clea was definitely getting loaded again, something she couldn't hide—not from me, anyway. The first sign that a reformed addict has lost her sobriety is when she starts dropping clues about the amazingly powerful effect an over-the-counter anti-itch pill had just the night before on her "virgin system." An even stronger indication of a slip is when said addict volunteers how the synergistic combo of, say, Robitussin—for that nagging, three-week-long cough—with Wellbutrin (Clea and I were of the non-Nazi sobriety school that didn't consider drugs for depression or OCD to be taboo) managed to produce actual stumbling and slurring of words. Incredible but True! AA's *Believe It or Not* . . . By making such faux-naïf observations public, the dope fiend craftily seeds the ground—or clouds, if you will—to justify the coming shitstorm.[6] So it was with extreme

---

[6] I always find it amusing when actors maintain they got hooked on painkillers because of bone breaks, neuralgia, and herniated discs, or began using speed to cope with the punishing hours of film shoots. Why is it that no one ever comes out and says, "I love the way it makes me feel! Stronger and prettier, smarter, sexier, luxuriantly numb! I hate myself less! I'm not afraid of terrorists! I can even love *you*, and the whole god-abandoned world!"

skepticism that I greeted Clea's casual announcement that she'd tripped on a rug and fallen down the night before (hence, the subtle limp) due to the totally bizarre and unexpected effect of mixing Zoloft, Benadryl gel caps, and Allegra-D. She caught my glance—really more of a grimace—my palpable displeasure giving her enough of a reason to cease and desist our get-togethers at the Sepulveda gym. Brunch at Hugo's was out as well.

I took a deep breath and told myself to stop the judgy, codependent nonsense. I could barely manage my own life and had no right or reason to micromanage hers. What was all this about, in the last analysis? Residual jealousies vis-à-vis Thad? Or maybe I was the one who wanted to get loaded—and resented her easy, guilt-free indulgence. Maybe I was the one with the death wish.

Then I told myself that was bullshit. She was fucking up big-time and I wasn't going to be there to pick up the pieces.

WARDROBE WENT ALL OUT: CLEA wore a diaphanous tunic, a madcap yet demure rip-off of a widely publicized haute couture design which had appeared on Parisian runways just two weeks before. How strange, seeing Thad and Clea stand together with transformed, angular faces that, while not exactly gruesome (perhaps I'd grown accustomed), were still within shout-out of an atavistic nightmare. It was as if I had donned special glasses, affording a view of the ordinarily imperceptible "alien" dynamic that lay just beneath the surface of any chemically complex, long-term, passionately erotic alliance. I wondered how Miriam and I would look, through the same magic spectacles. Probably nowhere near as interesting.

We were pondering whether to have the strawberry shortcake or peach cobbler à la mode when Nick Sultan, our properly English director, arrived with a tray of meat and potatoes. He diffidently asked if he might join us (directors always seem to begin their meals just as everyone else is finishing). Not wanting to be rude, we obliged.

"That was *such* a great scene," he said.

He referred, of course, to the moment in which it was revealed that our own Ensign Rattweil was none other than a Vorbalidian prince in exile. See, Thad's father, the king, was near death; hijacking the *Demeter* was the family's way of bringing the runaway royal home to take care of unfinished business—i.e., the sticky wicket of succession to the throne involving his nasty twin, Prince Morloch.

"I was in *tears*. You were *brilliant*." Gentleman that he was, the helmer hastily included Clea and myself (glimpsewise) in his encomia. "I'm *so* glad you're doing the show," he said, now strictly addressing the famed guest star. "You wouldn't *believe* who's addicted to *Starwatch*. It's *bizarre*." The last, accompanied by a fuller glance in my direction, as I must naturally be the residing expert on the cult franchise's global appeal.

"I know," said Thad. "I read somewhere that Rumsfeld's a fan."

"Yes!" said Nick, gleefully. "I'd heard that! And *Dylan*! Dylan's supposedly obsessed!"

"Wow," Thad said, without irony.

"David Sedaris is very big on it."

"Really."

"Oh yes. And the girl who wrote—not *Adaptation* but . . . *The Orchid Thief*. And who's the *Atonement* writer?"

"Ian McEwan? You're kidding."

"McEwan! Yes. *Big*, big fan."

"Well . . . I'm shocked!" said Thad, in dismay.

"By the way, I hadn't told you, but I thought you were absolutely *amazing* in *Quixote*. Brilliant!"

"Thank you. Working with Terry is an 'experience.'"

"Gilliam! *There's* a wild bloke!"

"He's *very* wonderful."

"A *mad* boy but a wicked talent," said Nick. "And great good fun. We worked together ten years ago, in Scotland." Thad didn't bother inquiring further. "Did your father ever see the show?"

"I don't think so. Dad didn't watch much TV. But you never know!" he exclaimed. "I could be wrong—Jack Michelet may very well have been a closet *Starwatch* fanatic! Right up there with Ben Stiller, Naguib Mahfouz, and Susan Sontag! Could've been"—this, à la Charlie Chan—"Numbah One Fan!"

"I guess," Nick conceded, "you don't become that prolific sitting around watching the telly."

Thad registered the innocent comment as a dig: *performing on the telly was an existentially malignant exercise.* You might as well be a clown with leukemia.

"I hear you've written books," said Nick. "Novels, right? To me, that's *absolutely* the toughest thing. And to write in the shadow of that *man*." He grinned, shaking his head. "Bit like being a sherpa to Hillary."

"Our styles are pretty different," said Thad politely, gathering his tray to leave.

Clea's face was like a Tornado Alley weather vane—the tremble before the wild-ass spin. "Does he mean Hillary Clinton?" she said with a fake smile, buying time so that some of us could make it to the storm cellar.

"Rather like me having John Huston for a father—to put it in filmic terms." Nick shoveled up peas, potatoes, and a fatty square of pork chop. "Tell me, though, didja feel a lift with his passing? I don't mean 'glad.' It's just that, well, personally, I was so *competitive* with me old man. Most sons are. And he was no genius, thank you—thank *God* for that! Not that *I* am. Compared to him, *maybe.* A haberdasher, he was. Good at what he did, worked on Savile Row.

Never saw a *thing* of mine, not even a student film. S'pose he was competitive as well, maybe more so. What I'm driving at is: was it a lift, Thad? Is it *easier* now that he's gone? In the sense of, well, d'ya find you're doing a bit less shadowboxing?"

"Not really."

"I don't mean to psychoanalyze! Probably projecting a bit—still working out my own stuff. When I was in college, I read a book of his called *Chrysanthemum.*"

Again, Clea blacked up. Noticing her mood change, Thad grew strangely perky. "Glad to hear it! It's not one of his better-knowns."

"True," said the director, matter-of-factly. "Can't say why."

"There *are* some rather explicit passages," said Thad. "Almost pornographic, don't you think, Clea? A few of the libraries tried to ban it, stateside. A town somewhere in Ohio actually had a *book burning.*"

"Don't fuck with Ohioans!" said Nick. "Did an Old Navy shoot there once, don't ask me why. Lovely college, though—Wexner? Wexler? Spoke to a film class; gave me a brickload of coin. There's money there but it was dull. Thuggish. Middle American, right? Not for me. I'm a bit of a mad boy, like Terry. I'm *dying* to do a feature." He rubbed his hands together, like a hobo at a trash-can fire. "TV's fun but you're a bit in the box. It *has* grown up, with cable and such. I mean, it's what Dennis Potter was doing thirty years ago, hunh? Hard to watch your mates pass you by. Tony Minghella and the Scott brothers—those were me mates! They threw me some commercials—they're the kings of that world—but I won't spend my life on cranes swooping down on a fucking *Lexus.* If I want to give a BMW a blow job, I'll do it in the privacy of my garage, thank you very much! The really *great* thing about TV is it's so fucking *immediate*—I don't have to tell *you*—doesn't drag on a year or two, like film. Still, I'm chompin' at the bit. There's nothin' like the movies!" He paused to shovel in food. "But they kill you if you're 'askew,' right? If that's your sensibility. What'd they do to Orson Welles? *It's All True.* Ever see that? The studio fucked him in Brazil while they mutilated *Ambersons* in L.A. That's how they reward you if you're 'askew'! Still, I'd love to have a go at *Chrysanthemum*. It's one of those pieces I dread picking up *Variety* to see it's snapped up by someone who's going to mutilate it—or worse, do it justice!"

He laughed heartily at the last remark.

"I'm gonna go have a cigarette," said Clea, then left.

"I was wondering, Thad? Have you written for the screen? Have you thought about it?"

"Well, yes. But I don't suppose I've made a serious effort."

"Might you consider adapting *Chrysanthemum* to film? I'm bloody serious, you know."

Thad's face froze in a creepy smile; I chose to intervene.

"You know, Nick, I'm pretty sure my father has the option on that."

"Oh yes, I know! And we've talked about it, Perry and I—we've discussed it. Casually, at first. When he found out how passionate I was about the property . . . well, that *he* owned the option turned out the most *amazing* thing. Magical, really. I mean I can't even remember, we were talking and it just came out of nowhere. He didn't mind the idea of attaching me to it, on a handshake—that's how *I* like to do things. How your dad operates too. S'pose that's how he's gotten all this way, right? When I suggested *Thad* have a go at it, he thought: Brilliant! We were having a coffee and Perry said your agent—she's called Miriam?—he said Miriam had already been in touch about novelizing 'Prodigal Son.' I thought that a tragic waste! May as well put you to work on something epic, something decent, right? Something really *brilliant*."

WHEN THAD LEARNED OF MIRIAM'S scheme, he seemed too weary and disgusted to be angry. I watched him go through the motions of confronting her at the hotel, where, like showbiz gypsies, it was our custom to indulge in a nightly room-service supper, regardless of the prevailing hunger or mood. Miriam shrank while Thad shook, rattled, and ultimately rolled the offensive, well-meaning gesture off his back with a shrug. It was my sense he knew there was a large part of Miriam that might never understand him yet would do anything to aid, comfort, and support. She was true blue and for that, he could never fault her. He was also well aware she must have been as frustrated by his miserable luck and rapid-cycling, self-defeating nihilism as he. After all, it was Miriam who'd stayed in his corner through the years, even when it wasn't profitable, which now it seldom was. They had known each other forever—she'd been closer to his folks than any of his friends—and one of the things he appreciated most was how she had never evinced interest in becoming professionally involved with his father's business. There had been opportunity; Jack Michelet was famously persuasive, one time suggesting out of sheer spite that Miriam become his agent too. She turned him down cold. Her allegiance was total.

It was a cheap psychological insight, but I suppose he'd transferred ambivalence toward his mother onto Miriam. While my encounter with Morgana—tetchily ennobled by widowhood—was brief, the description of soul-killing ice queen didn't seem to fall far from the mark. (Not that Miriam shared any of those qualities; on the contrary.) I tried to imagine what it would have been like to be despised by both dad *and* mom. It'd been my experience that in these United States, sons take it for granted that fathers are useless, absent, or malevolent; if not a cipher, the prototypical American patriarch is almost certain to be a disgruntled knight, jousting with underequipped offspring in never-ending phallocentric battle. (Per-

haps I've revealed more of myself than intended.) Male progeny
come to expect their martyred mom—a victim herself—to be waiting in the wings with smelling salts, hot towels, and tears of sympathy for her best and brightest. Yet, when Mother herself is hostile, a
boy is in danger of becoming a kind of orphaned enemy of state. In
Thad's case, things were even worse, as he'd been scapegoated by his
twin brother's death; a kind of walking, wounded repository for Jack
and Morgana's displaced rage and sorrow. Maybe it would have been
like that anyway, even if Jeremy Michelet had grown up to fulfill
whatever lush promises were envisioned—some deep, chromosomal
karma already in play, the acrimonious troika fated to beat the feckless pariah to death the way chimpanzees sometimes do their own—
beloved alpha twin already well on his way to joining his folks in
rapturous filial abomination, their formidably contemptuous blood
united in sensual loathing of that dead-ringered excrescence called
Thad Michelet, shat out nine minutes (upside down, no less, and
blue in the face) after the Chosen One.

— • —

It was with mild surprise that I found myself pumping Miriam for
historic details re: the House of Michelet on the morning I drove her
to LAX (a Thursday toward the end of the two-parter's first week of
filming; I was on hold till after lunch). I was trying to glean the look
and feel, the *fabric* of Thad's early life. It was uncharacteristic of me
to have the energy for such a campaign—a welcome distraction
from my usual self-involvement. Subconsciously, I suppose work
had already begun on this very narrative, the writer in me instinctively gathering pigment to make a fireside portrait of the artist as,
well . . . a man.

"You met Jack Michelet at Yale?"

"Uh-huh."

"I thought you met him through Thad."

"Uh-uh. I was a student there. He lectured."

"Right. And . . . so you—did you . . . interact?"

"There was a Q and A, then we took him to dinner."

"Right."

"What's with 'right'?"

"What do you mean?"

"You keep saying 'right, right'—"

"So? I'm within my rights."

"You are *such* a dufus." She laughed and lit a cigarette. "*No,* I didn't sleep with him, if that's what you're crudely angling at. Which I *hope* you're not because that would be *really* offensive." Then, apropos of nothing: "Do you think they're going to blow up the airport today?"

"I think that's scheduled for later in the week."

"Oh! I forgot to ask what you thought of Miss Clea's big idea." I shook my head. "The TV show—she didn't tell you?"

"No."

"It's probably a surprise."

"What."

"Maybe you should hear it from *her.*"

"Come on, bullshit. What is it?"

"She wants to do a sitcom with Thad. Not a sitcom but more like a 'dramedy'—is that a word? A smart improv thing, like *Curb Your Enthusiasm.* That's what *Clea* said. About what it's like to have a famous mom and dad. She and Thad would star but I'm not sure she meant they'd actually play *themselves.* That part sounded kind of too 'reality show.' But I think she thinks they could get away with having, like, famous *fictional* parents, with fictional vocations. I mean not, like, a big movie star and a famous writer but maybe famous in some other field. She wants to pitch it to the networks while Thad's still here. I *like* it. I mean, if it's done like Larry David, I think it could be really great."

—·—

After we finished shooting that day, I stopped by Clea's dressing room.

I mentioned hearing about the celebrity offspring project from Miriam. I was actually kind of hurt she hadn't brought it up—we always hashed over dumb ideas together—but Clea prattled on, coolly ignoring my sulk. (All peevishness aside, I thought the idea was exploitative and trivially bogus.) She caught my mood but neither of us wanted to go there. We knew we'd been in murky waters of late. As a peace offering, I asked if she wanted to hit the gym.

When Clea said she was having "sciatica" problems, I smugly asked, "Why don't you just tell me you're using again?"

"What?" Her face contorted in a loony smile, as if I'd gone psycho.

"Oh please! *Please* don't bullshit me, Clea. It's so *pathetic*. And *really,* really sad, OK? You've been doing *so great.*"

"Don't you fucking patronize me!" She gathered her energy before making an actor's choice to commit to a lie. "I've been in *pain,* Bertie. If that's *all right with you.* I've been to *three* acupuncturists and *four* chiropractors. I've had *two* MRIs"—I was wondering where she found the time—"and *no one* can figure it out, OK? I took *one empirin codeine,* OK? I was on a shitload of anti-inflammatories— *nada.* I can't sleep, all right? You *know* what happens when I can't sleep. I *freak.* I slur *words.* I can't learn my *lines,* I *panic* attack. *You're* lucky. You don't *have* those kind of problems. You're so fucking *blessed.* You know what? I may really *want* to. And I'm not saying I *won't.* But at the current *moment,* I am *not* getting loaded. OK?"

"You sure act like you are." I wasn't proud of proselytizing but the train had already left the station. "You need to be careful, Clea. People are gonna know. It doesn't *matter* if the reason is legitimate." (I gave her that.) "People aren't going to give a shit. You've worked too fucking hard—"

"Yeah, right!" she said, sarcastically. "It's so artistically *gratifying* to sit in a chair for ninety minutes and have four pounds of latex glued to my face! *Tell* me, Bertie: what's gonna happen if the *world press* finds out I'm taking a little *codeine*"—she spat the word out with supreme condescension, like it was a multivitamin—"to relieve some *shitty, intractable* pain. Is Katie Couric going to call, Bertie? Think they'll want me on *Dateline*?"

"Why don't you lower your voice?"

She kicked it up a notch instead. "Is your daddy gonna ban me from the dunking booth at the next *Starwatch* convention?"

I backpedaled, without softening my message. "I'm just saying you have to start going to meetings again. And you need a better doctor," I advised, indulging her fantasy of musculoskeletal alignment. "An orthopedist. Gita's the total maven—she'll find you one." I took on a somber tone. "And you have to be careful, Clea. You're with him *all the time*. Look: I really like your boyfriend but he's a major addict-alcoholic. I know it's hard not to use when you're sleeping together."

"You *know*, you *know*, you *know*," she mocked.

"Yeah well one thing I *do* know is it isn't great for you to be around that, twenty-four/seven."

She paused before blurting out, "You're fucking Miriam."

"OK," I said, with a dumb smile.

She was trying to gain a little control. I couldn't blame her for that.

"So. How's that going?"

"It's not really a steady thing. But fine. Thanks for asking." I waited a beat before reasserting my point. "I worry about you, Clea. I don't want you to disappear from my life." The cliché was on the treacly side but I meant it.

"Like, you mean, die?"

I stuck to my tough-love guns. At the risk of sounding like a Brentwood shrink, I said, "That's one way of disappearing."

"As if you would *know*."

A cryptic cheap shot—she was playing the dead-mother card.

"There's a lot I don't know," I said, Zen humble.

My equanimity infuriated her. She raced around the dressing room, throwing things into the duffel I'd bought her at Miu Miu. "As *painful* as it may be, Bertie, you are *not* my father—OK? You are *not* my father and you are *definitely* not my mother. You're not *Thad's* father, either." I braced myself, knowing the worst was to come. "Do you want to know who else you're not?"

"I have a feeling you're going to tell me, Clea."

"That's right, because nobody else will! No one has the *balls*—cause you're the son of the *great Perry Needham Krohn*. I'll *tell* you who you're not, OK? You're not *your* father—and that must *really fucking hurt*. That must fucking suck! And I know you're really *trying* to be? With all your fab little HBO projects?" Her voice kept rising, Valley Girl style. "And of course *no* one—none of your *pathetic, downtrodden friends*—can even *dream* of having a project but you, huh, Bertie? I mean, God *forbid* that *I*, the *loser queen*, should come up with an idea and go pitch a network! Without your blessing!" She peppersprayed the room with saliva as she vented. "And I *know* you're trying to climb out from under his shadow—and that's so OK. That's really OK! Cause you're a sweet kid, Bertie, and I love you and you've done a *lot* for me, but you know what? I would *never* judge you. Never! Because maybe one day you'll *succeed*. Wouldn't that be amazing? I would so celebrate that! Maybe one day you'll surpass the achievements of the great God and creator of *Starwatch: The Fucking Navigators*. Maybe you'll have a bigger house than *he* does, right in Malibu! Maybe you'll build it on *stilts* in the fucking *water* and block his view! Who am I to say? Who is the *fucking loser queen* to say? And who are *you*, Bertie? Who are *you* to say, and go judging my shit? Know what your problem is? You're busy monitoring my life when you should be checking your *own* shit. OK? Do you think you could maybe do that, Bertie? Do you think you could maybe find the time to check your own shit? And leave my shit alone?"

I FELT BAD ABOUT WHAT happened.

Anyway, Clea was right—I *had* been judging her. I felt like a jerk. I was genuinely worried about her sobriety yet somehow managed to come across as petty, hostile, and competitive. I had immediately gotten off on the wrong foot by dissing her TV idea. We'd never had an argument like that, and it didn't sit well.

Friday, around midnight, Clea called, crying. She said they got into a big fight at the Chateau and she was on her way back to Venice. I invited her over but she needed to pack for a Roosevelt Chandler event over the weekend, in San Rafael. At her request, the promoters had booked a room in a sleeper car on the Coast Starlight—Thad was supposed to have accompanied her but now she begged me to go. I was happy she'd phoned at all, and eager to repair the rift. The convention was on a Sunday; we could fly back that night. A car was coming at 7:00 A.M. to take her to Union Station. Clea said they'd swing by and pick me up.

— • —

As we entered the echoey terminal, redolent of another era, we saw him sitting at the end of a row of chocolate-brown leather Art Deco chairs.

Thad poked his head from the collar of his tweed coat with exaggerated contrition—no longer Chan, he was Chaplin now—and clutched a bouquet of roses. He wore a broad smile and his Movietone pantomime instantly melted her heart. I was glad of it because anything (especially at that time of morning) was preferable to having a scene.[7] Before I had the chance to discreetly bow out and beg off, Thad, with the inherent skill and muted enthusiasms of a concierge, confirmed his suspicions that I was more than a simple escort—I was carrying a small overnight bag myself—and had indeed been enlisted as

---

[7] OK, it was hard to stay mad at him. So I'm an enabler, I'll admit. Feel better?

Bruce Wagner

boon traveling companion and general shoulder to cry on. At that point, I *did* begin my retreat but he would have nothing of it. Ordering us to "sit tight," he strode to the reservation desk, returning some twenty minutes later to inform he'd secured a second deluxe bedroom on my behalf, "just two doors down from Mom and Dad."

Clea's eyes told me she was more than happy with the new arrangement. I had a feeling that my role as chaperone would calm the waters—besides, I was actually looking forward to the singular relaxation and magical musing time that only a train trip provides.

—•—

The deluxe cabins were on the small side but their solitariness made them feel more than ample.

After scoping out my new habitat, I serenely organized my things, like a fastidious man embarking on a long journey. Comfortably ensconced in my chair, feet propped on its opposing twin (a dinner tray sprang up handily between them), I faced northward, the bare bones of the *Holmby Hills* bible before me like a financial spreadsheet, ruminatively clutching the absurdly expensive fountain pen my mother gave me on my thirty-fifth. Leaving the station I felt surreal, like someone traveling alone without rhyme or reason. I didn't plan or expect to see friend or her lover until we reached our destination, some fourteen hours later.

A conductor collected my ticket.

A Central Casting porter knocked.

I asked for Diet Coke, a bucket of ice, and a few extra pillows.

I phoned Miriam, childishly eager to play "Guess where *I* am?"

(She relished updates on the Michelet-Fremantle soap.)

I got voice mail but didn't bother leaving a message.

I went to BlackBerry her, realizing with small irritation that I'd left the thing behind.

Rambling from the vast yard, I set chin on fist in classically informal meditative pose. Say what you will about Amtrak's chronic insol-

vency but there's something insistently, imperishably romantic about
a train. The sounds and smells and gentle rocking, the funhouse
ambling from car to car (and nostalgic memory of childhood it elic-
its), the pneumatic mobile mystery of it all more than make up for the
occasional derailment, electrical failure, toilet overflow, or death by
train vs. auto. A ride on the rails has never failed to awaken an
unbearable sense of longing, the whole mournful package—this
touching anthology of rhythm and blues—stirring a tenderness
within, enlivening me to the great, prosaic poetry that is our lot.

Somewhere around the Ronald Reagan Library, Clea's words
began reverberating in my head—"You're not your father and that
must really fucking hurt!"—her face dissolving first into Liz Taylor's
then Dorothy Malone's, a demented montage of *Who's Afraid of Virginia Woolf* and *Written on the Wind*. I was reminded of an AA meeting some weeks back where the speaker told a large crowd that if an
"adult child" didn't resolve his animosities toward a given parent, he
was doomed to *become* that parent, a pop platitude that still rang
true. I'd always been on careful lookout for overt signs or wonders of
my inner Perry Krohn, often catching the man's looking glass leer
amid so-called enlightened dealings with the ladies—the way I
tended to objectify or condescend toward, rage against, malodor-
ously charm, or smugly indict. (For some reason, I never focused on
traits I'd acquired from Gita—the empowering, honorable, nurtur-
ing ones, no doubt, of which Miriam pleasurably found herself on
the receiving end and wasn't shy about declaiming, with sweet sarcasm, "Without Gita, you would be a shit.") I think ultimately I
came to believe I had worked through the complex relationship with
Father, completed the course with honors, so to speak, and that my
behavior in the world was now perfectly *au courant*, dictated by an
independent, if flawed, self that paid no homage, heed, or mortgage
to the flawed being from whose seed it had sprung. See, I'd rejected
Perry's ethos and struck out on my own at a relatively young age,
pretty much escaping unscathed (that was what I told myself and

still believe it's for the most part true), returning to the fold of my own volition—or should I say Vorbalition. By her harsh comments, it was obvious Ms. Clea thought otherwise. If viewed in a colder light, I suppose there will always be some residual sense of impotence or jealousy regarding Dad's power and station. At least I consoled myself with the idea that I didn't suffer as Father did from Failed Artist Syndrome. But maybe I protest too much.

It was all trainworthy food for thought. It was possible Clea was working through her *own* father issues. I'd met Freddy Fremantle plenty of times at the house when Clea and I were kids. He and Roos were amicably divorced. He lived in Mandeville Canyon, a debonair talent agent rarely seen outside an amazingly tailored, subtly pinstriped charcoal gray suit—perhaps courtesy of Nick Sultan père!—a slim, suntanned *mensch* of ready, overwhitened grin who suffered a massive coronary infarct while visiting a client's film set in Rome. (At the time, if I recall correctly, Roos Chandler was already ten years in the ground.) Father and daughter were quite close and as I summoned his memory, along with those windy, sultry Bel-Air summer days and nights, I felt a pang of guilt—I was on a roll—over not having spoken to her about Freddy since we'd reentered each other's lives. I suppose that was another characteristic I shared with my dad, and wished I could exorcise: if a thing required delicacy of inquiry or effort, sometimes I elected to act as if it never was, willing it into emotional nonexistence.

Bucolic scenery overtook my sunlit berth—it grew leafier as we neared the coast—and the musing dominoes fell one to another until eventually Mother was struck. (Though she was no pushover.) I wasn't thrilled with myself for not having spent more time with her since she became, in the parlance of her fairly recent station, "nonambulatory," but my lapse was mitigated by the fact she was a proud woman who no doubt would have interpreted a rush of attention from her loving, characteristically standoffish son as a bit of an insult. For that reason, and because she was so fiercely independent, it was Gita who gave the impression of wishing to see less of *me*. (Though maybe I was wrong about that too; maybe I was wrong about everything.) I still felt badly because when I *did* speak to Mother, it was of asinine, mundane things like the general, obscenely ridiculous state of the world or my hygienically censored romantic life—all in tidy sound bites, with nary a nod to anything of sophistication or depth, not even a gentle probing of her own predicament nor the heroic shifts and adjustments it must have required: never a testing of waters to see if she wished to speak of anything that may have disturbed or distressed—mortality, say, or the general mortification of flesh, a subset being Dad's philandering and long-ago abandonment of his wife as a sexual creature, a wound at least now sealed and cauterized by the diagnosis and progression of her disease. Not that it was my role to play therapist or confidant. But it *was* my role to treat her as an equal or, rather, a superior being (which she clearly was), *not* as an old friend with whom I'd lost touch and on bumping into at a party felt shoddily compelled to bring up to speed. In short, instead of taking this invaluable resource for granted, my job was to be a good, righteous, compassionate son. Judging from my performance, I should have been fired and forcibly led from the building.

As I pondered these inadequacies, locomotive lucubrations got the best of me. My mood plunged as we approached Santa Barbara (it had taken three full hours). There was a sudden pounding at the door and I sprang to life, rescued by an ebullient Thad, who suggested the three of us adjourn to the dining car for lunch.

— • —

Late that night, I wandered from my cabin to the glass-domed parlor car exclusively designated for those traveling by sleeper. I fixed myself a coffee at the bar and settled into a couch facing the dark waters of the ocean. With a slight start, I noticed an ember flare within a bundle of clothing at the purplish settee's end. My eyes adjusted; it was

Thad. Huddled in wool, as if against an invisible onrush of elements, he held a glass in one hand and a flask in the other.

It was his turn to walk the shifting rails of self-reflection.

"Clea's asleep," he said.

"How's she doing?"

"She's amazing. She's really much more amazing than a person has a right to be. Trouble is, I'm not worthy of her."

The moon was nearly full. Occasionally I glimpsed the sacred ribbon of highway running parallel to the sea. I've always had a sense the Beat spirit of Highway 1, the wet, gusty, yellow brick promise of it, can never be adequately conveyed to those not reared by its banks. Possessing a majestic, quintessentially Californian indifference, it rolls and advances by hillock or high water toward the gigantine cliffs of Big Sur and beyond, rugged and celestified, graveled, gravid and golden, beflowered and embedded with the ghostly hitchhiked heft of 10 million hippies' hajj to the phantom mecca of the Haight.

It disappeared, swallowed up again—clickety-clack.

"My brother and I loved that movie *The Time Machine*," said Thad, pouring himself something stiff from the silvery filigreed flacon. "One day we actually *built* it—from a chair in Dad's study. Did you ever see that movie? Remember that red velvet *chair*? We fastened all kinds of shit to it: stuck a bicycle wheel to its back that we could spin. By the time we were finished, there were all *sorts* of dials and levers and throttles. Course, Jack was out of town at the time. It was his *writing* chair and I don't think he would have appreciated it! He was in Capri. They were making a movie of a book of his, *The Death of a Translator.* Alain Delon and Sophia Loren. Ever see it? Jeremy was going to visit—Dad, in Capri—and I was supposed to stay at home with Mother because of my asthma. I'd have fits in the middle of the night and couldn't catch my breath. Plus, I don't think Morgana and Jack were getting along. A minor detail! (They rarely did.) Oh but Jeremy *loved* the idea *he* was going to the 'Isle of Capri'—that's how he referred to it—and *I'd* be left behind. He

really was the Chosen One, you know. We were twins but *very* different. He was Pollux, the immortal; I was Castor . . . that's why it
didn't make any sense when he died. The gist of it was—at least the
way we overheard it explained to *friends*—the idea of separating
us—you know, the psychologists' fad at the time was this *separation
thing* with twins. Of course, Jeremy wound up going to school in
Switzerland, which actually would have been a torture for me—even
as a kid, I didn't travel well—but back then I was enormously jealous. It sounded so fucking glamorous! Come *on*. And I think it probably *was* glamorous . . . skiing around, doing all those alpine things
with coquettish principessas and future despots, wearing cashmere
cable knits, drinking cocoa or champagne or schnapps or whatever at
the foot of the Matterhorn, God *knows* what they were doing. I used
to tease Jeremy when he came home for the holidays—I was actually
pretty good at that—because he had this incredibly affected accent,
sort of Continental—we were only eleven or twelve, you know how
kids pick stuff up, to fit in—so many students at that school were
the scions of dukes or duchesses. Lords and royal lardasses. Jeremy
would say 'row'—'Mom and Dad are having a row'—and I
absolutely *savaged* him about that. Made him furious! When the fact
is, I was jealous. Hurt. *Violently.*

   "So we built this time machine the week before he left for the Isle
of Capri (he was on a school break and had flown home from
Switzerland a few weeks before to see Morgana). We used it to go
back to prehistoric times and *way* into the future. Must have been
charming to watch . . . if one could have hidden behind some bush
with an eight-millimeter camera—what I wouldn't give to see a
home movie of those two little time travelers! Do you want to know
the most amazing thing, Bertie? I don't even know if you'd call it
Freudian . . . but you know what time I wanted to go back to? Morgana, giving birth! I'm serious! I kept spinning the wheel and all the
crazy dials, saying, 'Oh! We're at the hospital now!' 'Oh! Now we're
in the delivery room!'—and I'd make Jeremy pretend Mommy had

her feet in the stirrups but this time *I* was coming out first. "But *I* was first, *I* was first!" he shouted, which was the truth, by nine legendary minutes. Or something like that. Jeremy went fucking *wild*. Because there I was saying we were going to *change* all that! He said we *couldn't* because it already happened and the rules were you couldn't change what already happened. The rules! Oh yes, there were rules. But can you imagine? The two of us going on like that?

"About five years ago, I was in a store in Manhattan. One of these side-street movie-memorabilia shops. They had it in a glass case—a beautiful copy of the time machine, an *authentic* one, an actual model from the movie. Beautiful upholstery, tuck-'n'-roll, soft, tufted, brushed velvet, tiny gold widgets . . . and that fantastic, whirring engine wheel! Whoever made this thing was a *genius* in miniatures. *Incredible* draftsman. I asked the nerd behind the counter if I could buy it and he said it wasn't for sale but he would give me the number of the guy who built it. Great! Fantastic! So I called and found myself talking to the *creator*. Went out to Coney Island, that's where he had his workshop. Bertram, I am telling you it was *unbelievable*. Here's this *man-child*, this sweet, lonely wizard surrounded by spare parts of all the fantasy machines he'd constructed for films—like that toymaker from *Blade Runner*. There was a half-built time machine on one of the drafting tables (there was a *ton* of debris, very 'Santa's workshop') and I was suddenly just so touched that my brother and I weren't the only aficionados. Apparently, there was this whole *secret society* . . . a worldwide fraternal order! And I really had to bend his arm—he said he was busy with so many things—the guy was very convincing!—but he finally agreed to build me one. I said, Take all the time you need. And I meant it. See, I knew he was kind of squirrelly and I wanted to make it easy on him because I understood his temperament. He wasn't of this world! He was an artist. I mean, if that's how you spend the bulk of your time, you're not fully on the planet, right? And what he was creating for me was this ephemeral—this magical mystery memory thing—how do the CIA say it? 'Eyes only.' *My* eyes only. A Caligari cabinet. Fabergé egg. I'm telling you, I was the ideal client—or 'patient'! That's probably the better word. And *man*, it was *really* expensive—I can't remember exactly how much, maybe seven or eight grand. But *totally* worth it. At the end of the day, I was going to have this *amazing* sculpture, this talismanic *fetish*. I thought it was a fucking bargain.

"So the months go by and finally I heard from him. 'Progress is being made,' he said. Funny-looking little guy—I wish you could see his face. But he needs more money. OK. No problem. I'd already given him an advance, right? A few thousand. So I send fifteen hundred. Then I wait and I wait—I must have waited another *year* because that was the deal, I said from the get-go I wasn't gonna hassle him, and I meant it. One day I call to see how he's doing and he says more or less the same thing: He's waiting for a *part*, he got sidelined by a big *studio* project . . . now I start to feel like I'm being had. I give him an ultimatum—still friendly, mind you—but I tell him I really need to have the little chair in two months' time. That's the deadline. Nonnegotiable. He says OK—but never delivers! I'm getting pissed off. He doesn't answer my calls. I'm starting to think lawsuit. So—and I can't remember the time sequence—I actually wind up going to Small Claims! To file. Can you imagine *me*, at Small Claims? You can't, right? It's insanity. I have no idea what drove me to that—I mean, I was frustrated, but still—anyway, after however many weeks I get a letter from the court telling me the person I sued was requesting a delay due to the fact that he was traveling on business. *Right*. A light goes off: something clicks and I realize that my fragile little model maker, my exquisitely tender *artiste*, is extremely well-versed in Small Claims! Knows the System, through and through! Been through this sort of action before—broken lots of hearts. Whatever. I don't give a shit. I become obsessed with justice being served. *I want my time machine!* The motherfucker's welshing on my *time machine*. And I'm, like, totally enraged! I'm serious,

Bertie! Part of me is genuinely galled. Because there I was, trying to reclaim some part of my fractured boyhood—and there *he* was, defrauding my innocence!

"It went back and forth: another date would be requested, and the tinkerer-con would delay—then *I'd* be unavailable and would have to go in and see the clerk to set another time on the calendar. And so on and so forth. And you couldn't do this shit by mail, you had to go *in*, right? This was pre-'online.' It became this bureaucratic ritual. Finally, the day comes we're both due in court but the asshole doesn't show. My moment of triumph! I thought that'd be the end of it—I'd win by default—but the tinkerer-stinkerer knew better. The judge rules in my favor but says his ruling could, most probably *would*, be appealed. He was actually tipping me to the guy's M.O., right? The judge was saying in so many words that I was involved with a pro. OK. So now we're talking maybe thirty-five hundred dollars that I've laid out in terms of advances, *plus* time spent filing, driving, parking—I actually kept a little leather satchel with receipts! You couldn't put a dollar amount on the raging and bullshitting that was going on in my head. Right? OK? Are you loving it, Bertie? I haven't even thought about this in fifteen years or whatever.

"So another eight or nine months pass—eight or nine months!—and the thing's fucking with me, mentally. I wasn't working so I've got *way* too much time on my hands, all right? He's got me turning into Lenny Bruce! I'm actually starting to get *paranoid*. I was on all this medication—lithium and shit—these were the pioneer days of bipolar!—but I'd stopped taking it for the reasons you always do and I started to drug a bit. That's the cycle. OK? And I'm getting more and more *fixated* on this fucker. We're getting closer to the legal endgame—is this not *fantastic?*—where the court's gonna have to rule against the tinkerer's appeal. Meanwhile, I've been doing all this reading—about stalkers and assassins. I'm not even sure how I got into that. But one of the books says sometimes the snapping point for these freaks is when they're humiliated by the court system. Like if a wife gets a restraining order against her husband and he kills her when he probably wouldn't have if she hadn't taken that final step, hadn't publicly *confronted*. I start to think (I'm also doing crystal meth, which isn't exactly helping my thought processes): what if this guy guns me down? Right at the courthouse? I mean, I'm a semipublic figure—I wasn't as known then as I am now . . . probably not too hard to find, though, right? You could spit Off-Broadway and find me in some equity waiver. What if this guy does a Stephen King—what was that movie with Jimmy Caan and Kathy Bates?—what if he kidnaps me and performs a little genital surgery? Or buries me alive in some sub-basement? This is what's going through my head, Bertie! So I go nuts a few weeks, looking over my shoulder, checking phone messages—then I start to think, *enough* already. We had a court date scheduled. Now, I wasn't sure if he was going to show, which at this point would have been worse for me, psychologically. He was probably out of options. Couldn't maneuver anymore. I do some serious thinking, and here's what I come up with: I'm gonna call the guy. That's right. I'm gonna call the bogeyman on the phone. Preempt him. I must have done a shit-load of coke and scotch and I don't even want to think what. And I finally call him up at like midnight—remember, by now, in my head, he's Arthur Bremer!—and I leave this message on his machine. He doesn't pick up. I'm relieved—sort of. Though part of me actually wouldn't have minded talking. So I say, See you in court. But nonconfrontational. I tell him I want to work something out— I'm talking to the *machine*—because I'm tired. I want to resolve it, *peaceably*. Totally whacked but trying to make sure my voice is friendly even though in the back of my head I'm worried he'll pick up in the middle and say, 'I'm gonna cut your dick off, stuff it in your mouth, and set you on fire! Put *that* in your time machine!' This is how psychotic I've become.

"We show up in court. And there he is, King Nerd—a white,

worried, harmless guy. We both sign some document saying we're going to work it out. He writes me a check for two hundred fifty dollars. And I don't give a shit. Fuck the money. And he's apologetic. Had this battered briefcase. Like me! A schlemiel. I actually felt sorry for him. Then I get this brilliant idea. *I'll ask if he can sell me the time machine I saw on his shelf the day I first walked in.* I don't even care if it's finished! I'll buy it, *as is*—for the thirty-five hundred I already gave him. But first, I need to ask if he still has it. I do and he says, Yeah. So fuck it, I'll get the sample. It won't all have been in vain. It'll even be funny, a kind of symbol of the folly of my great quest. So I say, Can I have that? For the two-fifty? It's actually thirty-five hundred but I say two-fifty. Then 'we'll be even.' And he says, No! Now, it wasn't so much that he didn't want to sell it that riled me—I mean, it was that too!—but I'm remembering the *way* he said it, like I was some rube who walked into Cartier to bargain them down over a necklace in the window. He was actually being smug! So I get this little smile on my face—at this point, I don't even want to ask *why* he won't sell it because the whole thing is like so piled sky-high with psychotic bullshit. *Then send me a Polaroid.* That's what I tell him—but still friendly, like, OK, you win. Right? I mean, it's so tragically *risible* that I thought a Polaroid would be a fitting souvenir. I asked if he'd take a snapshot—and all he had to say was yes, even if he never planned to—you know, my way of giving him a way out—and he says, No. Again! *He actually said that he couldn't.* In the same smug way: like I'm a tourist being reprimanded by a guard for touching the Rodin.

"On the way home from court, I wondered if the time machine I'd seen two years earlier had been a quickie mock-up, a cardboard plant, to lure me in. I mean, more and more the guy was like someone Ricky Jay would play in a Mamet flick. But to what end? What was the big score here? Thirty-five hundred dollars and a Small Claims hassle?

"A week or so later, I was recounting the story to Clea—this is a long time ago, we'd just started seeing each other—and I have this ecstatic revelation. Almost like a religious experience. I realize this man, this *tinkerer*, wasn't human. *The motherfucker wasn't real.* This wasn't my medication—or lack of it—talking. I came to the conclusion it was some kind of *entity* that was trying to tell me something. What it was trying to say was, you *can't go backward*—and you *can't go forward*, either. This . . . this schleppy *thing* was illuminating the arrogance of my aspirations, and the pain and suffering it had caused. I became *absolutely convinced* that if I tried calling the man's number again, there'd be a recording. That I misdialed—or it didn't exist. Not 'disconnected' but *nonexistent*. And if I visited where he lived, the little workshop would be shuttered or razed. You know, where you see the postman and he says, 'That place has been vacant for thirty years.' And I *knew* there'd be no record of our time in court—no paper trail. I didn't even want to look into it. I knew it all—and oh shit! That was *another* thing: I *lost the check.* For two-fifty. Never found the check. It fucking *vanished*. And to this *day*, Bertram, I'm a thousand percent certain my theory is sound. It's a *Twilight Zone* episode, OK? With a Zen twist. You believe in this kind of shit, don't you? How can you not? And it turns out—the moral of it—is one of the most beautiful things life ever taught me."

He paused, then said, "Do you understand, Bertie?"

I nodded.

He looked out the cold, dirty window into the dark.

"The week after we built our time machine, Jeremy went off to Capri to join my father. And that was where he drowned."

WHEN THAD SUGGESTED we find a way to occupy ourselves in quaint San Rafael during Clea's gig, she wouldn't hear of it.

She insisted on our presence in the auditorium during the tried-and-true cabaret-style tragicomic monologue that she performed prior to autographing photos, posters, and miscellanea, both Roos- and Clea-related, offered up by rabid fans. There must have been over 2,000 folks converging from God knows where (three of Roos Chandler's most famous films plus two obscure ones plus a rare home-movie clip were being screened) and I marveled at the organized industry of it. Clea's share of the take was a flat $35,000. The promoters couldn't have been happier with the bonus burger of her unexpected companion, Thad Michelet. In short time, the faithful flock miraculously handed over effluvia for signing—stills from *The Jetsons* and *Quixote*, that sort of thing. He was remarkably good-humored about it, I suppose still redeeming himself for his bad behavior of the night before.

We were back in L.A. around 10:00 P.M. The car dropped me off before ferrying them back to the Chateau.

AFTER HEARING ABOUT THAD'S BROTHER up close and personal, it seemed a morbid coincidence that Ensign Rattweil had been assigned a perversely devoted twin who'd remained behind with the Vorbalidian parents. The monstrous Prince Morloch was jockeying for the throne; for reasons of arcane galactic law which only the writers understood, Rattweil had been forcibly summoned from self-exile to bear witness to the royal succession. I should add that I made it a point to quiz the staff—had they been aware of the biographical detail of twinhood before crafting the teleplay? They swore they had not.

So it was with an air of bizarre anticipation that on Monday morning I found myself, along with Thad, Captain Laughton, X-Ray, and the android Cabott 7, loitering amid a barren landscape strewn with formidable-sized boulders—Soundstage 11's all-purpose blue screen wilderness. Cabott was compelled, in typically droll fashion, to inform us that instead of landing within the coordinates guaranteeing our arrival at the official Vorbalidian seat, we had instead corporealized in a wasteland, an error he attributed to the "most peculiar" qualities of radiation emitted by the Great Dome. We'd overshot the government enclave which, owing to its configuration when scanned from the ship, had the shape of a large white flower. As the *Demeter*'s resident wag and Earth world history buff, I—Commander Karp, rather—dubbed the buildings the Chrysanthemum Palace.

"Cabott," said the captain. "By your reckoning, how far are we from city center?"

The android glanced at a handheld device. "Around twenty thousand miles, sir."

"Pity," said Dr. Chaldorer. "I didn't pack my hiking boots."

Thad clocked the landscape with a dull shock of recognition. "I know this place—it's the Fellcrum Outback." When the captain asked him to explain, he informed it was ancient fighting ground. "Vorbalidian nobles often used blood sport to settle disputes."

"Curious," said Cabott, wrinkling his nose. "One of the most advanced of all known civilizations, engaged in gladiatorial combat."

He requested permission to reconnoiter soil samples. Laughton told me to accompany the major but remain within shouting distance. We exited camera right. The good doctor lazily positioned himself against a papier-mâché rock, of which there was a great profusion. I watched from the wings.

"What exactly happened between you and your family?" probed the captain.

"I'd rather not discuss it, sir."

"I'm *ordering* you, Ensign. By concealing your true identity, you've endangered a starship and her crew."

"I'm sorry, sir," said Thad, subtly flinching. "I never imagined they would—"

"I am not assigning blame. All the same, I expect some answers."

"I suppose . . . I never belonged." He plunged in without fanfare, delivering potential laugh lines as if abruptly from the analyst's couch—an unvarnished, marvelous choice that made him as watchable as it did vulnerable. "As the king's son, tremendous pressures are exerted. There are expectations. Responsibilities . . ."

"We all have responsibilities, yeoman," said the captain, tough yet avuncular. "Mine is the *Demeter* and her crew. That's what it means to be a grown-up."

"You couldn't understand," said Thad, wandering toward a clump of lime green stalactites. A touch of Monty Clift savvily crept into the stutter of sturm und drang. "There was no privacy—to study the things I cared for. No time to be *myself.*" A smile graced the captain with the realization he had engaged an exotic, overgrown adolescent. "The days and nights were empty, filled with mindless pomp and circumstance."

"I assume there *are* necessary evils to growing up as you did . . . though I have a hard time imagining 'pomp and circumstance' high on that list. May not a prince be able to choose how he spends his day?" asked the captain, slipping into the manneredly aggressive mode that had become a veritable staple of *Mad TV* parody. "He has merely to *assert,* to *demand*—"

"I am not my brother! He *revels* in the trappings of palace, the glory of his *subjects.* My father always said he was a throwback to olden times. Morloch is a warrior—his whole life has been a rehearsal for kingship."

"But *how,*" said the captain, with the sensual, stammering breathiness that was his hallmark, "did you come to leave a world that was your home? To give up your birthright as *prince* . . . for the corridors and engine rooms of a Legion starship?"

"I—I ran away," said the ensign, sadly. His father's shame was such that the royal court was forced to tell the people he had perished "while on what we call a Kuzda: a spiritual rite of passage endured by Vorbalidian males similar to the 'vision quest' of your American Indians."

Suddenly, the captain had newfound admiration, impressed by the "moral ferocity" it took for the ensign to give up family and monarchal inheritance in order to live as a free man.

"That," he said, "is true warriorship."

"I've had time to think about it, sir." Thad grew pensive, readying himself to walk the plank of one of those lowbrow-highbrow *Starwatch* soliloquies. "I've concluded it was fear that exiled me— fear that banished me from the kingdom of my life. You see, Captain, I was in love with a woman, and ran away under the cloak of 'integrity.' I was afraid I would abdicate and bring her disgrace. You cannot imagine what it's like to be born a prince yet know in your heart *you are not that.* Rather, you are a foot soldier of mediocre stamina, little ambition, and less vision: in a word, an ensign." Pause. "And that I have become."

"True," said Laughton, in full-bore Emmy throttle. (A few writers had converged just out of eye line to behold the harvesting of the fruits of their labors.) "I cannot. Nor can you imagine what it is like to awaken each morning a foolish, frightened boy who must convince himself—and his crew—that he is captain of a starship." At "Cut!" the crew applauded both men. We broke for lunch.

—·—

I ate barbecued chicken with a cute little gaffer. Upon finishing, I noticed a production assistant loading up a tray with assorted desserts. I assumed correctly they were destined for Mr. Michelet and told the P.A. I'd bring them to the trailer myself.

As I stepped into sunlight with my clumsy burden of sweets, Clea intercepted, steering me toward makeup. They were redoing Thad for the scenes featuring his twin—Morloch was to have a slightly harder, "Brechtian" edge. They held him captive in a big barber's chair while a rash of newfangled skinware was applied. His hair acquired extensions, some wrapped in the same aluminum foil that covered the peach cobbler and melting vanilla ice cream; he looked like something out of Ed Wood. The guest star was allowed a moment's respite so Clea could insert a spoonful of pie into his mouth before the gals went back to the surgical task at hand. An assistant director knocked at the door: he was needed on set. Another five minutes passed while cosmetic snake charmers called forth the cobra Morloch, then ten, then fifteen, the mood typically urgent, sweaty, and airless as walkies crackled outside and the nervous messenger hovered, fearing he'd be shot for the delay. Finally, the dark prince was released. Clea and I walked him to the soundstage, preceded by the A.D. as if by royal retinue. Occasionally, a bustling carpenter or grip whistled or shouted approbation of the ensign's charismatically toxic transformation.

Thad strolled abstracted to his off-camera mark.

Clea and I had a few minutes to catch up before shooting began. She said Miriam called with good news: Mordecai Klotcher had expressed interest in *The Soft Sea Horse*, and wanted to "get Thad in a room" with some hot young director. Clea delighted in adding that there was a nice response to the Children of the Famous idea when her agent floated it past a certain Showtime exec. More importantly, things had been going well with the couple since the big upset—the San Rafael excursion had worked wonders. (She thanked me again for coming.) I told her Dad wanted to throw a soirée for them at the house on Friday night, and was particularly looking forward to meeting Thad.

An A.D. shouted imperiously.

We scrambled to our positions. A makeup girl gave my boots a sheen of Fellcrum fairy dust.

The director called "Action!"

I entered frame, out of breath, followed by the android.

"A landing party, Captain," I said. "Headed this way."

"How many?" he asked.

"Two," said Cabott. "A male and a female."

A beat later, Morloch arrived accompanied by his consort, Ambassador Trothex. With glistening cobalt blue hair and tackily resplendent jewel-woven bodice (native to this far-flung quadrant), Clea looked breathtaking—and astonishingly like her mother.[8]

After introducing himself, the flamboyant prince apologized for our awkward arrival, noting "how even Vorbalidian technology could not circumvent the devilish molecular tricks played by the magnetic properties of our Great Dome." The captain didn't buy it, going on record that our forced visit flew in the face of established Jano-Kryag Convention accords.

Morloch approached the ensign. (Actually the script supervisor. Thad would shoot the opposing part later in the week, the two images ultimately spliced together.)

"How soft you've gotten," said Morloch.

"How hard you've remained," said the script supervisor. "What is the state of Father's health?"

"Your arrival will most likely finish him," said Morloch, wonderfully witchy.

"And—Mother?"

"A shadow. A wraith. A phantom," said the twin, gleefully chewing the blue screenery. It was fun as hell to watch.

As the scene continued I noticed Thad's features, even beneath the shell of appliances, weirdly soften. Then, as if in a dream, he stepped languorously off his mark.

"O graceful moon, I remember, upon this hill I would come full

---

[8] Throughout the day, I heard more than a few comments in that regard, in respectful *sotto* from the crew.

of anguish to look at you . . . and you hung over that wood as now you do, lighting it all . . . and yet it helps me to remember, and to count the age of my pain—"

It wasn't until halfway through the speech that some of us realized he'd gone "off book." The actor suddenly appeared woozy and I rushed to his support; otherwise, I think he'd have fallen. After a moment's recovery, he seemed embarrassed by his lyrical, improvised outburst. As the director helped us lower the fallen prince to a chair and the medic was called, Thad appeared to be in a fugue state. In time, the clamminess evaporated and color returned to his skin. He drew us in to explain that such spontaneous poeticizing (this stanza from a favorite, the venerable Giacomo Leopardi) sometimes foretold a migraine was imminent. He would try "the new medicine," he said, already prescribed for this very event—Clea confirmed the Zomig was in her purse. All he needed, said Thad, was to lie down. The medic arrived but he politely turned the man away. A fifteen-minute break was called.

Clea walked him to his trailer. I followed at a few paces.

She turned and whispered, "He wants apple pie and ice cream. Can you get some, Bertie?"

Arriving with the goods, I tapped lightly on the door. No response. Cautiously, I stepped in. I heard soft voices and warily proceeded. Clea was framed in the bedroom door with her back to me, partially blocking the view. Thad lay north to south and she ministered like a nurse, motioning me to bring the dessert.

I caught glimpse of his face, ruddy and alert.

"An ambassadorship!" he muttered, with charm. "You've done well for yourself, Trothex."

"Yes, darling," said Clea, sponging his forehead with a damp cloth.

"He took the pill?" I whispered needlessly.

She nodded.

"What kind of name is that, anyway?" he asked. *"Trothex."*

"Dumb," I said, affably. "A dumb name."

"Sounds like bleach," he said. His brow furrowed and he turned to Clea as if they were alone. "When I first saw you on the bridge"— I realized he had leapfrogged to the lines of tomorrow's scene— "looking out from the starscreen . . . all the years rushed back." She tenderly put a hand on his. "And I thought: How terrible that I never even said good-bye."

THE MIGRAINE DIDN'T COME BUT Clea worried nonetheless.

She confided to me something I already suspected: that our friend took a daily barrage of "meds" to control various manias, compulsions, and depression and that it was paramount he neither add nor subtract from the carefully calibrated chemical concoction as it might effect a harsh imbalance of mood. Clea had seen the consequences and it wasn't pretty. She was worried—aside from the Leopardian lapse, there were recent blips, dots, and beeps on her radar that she couldn't yet translate—so the two of us kept close watch. Gently, she asked Thad if he was currently taking this pill or that, careful not to antagonize, in the effort to determine whether to begin the begging campaign he not abandon the pills that *mattered*, at least not till the end of the shoot, a tantalizingly close yet shockingly distant ten days away.

Clea and I were old hands at caretaking—Mom had been a semi-invalid since my early twenties—and made a pretty good tag team. We made sure he was well fed and lightheartedly entertained but confined to his room by shooting day's end. While prudently maintaining a general policy against overstimulation, Clea considered the sexual act to be palliative and good for his soul, a natural antibody and witches' brew against the virus of soft-focus schizophrenia. (She took her custodianship with touching seriousness.) Every few days, Miriam called at a late hour in a sultry voice, as if catching mossy, musky whiff of Clea's carnal healing; though it was more likely she was trying to atone for the celibacy of her last brief visit. If she *did* bring up Thad, it was by way of signaling phone sex was over—the topic of his cracked psyche definitely broke the mood. She'd usually mumble something about "coming out there if things get too rickety" before slipping back into sexy sign-off mode.

The amazing Michelet had a new preoccupation—at least, new to us. He'd been contemplating a one-man show, which he'd already spoken to Mike Nichols about directing. Or so he said. Mr. Nichols was seemingly enthused. It would be the story of his life: his revenant twin, Zeus-like dad and ice queen mom—the whole shebang. Apparently it had been on his mind a long while but everything had coalesced during the trip to San Rafael. Just after our late-night parlor car confab, he'd had a powerful vision in the form of a disturbing image, nearly religious yet intensely theatrical: himself alone onstage, sitting at a table applying makeup "like a Gielgud or a Richardson" (*"not* Spalding Gray!" he added pithily) while intimately addressing his audience. The makeup, he added, was none other than a Vorbalid's, the epiphany being that a monologue encompassing his life would unfold as the cosmo-cosmetic layers were inexorably applied (or removed; he wasn't quite sure yet), until at performance's end he stood to face the assembly in the naked, poignant, transworldly mask of human comedy—agglutinized agony of all the lost and ruined years. He'd forever been attracted, he said, to metaphorical monsters and the tortured poetry of their lives—Chaney's Phantom, Laughton's Hunchback, Karloff's Frankenstein—and nonmetaphorical monsters too: the homely, sickly, myopic Giacomo Leopardi, whom Thad described as a lonesome boy who sequestered himself in his father's library, promising not to come out until he was "as great a poet as Dante." The operatic stageplay would be a unique chance to formally add his own unforgettably tender gargoyle to the canon.

While delighted to see him thus diverted and enthused, Clea and I were taken aback by the scope of his ambition. That he seemed intent on characterizing himself as a kind of Creature of the Black Lagoon caused a bit of shuddering on our part, alongside the realization that we needed to continue to voice support and encouragement, which was deeply genuine. There was no question the concept was brilliant in its macabre simplicity—a perfect vehicle to make use of a wide breadth of talents while at the same time proving wildly therapeutic. The raw honesty of the thing was, after all, what set it apart. I cringed and got gooseflesh at once, which made me think his proposal had the potential to be one of those breakthrough projects an artist is always remembered by. As we listened to him map it out, I grew more excited, playing off Clea's enraptured startles, pregnant hesitations, and bridefully unbridled enthusiasms. (Don't forget, I was her legal codependent.) Before long I had completely lost my head, giving my word to be first in the coming tsunami of financial backers.

"Do you remember *The Day the Earth Stood Still*? My brother and I *loved* Michael Rennie. How gay was Michael Rennie? We had total kiddie-porn hard-ons for Klaatu. We used to put on these little plays—I have all this written down!" He seized a disorderly sheaf of papers, some typed, some longhand, riffling through them with great devotedness as he spoke. "I was originally going to do a memoir but then I thought (and Miriam completely agrees): *Don't* do the perimenopausal Susan Cheever thing. I want Grand Guignol-in-the-round, the roar of the greasepaint, the stink of the crowd!"

"It's *so great*," said Clea, really meaning it.

Then *I* thought it—and said it—and meant so too. And do, to this day.

Thad said Clea and I should coproduce; there was much to learn from his old friend Nichols. (Years back, delays on the *Quixote* shoot had forced him to bow from the director's Lincoln Center revival of *Waiting for Godot*.) He began to pace, voicing concern that because of its autobiographical nature he might have to dip into *The Soft Sea Horse* for material. He was afraid of legal repercussions, should Mordecai Klotcher wind up optioning the book. Clea told him not to get ahead of himself.

Returning from the kitchen with a sack of chips, Thad assumed the posture of a suave extraterrestrial with an absurd French accent. "*I am Klaatu, from Alpha Centauri.* That's how my brother used to say it—*très* Brigitte Bardot. We'd do our little mise-en-scène in the garden. I'd be 'sleeping' and he'd enter stage left making the Theremin sound." He imitated the instrument's campily evocative pitch. "I'd open my eyes and he'd be standing there, beamed down from nothingness. Very *Starwatch.* What can I say? We were ahead of our time. I'd pretend to be shocked, then start to stammer and be a good Earthling host. *Uh, have you been traveling long?* Jeremy would say—*intone*—'About five months. Five of your Earth months.' *You must have come a long way.* 'About two hundred fifty million of your Earth miles.' He'd look around the yard—he was actually very good at the cosmic snob thing—he must have picked that up from his little Gstaad pals!—and Jeremy would say, 'What do you call this sector?' I'd tell him we were in a place called . . . *Martha's Vineyard.* One day we were doing our thing (I have it in my notes) and Jeremy said the *big* reason he'd journeyed all those millions of miles was—and *this* is fucking *genius*—'I'm most curious to board what I believe you Earthlings call a "yacht." It is my desire to explore the exotic Isle of Capri.' The exotic Isle of Capri! Priceless! *Oh,* he was good! Oh! He was *very* good. 'I wish to meet the fascinating specimens you call movie stars.' Jeremy could be a *devil*—he was a *smart* little fucker. He stands there saying he could tell by my aura I had 'what you Earthlings call asthma' and that he could easily cure me of this 'petty ailment'—but *not until he returned from visiting the Isle of Capri* where he planned to learn 'the ways of Hollywood moviemaking.' See, evidently, that was the main thing aliens wanted to know! How to make Hollywood movies!"

Thad smiled a weary, memory smile. Then, with casual elegance, he contemplatively tucked hands into pockets, already rehearsing mannerisms for his tour de force.

HIS ENTHUSIASM WAS CONTAGIOUS.

If we threw enough at the ceiling, something was bound to stick—for somebody. Besides, I could always use a creative kick in the ass.

I forced myself to work on *Holmby Hills*. Clea finished a précis for her children of celebs sitcom. Thad immersed himself in the one-man show, which, seen through the lens of my own collegiate dabbling in avant-garde, already looked like some sort of outrageous classic-in-the-making.

There were lots of irons in the fire. In addition to Miriam's misguided efforts on Thad's behalf to novelize "Prodigal Son" (she was actually making headway), Mordecai Klotcher was drawing up an option on *The Soft Sea Horse*. As if that weren't enough, Nick Sultan was in hot pursuit of making a deal for the actor-author to adapt his father's novel to screenplay form. I kept forgetting to ask Dad—perennial holder of the *Chrysanthemum* rights—if Nick was really attached or if he'd ever broached the idea of Junior's involvement, as claimed. (I guess part of me didn't want to know.) It was all pretty incestuous—not that it hadn't been from the beginning.

On a typical day, Mr. Michelet catnapped in a lawn chair in front of his trailer while Clea and I took over the bedroom, ostensibly to work on one of a thousand or so projects. The truth was, I had begun a leisurely read of the out-of-print *Soft Sea Horse*—ordered online just after the funeral, it had finally come—while Clea obsessed over *Playboy*. The current issue contained a witty photo essay by David LaChapelle featuring an old friend of hers, *also* the daughter of an icon of silverscreen, albeit one still living. Hefner's people had a long-standing, lucrative offer on the table and with each new issue Clea contemplated blowing out the candles of her birthday suit afresh, before there were too many.

We were thus engrossed when inquiring voices disturbed our peace.

"Thad? Is that him?"

"Of *course*, it's him. They said it's his *trailer*."

The first again, louder: "Thad!"

We rushed forward and there they were, figures in a scary dream: Morgana Michelet and Mordie K, at the foot of the trailer's entry, cautiously ogling the cubistic Morloch as fussy merchants might observe a transient dozing in the vestibule of their shop. Her eyes lit upon us as we appeared at the door; smiling awkwardly in our futurama getup, we felt the full sting of Morgana's phaser, set eternally on Humiliate. Just then the sleeping Vorbalid stirred from his psychopharmacologically induced haze and, blinking rapidly, sat up with veteran professionality to exclaim—strand of spittle brocading his mouth—"Mother!"

— • —

"Freak!" cried Klotcher's great-nephew, in admiration of Morloch's impressive deformities. "That is *so cool*."

Clea stepped between Thad and the boy, as buffer.

Morgana gaped at the ambassador, not yet recognizing the girl underneath. Finally, the old woman eked out "Clea?"—like a dowager discovering that a new society friend was a sales assistant at Walgreen's instead.

"Hi," I offered, lamely bright, extending a mitt in the direction of Mordy/Morgana. With no takers, the hand retracted. In its place, I tendered a pathetic reminder—"I'm Bertie Krohn. My father cre-

ated the show"—that we'd met on the Vineyard, blah. The M & Ms'
mouths widened but still said nothing; I suppose they were in shock
though I wasn't quite sure why. Standing in uniform, I felt a fresh
wave of foolishness, as if me and my compatriots had been caught
playing dress up. Or strip poker.

"Vorbalids!" shouted the horrid, gleeful boy.

I flashed on what it would be like to hit him so hard in the chest
that he'd belch blood and expire at the moment of impact.

"It *is* you," smiled the producer, eyes crinkling like the Tin
Man's. "I was beginning to think we had the wrong galaxy!"

"What are you doing here?" said Thad, now awake enough to be
bemused. He addressed Morgana but Klotcher answered instead.

"Didn't Miriam tell you I was dropping by?"

"That looks *shitty*," said the unstarstruck child, scrutinizing
hours-old peel at the neck of our latex-grafted prince.

"I didn't know you were in town," said Thad to his mother.

"I'm taking portraits," she finally answered. "For my book."

"You're kidding," he said. (Curdled smile.)

"I've only been here a few days—at the Peninsula. Mordecai rang
up and said he was coming to see you. I hope you don't mind me crashing the party! I thought we could all have dinner tonight at L'Orangerie."

"How long does the makeup take to put on?" asked the boy,
running thin, dirty fingers over the polyester hem of Thad's royal
tunic.

Clea swatted his hand away; he silently mouthed Fuck You.

"You knew I was out here," said Thad. "I thought you'd have
called."

"I didn't know how to reach you!" said Morgana. She talked too
loud.

"How long does the makeup take to put on," the punk testily
implored, giving the fabric a yank.

Thad obliviously shoved him, hard enough to put an end to the entreaties. Morgana looked as if she might reprimand her son but begged off when she saw no real harm had been done.

"What do you mean, you didn't know how to reach me?"

His sneer reconfigured itself into a kind of fluorescent incredulity.

"You didn't tell anyone where you were staying," said Morgana.

"I *always* stay at the Chateau. You *know* that. And *Miriam* knows—"

"Well, I don't know how to *reach* Miriam. How would I? And believe it or not, your lodgings are not as legendarily known as you might think. But here I *am*, so what difference can it possibly make?"

"I didn't mean to intrude while you're working," said Klotcher conciliatorily, mindful of the tension between the two. "I thought Miriam gave a heads-up. She must have told *someone*, or there wouldn't have been a drive-on."

I eased my way back to the bedroom while Clea protectively remained. I had planned to leave but, after retrieving my things, hung back to listen.

"I've been taking your mother around with my realtor."

"Oh?"

"We looked at a fabulous horse ranch in the Malibu Hills," said Klotcher. "Twenty-two acres."

"Lovely but *not* for me," said Morgana.

"I think it was once owned by Bo Derek."

"You're moving here?" said Thad, further dismayed.

"Not on your *life*," said Morgana. "It's a nice way to see the city, though—it is *such* a luxury to look at property knowing you have absolutely no intention to buy!"

"I want to meet Cabott 7," said the boy.

"I'm sure the feeling's mutual," said Thad. "But I'm afraid the court has ruled against the android having contact with minors. Stipulation of parole."

"What's parole?" asked the child, faintly flummoxed.

Klotcher guffawed while Clea nattered about how nice supper at L'Orangerie would be. The little shit harped on *What's parole* until Morgana set him straight.

"My son has a warped sense of humor and should not, as a rule, be taken seriously."

"Are you going to be a regular?" asked the boy.

"No," said Clea, protectively. "He's guest-starring."

"You should be in another *Jetsons*," he said, like a pint-sized agent.

"Aren't you meant to do something in La Jolla?" asked Morgana. "A play?"

"Postponed," said Thad—prevaricating, as they say. Suddenly he grimaced, as if discerning great hooves of headache kicking up dust in the distance.

"Can I see the ship?" asked the boy.

"He wants to see the ship," said Klotcher.

"Go for it," said Thad. "Anyone hassles you, say you're my guest."

"I want to meet Cabott 7."

"I told you. He's not allowed around minors."

"Thad!" admonished Morgana.

"But why? *Why* isn't he?" pleaded the boy.

"I *said*. Major Cabott's not allowed around minors because he's a pedophile. In fact, that's what we call him on the bridge—Major Pedophile!"

"What's a pedophile?"

"Those are androids with *very special* powers. Android priests— machine-men of the cloth! Now go bother someone else."

Klotcher laughed and Morgana clucked in disapproval as the child dashed out.

"I'd like us to have lunch on Saturday," said the producer. "Can we go to the Ivy on Saturday? I read your book . . . and so did Mikkel Skarsgaard. Do you know his work? He's *very* intrigued. Miriam didn't tell you about this?" The boy shrieked for his great-uncle, making a general ruckus. Klotcher left to find him, with a parting shot to Thad: "See you on the bridge!"

"Who the fuck is Mikkel Skarsgaard," asked Thad of Clea.

"A famous Danish DP. It's good."

"*What's* good?"

"It's good that he read it."

"Why is that *good*?" he said, annoyed.

"Because he's really hot."

"Oh goodie, he's *hot*. He's hot hot hot!"

"And he wants to direct."

No one said anything. I was about to come out. I assumed his mother had wandered off with Klotcher. I hesitated. More silence, then Clea entered the bedroom without warning. We heard Morgana return to the trailer—and gave each other a look. The fact we'd have to pass by them in order to exit had a paralyzing (and alluringly voyeuristic) effect. We intuitively sensed a primordial mother-son spectacle looming.

"Awfully small, this trailer, isn't it?"

"It's television, Mom."

"I would think they'd at least have found you something bigger. Don't the agents tend to all that? Miriam—is she as effective as she could be?"

"Miriam's not my agent, Mom."

"She isn't?" said Morgana, baffled.

"She's my agent for *books*."

"Then she *is* your agent."

"Not for TV or movies. Just books."

"Well, maybe you'd do better to go elsewhere."

He let that one go.

"You haven't done any films lately, have you, Thad."

"I don't know, Ma. Have you seen me in any?"

She let *that* one go.

"Are you really out here taking pictures?" he asked suspiciously.

"There were a few legal things I had to attend to connected to the estate. As it turned out, your father owned a condo in Century City. Another little secret," she said ironically.

Since his mother had opened the probate door, he decided to step in.

"There's some stuff I wanted to talk to you about. I was going to wait, but—I wanted to ask . . . if Dad made any provisions."

"That's what I'm telling you. The lawyers are going to be calling."

"Calling?"

"That's what I said. You'll have to ask the lawyers."

"Because I could use some help! The IRS thing, the 'offer and compromise,' or whatever—the thing my accountant was working on didn't come through."

"You told me that—at the funeral."

"I thought I'd be paying pennies on the dollar. That's how he represented it—"

"You told me, at the Vineyard."

"—but it just didn't happen. I might sue the idiot for malpractice."

"You can't sue the world, Thaddeus."

"He *never* should have repre—you start having these *expectations*. Anyway, I made a deal, with the government. My *accountant* made a deal, but it's *usury*. It's like thirty eight thousand a month, for *five* years. I may as well have borrowed from the Mob."

"You should have thought about that when you didn't pay taxes."

He let that one go too. "So what do the lawyers want? Why are they calling me?"

"About Jack's will."

Clea and I gave each other a look again.

"So, who you taking pictures of?" he asked, forcedly casual.

We were actually now spying on them through a crack in the

door; a bit insane. Morgana gave her son a blank look. She knew exactly what he wanted from her, but sometimes did the vacant-look routine, just to make him "work."

"For your *book.*"

"Oh, I've forgotten their names," she said, bullshitting. "Someone . . . wait a moment. He wrote A *Staggering Work of Genius.*"

"Dave Eggers?"

"Yes. Oh—and another: David Wallace Foster? Or maybe it's David Foster Wallace."

"Foster Wallace," said Thad, quizzically. "He was at the funeral. I didn't talk to him. Why was he at the fucking funeral?"

"Pretty soon," she said, ignoring his ire, "your mother's going to have to walk around with Post-its glued to her forehead."

"Where are you going to shoot them?" he asked, like an undercover Fed consorting with an assassin.

"Wallace Foster or Foster Wallace teaches nearby. *Relatively.* Someplace called Pomona. A lot of these colleges *pay,* Thad. Irvine too. Big, big budgets. They're going to drive me. Evidently they give him *millions* to teach. You know, he was a great fan of Jack's—they used to chat on the phone at indecent hours. Alice Sebold teaches there too. Her husband's quite well known, as well. A novelist. They're both bestsellers. I'm going to do both of them, then fly to San Francisco for Eggers and Michael Something."

"Chabon?"

"Yes. He won the Pulitzer. And I believe he makes quite a living writing screenplays."

"Jesus," Thad muttered. "Mr. *Spider-Man 2!*"

Long, chafing pause.

"Why don't you do *me*?" he asked.

"What?"

I could see her face contort, as if he'd said something in a rough, dead language.

"Can't you take my picture?"

"Well, of course I could," she said emptily.

He snickered before saying, "Then why *don't* you?"

"I doubt the publisher would allow. These things aren't my choice, you know."

"Why not? *You're* taking the pictures, aren't you?"

"They give me a *list*—"

"It's *your* fucking book, isn't it?"

"Let's not get *overblown*, Thaddeus. *Yes*, it's my book but it's *their* decision. We've been doing it like this for years, you *know* that. Anyway, it's appearances—how could you be included in the series without cries of nepotism?"

"Of course!" he said, sarcastically. "There would be a public outcry! Not to mention I'm not *remotely* in the League of Superhero Writers! *The great Alice Sebold*," he sputtered. "She's right up there with Virginia Woolf! Maybe I should go get myself *raped* then write a *slender memoir*. Parlay it into a tender little *porn novella*—with *me*, the adorably sodomized angel, high in the sky! Throw in a decapitation—decaps are all the rage! Oh, boo hoo hoo! Readers and Book Clubs'll love it! Yes! If I get myself *fucked up the ass* and *beheaded*, with my heart yanked from my chest and eaten by some teenage Liberian warrior—no, wait! Not a Liberian, a *librarian*. There's just my head left, upchucking lyrical little monologues . . . The publishers will *line up* for the advances!"

She composed herself during his fit.

"The writers on the list are widely read, Thaddeus, in the popular sense—"

"Have *you* read them, Mother?"

"Of course I haven't. You know I don't read."

"Then how do you *know* they're widely read?"

"That's a nonsensical question. The publishers have that information—BookScan, it's called. It has *nothing to do* with my having read them or not."

"Have you read *my* books, Mother?"

"Yes," she said. "I have. Don't be an ass."

"You *haven't!*" said Thad, smiling imbecilically. "You haven't read *word one.*"

"I think I've had enough." She made a move to leave.

"If you *have* read my work, Mother, I am *deeply impressed.* Even if it's only two paragraphs. OK? OK. But tell me: having digested my *oeuvres* throughout the *years,* what do you think? What thinkest thou of my *lit'ry gifts?* What dost thou *thinketh.* I'm serious, Morgana! Because I never asked. We've never really had this conversation, *have we?* And it's healthy! Am I up to Alice 'Rape Me' Sebold's standards? Or Professor David Pomona *Wall-ass?* Do *you* feel I'm *worthy* of being included in your vanity project? Forgetting the publishers for a moment. Am I worthy of the pantheon, Mother?"

"What *I* think isn't the point," she said curtly. "I've already told you that."

"You're dodging the question!" he said, radiantly.

She grunted. He clapped his hands with infernal delight.

"Ha! I'm not *worthy,* am I—wasn't that always the bottom line?"

"In your mind, perhaps."

"In my mind."

"That's right."

"By the way, who reads these books, anyway?"

"I *told* you, the publisher makes the decision—"

"I mean who reads *your* books, Mama? How many have you done, seven? Seven books! I suppose people don't really *read* them— they just look at the pictures. Like *Hustler* or *Maxim* . . . and all remaindered, just like me! Don't you see? We share a common bond! In fact, I think *you've* been out of print longer than *I* have! Why are they even allowing you to publish? How did you manage to get a deal? Did you tie it in with Dad? No shame in that. *I want your agent.* Are you paying *them,* Mother? Are you paying for publication and they're slapping their name on it? That's OK. I should do the same. I *will* do the same. Whitman self-published—Emerson too.

We're in a happy league: the League of Superhero Remainders!
C'mon, Tammy, tell me true. I *understood* why they let you take your
little snapshots while Father was still alive; it was always under a
Harcourt imprint. A bone they were throwing ol' Black Jack, no?
But aren't you worried, Morgana? Aren't you worried the cottage
industry is gonna fold up its tent? I mean, now that the money
train's *a-molderin' in the grave*—"

"I don't appreciate this! I don't appreciate *any* of it," said Morgana, finally gathering up her things. "You can go fuck yourself,
Thaddeus!"

"Mother, wait! You're *misunderstanding*. No disrespect! What I'm
saying is, if no one's buying this incredibly *contemporary* coffee-table
anthology of literary portraiture *anyway*, then no one will even notice
if we stuck in a photo of *little ol' winemaker me*."

"It'd be self-aggrandizing," said Morgana. She was trembling,
and nearly at the end of her tether. "That's how it would *appear*."

"Who *cares* how it appears?"

"All right, Thaddeus," she said, at breakpoint. "I'll *take* your picture! Grab a Polaroid from a makeup gal—let's do it! Right now!
We'll just 'slip' it into the book like you said and no one will ever
notice!"

"Great! Perfect!" She'd called his bluff and Thad was suddenly
tamed. But he needed some serious de-Vorbalizing. "Just let me find
one of the girls to take this shit off my face . . . we can do it in front
of the blue screen—and digitally insert Yaddo later on! You'd be surprised at what Photoshop can do," he said, excitedly rubbing his
hands together. "I'm *telling* you, your editor's asleep at the wheel! I
think it'd be great to be on a page between Franzen and Cunning-
ham—the prick and the fag."

"Right! You don't even have to get out of your makeup!" Suddenly, she crumpled, tired of the sport. "I'm going to leave now.
Mordecai and I are having lunch."

"Aren't you going to take my picture?" he said pathetically.

"I said I would. But some other time."

"Liar!"

He seized her wrist and she shouted, "Let go of me!" Clea and I rushed in. He'd pinned her to the Naugahyde couch, and Morgana broke free as I went to subdue him.

"Someone get me a Polaroid!" she shouted, a carbonous edge to her voice—as if drawing that special sword reserved for the occasions her husband became dangerous. She shoved Thad away, snatching her purse from the floor. "You—you—*crazy man*. Go! Stand on the bridge of your *rocket* and I'll take a picture! I'll take a *thousand* pictures of you in that . . . Halloween costume! Of you and *all* your little fools! Your *girlfriend*," she snarled, "the slut who fucks for dope, like her mother did!" (Clea cried out, as if stabbed.) "*Go, Mr. Vorbalid, get the Polaroid! I'll show it to Deepak Ghupta and he'll say, 'Who is *this*?' And I'll say, What's the *matter*, don't you *recognize* him? That's my *son*, Thaddeus Michelet, the genius! And Deepak will say, 'Oh, forgive us! How *wonderful*. You know, we have to admit we weren't going to publish you because you're a *widow* and a *hack* and a dried-up *cunt* but now that you've given us the gift of your *famous son*, forgive us, Morgana! Because *everyone* knows Thaddeus Michelet—didn't he win the Pulitzer? Didn't he win the National Book Award?—every *schoolkid* knows Thaddeus Michelet! He's a bestseller, he's a household *saint*, they even recognize him when he's all dressed up like a green man from outer space! Thad Michelet's a *genius*, like his *father*—*better* than his father! We'll put him on the cover, Morgana! Why don't we put him on the cover of your piece of shit book because that way we'll sell a million! What a *coup*. Oh thank you oh thank you, *fata morgana*, dried-up widow-cunt that you are, because now we can publish your amateur-hour book!' And I'll get down on my knees and suck Deepak's cock—I'll suck everybody's!—just like Clea would—saved by my genius son, my genius son, my genius son!"

The old woman ran out.

CLEA LATER TOLD ME THAT the lawyers had indeed called and because of Thad's schedule, made arrangements to drop by the Chateau after dinner. We took their thoughtful urgency as a good omen.

She added that while her lover said he was trying not to fantasize about any provisions his father might have made (cash or real estate seemed unlikely), a bequest of books, paintings, or correspondence would still be of enormous value. It was a revelation that over the last few years father and son had come to terms during late-night bimonthly phone sessions—squeezed in, Thad joked, between Jack's calls to David Foster Wallace—in which the old man showed distinct signs of mellowing. With the pending powwow, Thad couldn't help but allow himself to imagine paying off the IRS or at least getting a handle on that part of his life. He even apologized to Morgana for his behavior on the soundstage, laying it off to the stress of "recent financial pressures." Again, he asked if she had any inkling of what the attorneys were going to say, but she claimed ignorance.

I made it a point to talk to Clea about Morgana's scabrous, trailer-trashed diatribe. I felt like an asshole for letting her get puked on like that. At the time, Clea was visibly shaken but now just shrugged it off. "Morgana didn't like me from the gate," she said. She always assumed it was one of those incesty, jealous mom deals. Moreover, "Mad Morgana" had long suspected her of a dalliance with Jack, as she suspected *everyone* (for good reason). She was the queen of ball-busters, Clea reiterated—the only one left standing when "ol' BJ" decided to finally take a wife. "Rage is her thing," said Clea. "Stick around long enough and she'll come after *you*."

No thanks, I said.

—·—

I had the afternoon off (Thad and Clea were shooting their big scene at the Chrysanthemum Palace) and went shopping at Maxfield's.

Gita's birthday was coming up. I got her some vintage Hermès jewelry, which she loved more than anything on Earth. I hit the gym and was done around 7:00 P.M. I headed for my parents' to spend time with Mom. Her doctor had either reduced or increased the strength of her meds and she'd been having a tough time of it. Carmen made us authentic Trader Vic's "snowball" sundaes (a woman of many talents) that I brought to Gita's bedroom with leopard-spotted caviar spoons. We wound up dishing minor celebs and talking the usual shit about Dad. We watched *Investigative Reports* awhile before I split. I was going to hop on the 405 but instead, as if guided by unseen hands, hung a left, heading east—straight to the Chateau.

Arriving at Thad's door, I suddenly remembered the suits from Century City. I stood outside and listened for a sign but all I could hear was Norah Jones. I knocked, waited, knocked again. In time, Clea answered, fully dressed. Gave me a hug. I smelled liquor and Listerine on her breath.

The lawyers showed up a few minutes later, apologizing for their tardiness. An "emergency" had come up.[9] Introductions and pleasantries were endured while Clea served a choice of sparkling or flat. One of the men actually consented to a beer—an elder partner—and I thought that a good sign too. Mr. Michelet appeared from the dark recesses in his expensive bathrobe, fastidiously shaven, without the usual trace of makeup at the collar. He had a buoyancy about him, a lilt in step and spirit, like he'd slapped on hopeful aftershave.

There was a lull, then the visitors' eyes cued me to leave—ready to get down to business. I stood but Thad overruled their motion. Our ménage à trois was thus decreed street-legal. I was family now, privy to the conditions of probate.

"The will *is* a bit unusual," said the key man, clearing his throat.

"Dad was an unusual guy," said Thad, trying to be cool.

[9] In Hollywood, whenever agents or lawyers are late, they play the "emergency" card.

The lawyers assented and laughed uncomfortably.

"Essentially, he has left you a very large amount . . ."

"A *very* large amount," affirmed a cohort.

"But there's a strange provision, which may be prohibitive."

Thad's smile brightened like the surface of a balloon before bursting. "Prohibitive?"

"Your father's will stipulates that you receive ten million dollars—"

"My God," said Thad, as Clea and I stopped breathing.

"With a *condition*. The condition being that the amount is triggered when one of your books appears on the *New York Times* bestseller list."

Thad glanced at Clea, then me, as if having heard a joke he couldn't parse. "Can you repeat that?"

The key man did, to the same effect.

His cohort, wishing to take the edge off the moment, said, "I guess your father's intentions were that you use your gifts to write something either very *commercial*—a John Grisham, or what have you—a *Da Vinci Code*—or something artistic, with crossover appeal."

"*Bergdorf Blondes?*"

Another colleague chimed in. "Not *Bergdorf Blondes*. Like *The Corrections*. Remember the guy who pissed Oprah off? Didn't that make the list?" He turned toward Clea as if she might know. "Some years back? I'm pretty sure it did. My theory—it's only a theory!—is that Jack was thinking of this as an incentive, a goal to work toward. A *reward*, if you will."

Thad started to laugh. It was a dry laugh, nearly a retch.

"I'm a *big* fan of your films," said one of the men. "But I have to say I wasn't aware you wrote *books*. When I jumped on the Internet, I was *very* impressed. Now, I'm not exactly sure how many you'd have to sell to get on the *Times* list—"

"I'm having a paralegal research that."

"It's a bit of a labyrinthine process. I mean, they definitely have their own logic."

"They have their own *country* over there!"

"But I think it's actually *doable*."

"Did he specify fiction or nonfiction?" said one to the other.

"Fiction—I believe."

"It was *definitely* fiction," said the one who referenced *The Corrections*.

"I don't think it's as high as you would imagine—in terms of sales."

"To get on the list."

"It's *definitely* doable. God knows your dad was on that list enough—"

"Though not as much as a person might think. It's not a cakewalk."

"It was clearly his fervent wish that some of his good luck and good fortune rub off."

—·—

Though after midnight on the East Coast, I phoned Miriam on the way home. She was enraged when I recounted what happened. She said Jack Michelet was a sadist who looked forward to striking yet another blow at his son—this one, from the grave. We didn't talk very long because she wanted to call the Chateau and check up.

As I walked inside the house, my cell phone rang. Miriam had spoken to Clea ("Thank God she's there") and Thad was fast asleep—his traditional reaction to upsetting news. Luckily, he didn't have to be at the studio until ten.

In the morning, I went for a jog on the beach. Black Jack's ghoulish machinations put Dad in a better light. (No shit.) Perry had his callous side, to be sure, but was never willfully cruel, which I've always considered among the most deplorable of sins. I couldn't conceive what it would be like to have a parent as full-time predator. It reminded me of someone who spoke at AA a few months ago, a man who trained attack dogs for a living. He said he wore protective gear but when the dog bit down it was important to keep your arm moving; that way, the animal tended to refocus and attack elsewhere. If you didn't stay mobile, the teeth sank dangerously down, even through wadded layers—point being, it was a fair metaphor to describe growing up in an alcoholic household. I imagined Thad dodging and feinting, tooth and muzzle upon him year after year, *still* dodging, *still* feinting, reeling from roughhouse burnout, adrenals spent—taking the infernal, foul-breathed blows even after a gaggle of vets had supposedly put the miserable beast down.

ON THE WAY TO WORK, I phoned the Chateau.

No answer in the room.

I tried Clea's cell—10:00 A.M. on the dot—nothing.

I feared the worst.

This time, as I drove through the studio gates, she picked up. Boisterous laughter on the other end affronted my ear. They were in Thad's trailer, having breakfast with some of the cast. I was ordered to join them, "warp speed."

When I got there, Clea, Cabott, the captain, and X-Ray were enrapt by one of Thad's gossipy pornographic anecdotes, this, regarding a Broadway diva of "uncertain age." He looked cheerful and wide awake, eyes clear as bells. Just as the story ended, we heard the A.D. walkie—"OK, everyone, *we are back*"—and the raucous laughter continued in choppy waves while actors drifted out. Nick Sultan, tucked out of sight in the kitchen nook, was the last to leave. The director gave a thumb's-up and smiled as he brushed past, heading for the set.

"Bertram!" said Thad, giving me his full, warm attention.

I was amazed by his powers of recovery. Though I wasn't exactly Dr. Phil, it occurred to me his ebullience might have been masking a dangerous mania, soon to show a savage, darker side. Still, I clung to the possibility Thad's lightness of mood was some indicator of mental health, say, the nimble instincts of a survivor that had allowed him to flourish, more or less, through the years of horrible abuse. At first, I thought the celebratory air was due to Clea's earlier announcement he'd been "green lit" to adapt *Chrysanthemum* to film.

But that wasn't it—that wasn't it at all.

"Did you *tell* him?" he asked Clea.

She shook her head pridefully, like a child who'd kept the biggest secret in the world.

"Tell me what?"

"You will *not believe* how *perfect* this is!"

"It's *incredible*," said Clea. "And it was *Miriam*—Miriam's idea! Miriam is a *genius*."

"*Tell* me." I was a child now too.

"Miriam *is* a genius," said Thad, peremptorily.

"She called this morning with this *amazing* concept."

"A brilliant fucking *stratagem*."

"Bertie, you won't *believe* it . . ."

"You guys are killing me—"

"Tell him," said Thad, coolly delegating.

"She was up half the night—ohmygod, I *love* her! She was *so pissed*. Miriam *really hated* what Jack did—"

"*Beware Miriam, when pissed,*" Thad intoned. "There's hell to pay!"

"—I mean, with the will." Clea was loaded. Lag-timed.

"*Total* fucking warrior. A killing machine!"

"She kept thinking there was some way *around* it."

"And she *aced* it! She *totally fucking* aced it."

"But how?" I said, beaming—happy *they* were happy.

"She went online, right?" said Clea. "And looked up all the *New*

York Times' bestseller lists—for like the *last ten years*. And you know what's there?"

"Can you guess?"

"What's on the list?"

I shook my head, stumped.

"There are *twelve Starwatch: The Navigators* titles! Twelve!"

I wasn't comprehending.

"Don't you *see?*" said Clea. "The total *genius* of it? If Thad novelizes 'Prodigal Son'—there's no *way* they're not going to let him—and if 'Prodigal Son' gets on the list . . ."

"Miriam found the cosmodemonic loophole, honeychile!" Thad jigged, arms akimbo, crooning: "Supercali-*fraga*-listic-expi-ali-*doh*-cious, *pay*-day on the *Fell*-crum Outback *won't* be so a-*tro*-cious!"

"It's the Vorbalidian Quick Pick! The Great Dome Super Lotto!"

"Wham! Bam! Thank you, Dad!"

"Bertie, can you *believe?* Can you believe how *genius* that is?"

"We're in the money! We're in the money!" He hooked his arm in hers as they polka'd round the cramped trailer, knocking into paper plates, sending breakfast burritos spilling to carpet, disgorging scrambled eggs and onions like the innards of a wormy piñata. "We've gotta lot of what it takes to get along!"

IT WAS THE END OF the second week. Five more (shooting) days, and we wrapped.

I had Friday off. I met a girl at the Wednesday night AA meeting in Brentwood (the supersized Pacific Group) and she invited me to Ojai, for pottery lessons. Sounded like fun but I declined, opting instead to hang with Mom, who by now was rightfully suspicious of my recent attentions. So be it—the Benedict house was conveniently located should I feel compelled to wander over to the studio after a visit, which I invariably did . . . [10]

I stood in the soundstage's cool, dark wings, watching the reunion scene between Thad and his parents. A great throne had been carried in by docile attendants with human bodies and canine heads; possessed of a shock of white hair and frail gait, the king still mustered regal authority. The wife entered on cue, pale and submissive, in blue toga-style robes. Thad still wore his ensign's uniform. He stepped awkwardly—boyishly—forward. With intense effort the king stood and held out his arms. They embraced. The traumatized queen stared into the void.

"Welcome home."

"Thank you, Father. Are you in pain?"

"Not so bad today." He steadied himself against the throne. "Your mother is grateful for your return. She will soon find words. It was a terrible blow when you left."

"What?" said Thad, breaking character.

The actor who played the king was confused, repeating his last line as a cue.

"It was a terrible blow when—"

Thad frantically looked off camera.

"I'm not—where's the script girl? What are the lines?"

Nick yelled "Cut it" and came over with the woman, who read from her thick leather binder the same line the king had given, followed by the ensign's expected response.

"Was that a *joke*?" interrupted Thad, throwing the actor a resentful look.

Nick edged him away from the others.

"What's going on, Thad?" he quietly asked.

I walked closer, in case I might be of any help.

"I *heard* him *say* it," said Thad.

[10] An obsessive, repressed, dysfunctional threesome is more work than it seems. Trust me.

Nick told an A.D. to get the medic.

"No—wait a minute!" He shook off the director's grip. "*No memory of having starred atones for later disregard or keeps the end from being hard—*"

"Thad? What's going on?" I said, gingerly.

While puzzled to see me standing there in my civvies, Nick was clearly relieved to have an ally.

"Your friend is sick."

I took Thad by the shoulders and asked if he was OK. In the most transient, intimate of moments, I watched him assess the terrifying enormity of what had just happened—being victimized by hallucination—then move to mentally tourniquet the event, laying the queasily idiopathic horror of it on that old saw "premigrainous condition." He informed us that his "classically anomalous proclivity for visual and auditory ephemera" (a smoothly clinical, amazingly believable rap) had actually been studied in teaching hospitals and likened by "the headache boys" to petit mal seizure.

"Let's get him to an ER," said Nick, which I thought to his credit.

"No—no need, but thank you. I can give myself a shot."

"Is that something you have with you?" asked the director.

"In the trailer. Really, Nickie—thank you but it's not a problem."

"Will it make you groggy?" wondered the solicitous actor-king. Politeness and hushed tones ruled, as if we had hastily gathered on a tarmac in the wake of a minor civic disaster.

"No! They're vasoconstrictors. Let me go do my thing then we'll finish the scene."

I offered to walk him to the trailer but Nick held me back, sending the First in my place. The director desperately sought reassurance—as if I were the "brain man." He asked if I thought Thad was going to be all right; I joked that we should arrange a consultation with X-Ray. Nick wasn't amused. As I rushed to catch up, I heard one of the grips say, "Piece o' fuckin work." Another rejoined, "Guy's nutsoid."

— • —

When a very upset Clea arrived at the trailer, I told her that he gave himself an injection and we should probably let him sleep it off. Things were obviously running behind; the pressure to complete his scenes was only going to worsen.

"What exactly happened?" she said, softly stroking his forehead with the back of her hand. He snored like an elf who'd gorged in a mushroom patch.

"I don't know. It's like he *heard* something—something he thought the actor said."

"Oh shit."

"Part of the migraine thing?"

She shrugged her shoulders and I got the feeling Clea knew more than she let on. "He takes this other medicine," she said. "Maybe he's not taking his other medicine."

———— • ————

They shot around him, so he'd have more time to recover. Thad refused any attempts by production to have him examined by a doctor. Clea and I were the only ones he allowed in his trailer. (I chose to stay away.) She gave out the occasional bulletins—he was resting, he was much better, he was going over his lines—that sort of thing. Meanwhile, Nick and his A.D. huddled over a folding board of colored strips, deciding which of Thad's scenes might be shot after lunch. The actors were naturally concerned. They asked how he was and I did my best to downplay the trouble, becoming the de facto spokesman for that insidious nemesis, Migraine.

Thanks to the writers, the show went on. By now they'd contrived for the entire bridge to be jailed by Morloch—but that was only the half of it. The gravitational pull of the Great Dome had worked an outlandish effect upon our crew. Suddenly realizing he hadn't yet had a single impulse to escape, the *Demeter*'s normally testosterone-charged captain came to the conclusion that he was losing his sap—and the will to command. Laughton complained of feeling "vulnerable," holding our captors responsible for confounding new emotions that washed over him "as waves upon shifting sand." His voice trembled, Hamlet-like and positively premenstrual; it was all he could do to keep from busting into tears.

The android was having problems himself. The unexpected incarceration (among other dilemmas) required urgent analysis yet Cabott had undergone a curious degradation of deductive powers. "In the past," he said, clinging pitifully to the painted plastic bars of his cell, "I have enjoyed my solitary time by solving Holstrum's Conundrum—visualizing the beauty of its axioms. Most peculiarly, I've been pondering the formula for days now, unable to make even the slightest headway . . . yet, somehow—the mere fact I am stymied seems to have caused me . . . irrepressible glee!" He shrieked and twittered like a hyped-up fembot.[11] "A veil is lifting from my eyes," said Cabott, seized by a mystical vision. "There's so much in the universe to *see*—to touch, smell, hold, *feel*. When I think of all the time wasted on . . . *mind games* and logical one-upmanship—I want to *live*, not *think*. I hereby send Mr. Holstrum and his precious conundrum to hell!" He tossed back his head like an amateur-hour Nijinsky, throatily declaring. "*Love* is the glue of God, not *logic*, but love! Love! Love! Love!—"

I won't bore you with further details. Suffice to say that my character, Commander Karp, disgusted and ashamed over past chauvinistic behavior, not only vowed celibacy but a lifelong penance wherein he promised to resign from his post on the *Demeter* in exchange for citizenship on a rough-hewn planet famously known for the asceticism of the religious order that had adopted its name. I turned to an adjacent cell in an attempt to engage Dr. Chaldorer; unfortunately, X-Ray was far too disturbed to take confession. Staring into space with dead,

---

[11] I should note our ensemble was giddy from stepping outside the box of their usual shtick, and that "Nickie" Sultan had no great desire, or ability, to rein them in. There was no shortage of Hamlet *or* ham.

weepy eyes, he proclaimed he had never been a true healer—he was just a "mechanic" who knew "how to oil the parts" and nothing more. The diabolical Dome (and those devilish writers) had forced him to admit to something he'd never told a living soul: in his first year of practice, he lost a twenty-two-year-old woman on the table because of a dubious judgment call. "My arrogance killed that young girl—she had a husband and a little boy! How fitting: the Star Legion's star butcher, finally behind bars where he belongs . . . where he should have been confined—long, long ago!" The oaths he uttered, which were more than Hippocratic, played havoc with his mascara.

I was glad the migraine, or whatever the hell it was, forced us to get those ludicrous set pieces out of the way. Thad and Clea's scene was slated for late afternoon, a good thing because the medication had left him subdued; he turned in an adroitly skilled and elegiac performance, and Nick Sultan was a happy man. Directors can be nervous individuals; Nick must have spent the better part of lunch strategizing with his agent, various producers, and casting gals over worst-case scenarios. Of course, everyone knew the "situation" wasn't Nick's fault—but you know what they say about crimes being committed under one's watch.

The thrones of king and queen were empty. Thad and Clea loitered in the palace hall, alone save for dog-headed sentinels in rigid attention. There came a moment of awkward intimacy when Trothex uncomfortably confessed that she and Morloch had been—were—a couple. As testimony to his skill as an actor, Thad's very skin seemed to color with the crude complexities of what she had shared. Just then, Morloch (a double whom Thad would later replace, digitally) entered with wolfish royal retinue.

"It is done!" the stand-in exclaimed triumphantly, referring to whatever internecine machinations. "The people demand it!"

With the rotten taste of a romance betrayed still in his mouth, the ensign selflessly switched gears. "I insist you release the others—at once!"

"All issues will be settled in the Outback."

"I do not understand. . . ."

"Then I shall make it clear, brother dearest! We will fight with our hands[12]—in twenty-four of your precious Earth hours. Forewarned is forearmed!"

The stand-in for the demon prince froze as the camera pushed in on Mr. Rattweil. After what seemed an eternity, the director "cut"— evidently, Thad forgot his final line but Nick was thrilled nonetheless. They would do a pickup.

Camera reset.

The First ordered everyone to settle.

"And . . . action!"

Again, the lens pushed in on Thad as he peered off, his gaze lost in the tarry, starry depths of the Outback.

"I am home," he said.

We wrapped the day.

MIRIAM SURPRISED US BY FLYING out early. She phoned on Friday evening to ask if I wanted to have a drink at the hotel; she was staying at Shutters for the weekend, "as a treat." She would check into the Chateau on Monday.

I was at the club when she called. I finished my workout, showered, and drove to the beach. When Miriam opened the door to her suite, she was in a thongy Victoria's Secret number. Drinks were postponed. I'd never seen her this passionate—not even the first

---

[12] In one of the writing staff's aggravating Shakespearean asides, Thad interjected, "Forever a duo, we shall have a 'duel' death."

time we fucked. It was more than exciting because the funny thing was, if I really thought about it, I couldn't recall a woman in the past five years who *seriously* came. I somehow remembered the girls of summer being more vocal, spontaneous, lubricated, what have you. Lately, I connected an overall waning of erotic impulse not just to growing older but to my unthrilled partners themselves. (A friend had palmed off a couple of blue, baseball-diamond shaped Viagras which I'd yet to try; a watershed moment I was willing to postpone.) Anyhow, my unhappy assessment of the current state of affairs—at least my own—was that sex seemed to be in a sort of cross-culturally, dumbed-down, or should I say numbed-down, state. As if the whole world had forgotten how to climax, and was content merely to grope its way toward the funky, muddled, middle-aged light at the end of whatever tunnel it found itself stumbling down.

A few hours with the new, improved Miriam shot my depressing little theory to hell, and it wasn't just a reinvigorated sense of my own powers: something elemental had been aroused that was instinctively attached to making babies. It's incredible how simply we're wired. In the days that followed, Miriam became my A1 breeding candidate, alpha bitch and repository of all manner of marital fantasies. I imagined us betrothed in elaborately catered affairs in Angkor Watt or New Zealand, lovingly captured in the *New York Times* Weddings/Celebrations section. Dad would happily pay through the nose; the bliss of it might even heal Gita of her tremors, allowing her to walk again. (Sorry, folks, but it's true—at the root of everything is the need to please one's parents.) Miriam would be a few months pregnant during the ceremonies, a saucy *zitz* and added delight to the gathered tribes. Oh, did I mention those tribes would be flown in by chartered jet? Knowing Perry, elaborate trust funds would already be in place, ensuring cushy futures for hordes of children, as Miriam would undoubtedly prove herself to be in possession of a shockingly fertile womb. HBO would pick up *Holmby Hills* and I'd settle into "the life," that of a proper man and mogulian force to be reckoned with. I'd give great amounts to expunging this and that disease, enshrined and honored at black-tie galas, *just like Dad.* How would Clea react? Sure, she'd be hurt—at first. There'd be some fireworks . . . where's the fun without fireworks? Besides, Miriam totally *got* it, understood from the beginning that Clea and I were contentious, harmlessly amorous siblings. To soften the blow, godmotherhood would thus be conferred. Clea would prove herself a natural, spurred on to drop a few kids of her own (by anonymous donor). If it was too late, I'd spring for a Mongolian, hiring a pro to arrange trips to orphanages and facilitate paperwork.

That's how I walked around—wearing the scent of Miriam's ovulations like a dreamy cologne, in full acceptance that the tidal tug emanated from the dictates of social order, not soul mate. But sometimes they seemed damn hard to tell apart.

WHEN THAD'S LUNCH WITH MORDECAI and the Danish DP wannabe director was canceled, Clea got it into her head we should all go down to Disneyland. It'd been a rough week and she thought it might be "fun" to get him out of the Chateau and "into open air." I hadn't been to the Magic Kingdom in years; the escapade jibed perfectly with my second adolescence (courtesy of Miriam). Still, I was surprised at the level of Thad's excitement when she floated the idea.

When we arrived in Anaheim, he suddenly got excited about California Adventure—so instead of going to Main Street, we hung a right. Friendly guards cursorily searched the girls' handbags then pointed us toward the truncated Golden Gate Bridge that served as the corollary theme park's entrance.

A sense of horror quickly descended.

There was nothing but wide-open spaces filled with porcine, handicapped families tooling around in rented, motorized tricycles. In place of attractions, an onslaught of shops—vast franchised plains of promotional material that looped back on the World of Dizleenan like a nauseating Möbius strip. Wall-to-wall music of the overamped John Williams variety piped relentlessly through invisible speakers, inflated and gaudily anticipatory, a sound track typically heard over opening (or closing) credits of a Spielberg extravaganza; everywhere you turned the orchestra strained toward something massive yet all one encountered were sprawling boutiques, screaming toddlers, and crippled fatties in PC motorcarts. Clea wanted to go roller-coastering and finally, miles away, we spotted "Mulholland Madness." Weirdly, the point of the ride was to simulate what it would be like to speed around Mulholland Drive. There was a long line but a "cast member" (translation: wage slave) signaled us through, having cheerfully recognized Thad as a VIP. It was lame enough to see a replica of the Manhattan skyline in Vegas, or the Eiffel Tower in Orlando, but something else entirely to take a forty-five-minute sojourn from the Chateau in order to be whipped around a simulacrum of my native Mulholland. Soon, no doubt, there'd be a new wonderland—a mini-Disneyland within the park itself, a glorified, edited version of the Happiest Place On Earth™, with tinier boutiques filled with bitsy souvenirs. Secondhand reality was hot! I thought about my faux-*Dynasty* project, *Holmby Hills,* and got even more dejected.

As my mood grew more cynical and downcast, Thad became contradictorily energized. He tugged us this way and that, as if burning off the nervous energy accumulated during the week. He and Miriam walked arm in arm, chortling about her brainstorm to make him a bestseller. (I was genuinely glad to see him upbeat.) Then he'd hook up with Clea and off they'd go while Miriam and I strolled among the meat puppets, dissing Black Jack Michelet. She was resolute her plan would succeed, giving Thad the last laugh. She wanted to huddle with Perry for his blessing and approval; I told her I would seriously lobby the cause. Basically, I'd agree to anything she asked, which had nothing to do with the fact she was my potential wife and the mother of my children, nothing to do with the fact at that very moment she had arched her neck to inhale the scent of my inner ear, nothing to do with the fact she was joyfully showing off the sun-bleached hair on her forearms, parading them for my delectation, and that her eyes witchily widened when I brushed her thigh and kissed a strawberry wedge of lip (in full view of grimy-costumed Cast Members, and the riveted toddler-spawn of a paraplegic dad)— and certainly nothing to do with the fact I found her crusade to get Thad his millions to be heroically sound, just, and true.

Eventually, we *did* find a ride I enjoyed.

Miriam and I sat in little steel gondolas that faced an IMAX screen, approximating what it felt like to hang glide. Soaring over a montage of river, mountain, and gorge, we clutched at each other with desire and wonder while the gondola swayed and surged in a warm, slyly generated current of synthetic Santa Anas. (At last, something worth the $47 park entrance fee.) She gasped and excitedly pointed—for a rapturous moment, our old friend Death Valley, and Badwater too, lay below.

Just when I thought everyone had had enough and we could hightail it back to lotusland for an expensive lunch, young Michelet caught sight of a heinous sidebar village called the Hollywood Pictures Backlot. In the last hour or so, I'd caught fans staring; once or twice a family approached to have their picture taken and Thad obliged, for which the three of us were skittishly grateful. (He actually seemed to enjoy the attention.) Strolling deeper into the Backlot, he thrust a theme-park brochure in my face, stabbing his finger at the captioned ride he was dead set on buying tickets for. According to the description, the miniature limousine (set on little railroad tracks) took starstruck groups on a Mr. Toad–like tour of "the Hollywood experience of casting offices and premieres." It *did* sound amusing, very Nathanael West, and Thad was miserably deflated when we arrived to find it shut down. We made inquiries to a ubiquitous Cast Member but the pimply girl said the ride had been closed for "voluntary safety issues," whatever *that* meant, and no one knew when it would "relaunch."

Thad just stood there, staring at the moribund attraction, as if he could will it to life.

Clea headed toward the candy superstore—she was jonesing for double-chocolate truffles—when our disappointed friend, ever-vigilant, spotted the "Who Wants to Be a Millionaire?" Theater. I groaned. The line was a block long. "We *have* to go!" Thad shouted. "Don't you see? I can pay off the IRS! I can finally pay off the fucking IRS!"

My mood plunged further, if that were possible. I hate to be dramatic but there was something so creepily apocalyptic about it—I wasn't even sure *Millionaire* was on the air anymore. Not that it mattered. Disney evidently fucking owned it and was going to fucking milk it for all it was fucking worth. When I was a kid, there was Tomorrowland, Tom Sawyer, and the glorious, snowcapped Matterhorn; now, it was all about replicating whatever syndicated hits had metastasized under the corporate umbrella. I had one of those "If this be our culture, let it come down" moments, and muttered as much to Miriam, who said I sounded like an intern at the *Voice*. I thought it was more *Fahrenheit 9/11*, but what the hell, I liked being put in my place. That's what wives were for.

It turned out the theater was full because everyone was eligible to win a three-day cruise and Americans really love winning shit. That probably isn't fair. I should have said, Americans really love *standing in line* to win shit. The host came out. Someone must have tipped him because he pointed toward us and said "we have a VIP in the crowd today." The audience applauded while our boy Thad-libbed; they laughed but something didn't feel right. Miriam shushed me for being a curmudgeonly paranoid.

Questions flashed on huge screens and whoever gave the fastest, most accurate response was moved to a center-stage "hot seat." ("Answer buttons" were on back of each chair.) Thad was nothing if not competitive; it suddenly occurred to me that he *really* wanted to win. Things went from bad to worse when he couldn't make headway. The questions were easy but they made sure to lob the occasional high ball, leaving you clueless unless you happened to be conversant with the inventory of the entire merchandisable Disney universe. Thad began to curse. It was funny for about ten seconds then some triple-chinned cracker objected to his language. Thad told her to shove it and the hubby didn't like that one bit. Clea and I began to tug at both sides, as both reprimand and cue to leave.

The master of ceremonies asked the hot-seater, "Where would you be most likely to find a denouement?" The answers flashed onscreen, with annoying musical trills:

1. **In the bathroom**
2. **In a story**
3. **Under the hood**
4. **In a salad**

The mispronounced word ("day-new-mint") had the contestant totally stumped. He used his "lifeline" to phone a Cast Member standing by somewhere in the park. After the employee answered, we could hear him hand the receiver off to a pedestrian. The Q&A was repeated and each time "day-new-mint" was enunciated Thad laughed so hard I thought he'd have a heart attack—it was that violent. After much deliberation the hot-seater said, "I guess in the bathroom."

Thad literally fell off his chair. "You fucking idiot!" he shouted. "Yes! Of *course. That's* where you find a *day-new-mint*—in the *shitter,* with your elephant-legged wife and waterbrain daughter! Sucking each other's pussies!"

Needless to say, we rushed him out at the very moment a squad of terrified Mouseketeers, poorly trained in militia-like maneuvers, gave dogged, unspirited chase.

—•—

While waiting for the tram to take us back to the car, Thad bought the tiniest cup of Coke I'd ever seen. It was like something from a dollhouse but still cost $4.50—setting off another rant, this one with anti-Semitic overtones that managed to include Michael Eisner, Mel Gibson, and shouts of *"Allah Akbar!"* Clea told him if he didn't shut up, "we could very well be detained."

We finally boarded for the two-minute trip to the parking garage. I remembered how exciting it was to listen to the recorded voice accompanying that ride in my youth; how it evoked the genteel mystery and endless promise of a clean, well-lit, preordained world—truly, the Magic Kingdom. Now everything was different. The kingdom was Orwellian, the world was rotten, and the singsong murderous monotone of the man alternating product promotion with safety reminders only filled me with premonitory dread.

WE DROPPED THEM AT THE Chateau and drove back to Venice.

Miriam and I had plans that night. She went to Shutters to bathe[13] while I headed for the beach. After an hour and a half in the car, I felt like stretching my legs. I took along *The Soft Sea Horse*, intending to finish it on a boardwalk bench.

I was surprised at the unguardedness of the book's narrative. (I knew the title had been cribbed from the yacht that launched Jeremy to his watery death but subsequently learned it was a line from a poem of Jack's.) *Sea Horse* is the story of twin brothers, one of whom, an autistic "angel" favored by their glamorous film star father, drowns in the

---

[13] On Sunday, the four of us were supposed to have lunch at my folks' in the Colony. It was a busy weekend.

Aegean Sea during a visit to a film set. When the child vanishes and is presumed dead, the long-embittered wife flies in from Amagansett with the surviving twin. The "angel" reappears after the wounded family reunites, in the form of a seaweed-swaddled wraith. When the book was published, Miriam said Jack called it a "cruddy *Creepshow* of a novella, worthy of a trepanned Stephen King." He did everything he could to humiliate Thad in print. I'm no critic but I disagreed. To me, the novel was a fantasia that attested to a courageous, tender nobility. The reviews, though, were unkind and it sunk like a stone—or a boy— providing trivia for future unauthorized bios of the patriarch.

Thad was forty when he wrote *Sea Horse*. While the book showed promise, it was still very much a first novel—there are far greater sins. At the exact same age, his father had produced *Radiant Light, Come to Morning, Death of a Translator, Jonas and the Whale, The Man at the End of the Booth,* and so on, already winning a clutch of Guggenheims, Pulitzers, and National this-and-that's. (Dual citizenship would eventually allow him a Booker.) Michelet saw the runt's efforts as blasphemous exposure of family business, a tabloidal assault dressed up in the pathetic gown of magical realism which was then in American vogue, lazily diluted by its long, northern migration. His rage knew no bounds or boundaries.

I did some Netsurfing and found an interview Black Jack gave in the *New York Review of Books*, at the time of *Chrysanthemum*'s publication:

NYRB: Your son has written about Jeremy in his book, *The Soft Sea Horse*.

MICHELET: It's god-awful! So clearly an attempt to stab at me. What's galling is, his publishers know it. That's how cynical the game's become. I doubt they even read the manuscript, such as it is. The thing has no value whatsoever, except as literary curiosity. Please to put quotes around literary. It's obscene. All the needy stuff

one prayed to have gotten off one's chest a lifetime ago while bat-
tling acne. Or on the frigging couch. You write it, yes—of course you
do, but then you burn the pages. If you've got any sense! Look, we've
all done it, I've burned reams of juvenilia. But to *enshrine*, as a man?
The towering *stupidity* of it—that kind of unforgivable hubris. If it
were any *good*, I'd be the first to—hell, I'd haul it out like a piss-
proud grandpa and do the book fair circuit with him, kit and caboo-
dle. But see, I cain't, cause it's so much shite.

It was piercing to read.

The devilish thing was, I found myself suddenly blackjacked. With
the collegiate nonchalance of an armchair freelancer I dismantled
Thad's inferior prose, tropes and longueurs, stylistic shibboleths and
high-minded canards. There on the boardwalk, hard by clusters of
sinister halfway-house junkies and hardbodied skatergirls, I smugly
took him to task for daring to attempt a dissection of family tragedy
through the refracted lens of a borrowed genre that in order to tran-
scend parody would have required genius. I excoriated the man for the
grandiloquent gall of embarking on such a voyage, knowing full well
his ship would founder on remaindered shoals—*he had to have known.*
On that Saturday afternoon, dusk approaching, my blood and eyes
grew cold, and I seemed not to care a whit about the fortitude, the
sheer, steely gumption required for Thad to have taken up his own
dare. Then I wondered: Had I ever done anything equally ambitious
or recklessly poetic? Had the pathetic, unrealized, revenue-driven
scribblings of Bertram Valentine Krohn even faintly approached the
boldness of this monumentally disruptive, violent, seminal act? My
remorse compounded as I recalled Michelet's single-minded determi-
nation to devour his remaining son. How could anyone have survived
such a father? Or such a reader as I was turning out to be . . .

Yet the legacy of Jack Michelet's genius will outlive our days—
the ironic curse promised and delivered, it seems, by all *monstres
sacrés*. I stopped at the bookstore tucked behind the Sidewalk Café

and found a thin volume of poetry that put the old man in good graces again; I hated myself but what can be done? I wandered to the fiction shelf. The absence of Thad's novels alongside his dad's seemed a grievous wrong—an unmarked, looted grave, a desecration and ugliness perpetrated by that child killer, cannibal, madman. Thus I seesawed back and forth, pro-Thad, pro-Jack, pro-Thad, finally leaving the paper cemetery to take in the ambient exultation of seaside tourists, natives and buskers.[14] I was at odds with the carefree crowd, wading against their currents while stewing over the House of Michelet, surprised at how far off the deep end I could go when it came to other peoples' bad juju. Maybe it was the writer in me. But that sounds so—

Let me leave it at that.

MIRIAM GOT TICKETS FOR US to see a guru in Culver City.

She traded in her Taurus for a Mustang convertible. The wind was warm and gusty, and Meerkat[15] smelled of sea, sex, and rosewood oil: a stone summer groove. It was good to be on our own, away from "the kids" (that's what we called them). Though it went

[14] A moment oddly reminiscent of hours spent listening to NPR during the Iraqi invasion: the commentators' ceaselessly articulate, impotent point-counterpoints and my own irrelevant internal tug-of-war, syncopated to the jazz riffs bridging ads and pledge pleas.

[15] Knowing it may be cloying to some, I include the nickname out of breezy verisimilitude. Having gone this far—I think I've probably gotten footnotes out of my system, too—I'm afraid there's just a bit more to be revealed under the irritating file marked TMI: I had taken to calling her that after watching a show on the Discovery Channel, postcoital.

unspoken, we were half spooked about any craziness they might get into while out of our immediate supervision. Regardless, we made a concerted effort to chill. We felt like parents playing hooky from their A.D.D.'d brood, except in this case we hadn't found a sitter.

Tough titties.

The hall must have held a thousand people. There were a few celebrities—Garry Shandling, Cheryl Tiegs, Jeff Goldblum—nothing heavy. It was festival-seating, with everyone on folding chairs and lots of SRO overflow in back. A thin, leprechauney guy came out and spoke two hours, nonstop. I liked him right away. He said what I thought were typical guruish things but I really seemed to connect. He talked of that great stillness already in our possession from which truth and happiness emanate (yes, Badwater came to mind), a stillness we seemed intent on ignoring. Pain and suffering came from the inexhaustible need for money, food, sex. The guru said that merely becoming *aware* of the "forgotten stillness"—the stillness of the moment, the power of Now—was enough. "Why can't people see how simple it is?" he asked, and everyone laughed. Funny but true. Apparently, he'd investigated all manner of disciplines and "men of knowledge." One day, upon hearing a Zen master say "No thought!" the budding avatar realized he'd been deliriously happy the last few years for precisely that reason: he hadn't been *thinking*. (The audience laughed again.) Thoughts were like clouds, he said, the difference being that no two clouds were alike . . . whereas *thoughts* were usually the same. "The sky would be quite boring if filled only with thoughts," he said. The elfin sage jerked back his head, pointing to the heavens like an everyday Joe. "Look! Those two clouds are exactly alike." Playing the part of another curious pedestrian, he exclaimed, "Hey! There's that same cloud I saw *yesterday*—and the day before. Strange, but I saw it the day before *that*, too."

I kept thinking about Thad and his father. Was I becoming obsessed? I dismissed the notion as merely another cloud. Then others blew in on the horizon: the thunderheaded cumuliform of Clea and her mom . . .

the cirruslike wisp of Leif Farragon—you didn't need a weatherman (or a guru) to see the sky was filled with spirits. To my surprise I had truly begun to care about Thad, just as I cared for Clea, and Miriam too for that matter. They were the special creatures who had fallen for whatever karmic reason (to use the contagious jargon of the acolytes) into my orbit and I into theirs. I suppose I *was* obsessed—by making meaning of it all. Perhaps that was foolish. As the wise and ageless sprite spoke, I meditated on the brevity of life's duration and the significance of the drama that played out on one's personal stage. I don't mean to get corny or metaphysical but I couldn't help thinking I'd be derelict not to further investigate the path upon which my own heart had led me.

On the drive home, I told Miriam about my experience. I talked about finishing *The Soft Sea Horse,* all the miserable things I'd read that Jack had said about his son, and the crazy ambivalence I'd felt in trying to hash everything through—so very democratic, like an honor student mastering both sides of a debate. She smiled, rather gurulike herself, without entering into the fray; her way of acknowledging I was now a rarefield member of Thadwatchers (or Micheleteers), an adherent of the Inner Circle.

Instead of returning to the hotel, we made love at my house— though it sounds a bit convoluted I think at least *part* of the reason was to avoid competing with the raw ecstasies of the night before— when Shutters stripped and shuddered, an event whose tomfoolery probably imprinted itself upon the overpriced, designer-seashell-strewn aura of that room for at least ninety days. (A discreetly placed plaque should read: MIRIAM AND BERTIE DIDN'T GET MUCH SLEEP HERE.) A few minutes after we came, in simultaneous, symphonic ciss boom-bah, Miriam fired up a cigarette, sucked in a fog bank of smoke, and set to a little musing herself.

"I was thinking . . . you know—when you were talking about *The Soft Sea Horse.* I'm not exactly sure what Thad told you when you were on the train—and I know you've read the book, but some things didn't happen the way he wrote them. Like, he wasn't in Amagansett—or the Vineyard—when Jeremy died."

Knowing what I read was "fiction," I was still bemused. "But it said they came over to the island," I said, defensively. "After the drowning."

"That's what I'm saying. He wasn't *in* the States, he was with him in *Capri*. When it happened. Morgana was busy with a nervous breakdown—they finally put her in Silver Hill. Or somewhere. Lillian Hellman made the arrangements. I *think*. That's why Thad wound up going to Europe. What happened was, Morgana thought Jack was having an affair with Sophia Loren which he *completely* wasn't, he was screwing two *other* actresses on that shoot. And the set designer too! The twins were playing in the water . . ." She closed her eyes, as if projecting a legendarily lost film on the back of her lids. "And his *father*, that *mother*fucker, *blamed* him for it. As usual! I mean, he blamed that little guy if it *rained*. Jack thought it was deliberate. That was his theory! Some sort of *willful* act on Thad's part. The *asshole*. Bertie, can you imagine? The man was a shitty, shitty father, he *never* watched those kids, it was *criminal*, he was—a compulsive *pussyhound*. Anyway, it was just some creepy literary fantasy of Jack's, a Henry James thing. And later on, I think he was pissed Thad wrote about it because *he* was going to, *supposedly*, but didn't have the *stones*. Cajones? And he thought, *How dare he!* You know, *scooping* the big genius. Thad would *never* have been capable of hurting his brother, he *worshipped* him. But I guess capable and culpable are just a few letters off.

"Anyway, Thad got righteously blamed, and that's a heavy thing to get laid on you at that age. At *any* age! Jack just *poured* out his rage—the rage toward *Morgana* that he'd *always* had, I mean *way* before those kids were even *born*—they were nothing but . . . *burdens* to him—oh *right*, I know he was supposed to love Jeremy *so much*—that's part of the myth, OK? But you know, I don't even think it was true. Jack had a death wish—for everyone *else*, not for *himself*. So when Jeremy died, he probably felt whatever form of guilt he was capable of feeling and then he poured this *sick rage* on that poor, poor boy. It so breaks my heart, Bertie. It so breaks my heart!"

THE NIGHT PROVED A TONIC all around. On Sunday morning, Thad and Clea looked clear-eyed, luminous, and light of heart. I hadn't fully digested Miriam's cliffhanger about the twins being together that ill-fated day in Capri; my plan was to visit the Herrick Library and see what I could dig up. I wanted to hold a bit of fragile yellow newsprint in my hand, something the Internet couldn't allow.

But first, let me backtrack: we officially got busted.

See, everyone was supposed to hook up at Shutters around noon. The Dynamic Duo awakened early, fled the Chateau, and swung by Clea's to grab a swimsuit. When there was no sign of Miriam at the hotel, they naturally decided to kill time by dropping over to harass me; as they pulled up, Meerkat was just leaving. They clucked their tongues and said "Aha!" in grandly sophomoric pseudo-revelation.

Our pal had hired a driver, and I wasn't sure that was a good sign. Miriam wanted to run the Mustang over to Shutters to pick up a suit of her own but Thad insisted we take the Town Car on a "pit stop" then continue to the Colony. Clea was gung ho. She'd never been to my parents' beach house.

We piled into the Lincoln and, after a few minutes of ribbing on their part and half-assed blushing on ours, settled in for the short ride.

—◦—

My father bought the place twenty years ago and since then had acquired the adjoining properties (his modus operandi, as by now you know). The structure had endured a multitude of upgrades and add-ons in the Richard Meier mausoleum style—"ad mauseum," as Gita liked to say, otherwise cattily known as the School of Swiss Sanitoria. "Perfect," she noted wryly, "for your parents' mutual invalidism." The sand castle was a suitable showcase for Perry's outsized art and ego. I had pretty much left the nest by the time they moved in, and while I'm certain to have secretly—all right, maybe not so

secretly—coveted the general idea of a $15 million weekend getaway,
I was glad to note that for all its meticulous minimalism, in the end,
like an aesthetic black (OK, white) hole, the dwelling consumed
itself, and everything in near orbit. When I finally visited—already
in Berkeley and on the outs with Perry (Mom was inadvertently
tarred with that brush)—I realized for the first time just how much
money my father had accumulated through the years. My outlandish
disdain was tempered by the fact that Gita loved the beach: sun and
sea were therapeutic and rejuvenative. If that's what money could
buy, the house had been worth every penny.

Mars (short for Morris), the longtime, fortyish-looking sixty-
something majordomo, greeted us at the door. Dad was having a
massage and Mom was still asleep. Though just half an hour early, I
fitfully asked if my parents had remembered about brunch. Mars
smiled like a mandarin. Everything would be ready—he was cooking
the food himself—around noon. He suggested we take a stroll on the
beach.

It was a spectacular morning. Jerky breezes snappily rearranged
our hair and we chased each other around while rich, healthy dogs—
locals—leaped and barked. Since our covers had been pulled,
Miriam and I dared the occasional intimacy yet when Clea caught
my eye, I reflexively dropped my lover's hand with whatever casual-
ness I could muster. (It was silly but Meerkat seemed mildly
amused.) Thad gazed at the horizon with a kind of pilgrim's
poignant hopefulness, like someone with a fatal disease on the eve of
sailing away for a last-ditch cure. Clea spent a fair amount of time
watching him, not just monitoring moods but fixated on his essence
as an anthropologist upon a totem. He completed her in a way—I
was going to use "ennobled," the word I invoked for Morgana on
Black Jack's extirpation—but that wasn't wholly true, not in either
case. He *did* lend a kind of gravitas: she'd finally met someone whose
anchoring to this earth was more tenuous than her own. While Clea
always yearned for flight, she had voluntarily grounded herself for

this man—a lovely sacrifice. Though I'll never be certain, I think she must have already known she was pregnant.

Another thing that touched me was how sweetly anxious Clea was to see my parents again, this time in the company of her man. I'm sure she thought it legitimizing, making her more respectable to the world. If I'd had *my* wedding fantasies, I can only imagine what *her* feverish brain drummed up. She probably saw herself back at the Vineyard, fumigating ghosts of that haunted cliffhouse with a sage-burnt ceremony of sacred union. If that termagant Morgana were to deny permission, she knew the Colony would be readily offered (one helluva backup plan) and they'd be hitched without a hitch, vows exchanged in Chanel gown and bare feet over unnumbered grains of sand—which actually made today a kind of holy reconnoitering.

As we returned, the masseuse was leaving, an enormous folded leather table tucked under her arm with the ease of a yoga mat. Gita waved to us from the kitchen. Perry appeared, groggily post-shiatsu, with the newly arrived Captain Laughton and his (much) younger partner in tow. Dad gave all a generous greeting, with particular attention paid to Mr. Michelet, the informal guest of honor. As we entered the living room, Nick Sultan and his wife materialized at the front gate. Perry announced to Mars that "the door may now be bolted." Apart from the help, there were ten of us.

While I hadn't expected it, the addition of a few friendly couples was a relief. They leeched some pressure off. Of course it didn't hurt that the captain's fey, charming friend was slightly in awe of Thad, and not just for his film and stage work—he praised his novels and had the good sense not to bring up Jack. Whether or not he was sincere, he'd definitely done his homework, for which I was grateful.

Mom and Thad became instant partners in crime. She was always terrific with wounded souls and I think her being crippled allowed him to tap into the innate graciousness that played just beneath the surface of his cynical mask of social dysfunction. They were fellow Masons, funny and literate and conspiratorial—of the secret order of Those Who Knew. As the day grew longer they huddled and whispered, becoming even more fabulous and risqué. We gave them plenty of space. (I had a neurotic moment before reassuring myself Thad's scabrous repartee would stop short of any mockery of Father. He would never have been so crass.) For his part, Perry was pleased at the alliance; he never brought home much except riches, so he was satisfied not to take center stage, happy that *she* was happy.

Besides, he would soon shine during the Grand Tour. I knew it might be dicey but Dad was particularly eager to display various artifacts belonging to Jack Michelet that he'd collected over the years like so many big-game heads. He also knew there was business to be discussed, however obliquely: Miriam's odd proposal that her client novelize "Prodigal Son" for the *Starwatch* book series—I'd already primed the pump—and the more engaging idea of Nick Sultan's that the surviving son adapt *Chrysanthemum* to the big screen. In fact, Perry had invited the television director and his spouse for brunch out of the former's tenacious entreaties to package the shtick-fueled, intergenerational project. When I took Dad aside to briefly discuss, he said he'd have much preferred a "name" like Neil Jordan or Phil Noyce but had had the option for so damn long without incurring A-list interest ("A" for "Anyone") that Nick's passions were actually welcome. Besides, he said, if instinct had taught him anything, there was a lot to be said about going with what was in front of you.

I could tell Thad wasn't fond of the director and it wasn't hard to see why. Nick Sultan was one of those grating showbiz animals who couldn't take a breath without advancing some pet project or other. His American wife reflected the same naked ambition—an aging Gold's Gym rat, she must have thrown $40,000 at her teeth alone; exquisitely symmetrical, they gleamed like airbrushed headstones.

Though hardly saying a word, Mrs. Sultan possessed the boundless energy of a trained spaniel, one who could circle her tail (or her master's) ad infinitum, eating whatever amount of poo it took to get the job done.

When brunch was over Mars took latte orders, and that's when Dad made his move—like sweethearts, he and Thad adjourned on cue. I watched the others quietly wrestle with whether they should follow but strategically held them at bay, informing that my father's show-and-tells were heart-stoppingly tedious. I promised a scintillating private tour after espresso and desserts. They got the message.

As soon as they were safely engaged in frivolities (the captain's boyfriend thought he saw Sting strolling past and everyone ran to have a look) I sprinted in hot pursuit of host and honored guest, catching up in the library.

"Your father's firsts," said Perry, waving to a shelf of leather-bound folios. "Did Miriam tell you I hold the option on *Chrysanthemum*?"

"Yes," said Thad. "Mr. Sultan won't let me forget."

"He's interested in directing." I could tell by Dad's tone that he wanted us to know he was slumming by even considering the Brit. But another implication was at hand: Perry Needham Krohn's instincts never failed him. "I'm sure he'd do a fair job—he's certainly thought about it long enough. He's passionate, and I think that's key. If you have a passion, you're halfway there."

"Talent helps," said Thad drolly.

(A small, unvarnished dig that my father dug.)

"Talent *would* be nice. But Nick comes from British theater."

"They *all* come from British theater."

"Right—the RSC. Well if he can hack *Marat/Sade*, I'm hoping he's up for *Chrysanthemum*. Besides, you've got people like Rob Marshall hitting home runs, right out of the box. Nick's got great energy."

Suddenly he was cheerleading, which I doubt had been his intention. As if to stop himself in his tracks, he turned to ask what *I* thought.

"It's kind of hard to judge from his work on the set. I mean, it's a well-oiled machine at this point, right? A feature takes a whole different—"

"True," said Perry. He faced our friend. "What do you think of *Chrysanthemum?* As one of your father's books." A good, simple question which I'm sure gave Dad the fleeting sense he'd regained control. When Thad didn't reply, he added, somewhat awkwardly, "What's your opinion?"

"I've always had a special relationship to that novel," said Thad, without elaborating.

This seemed to please my father.

"Nick said it might be something you'd like to adapt."

"I didn't *quite* say that."

He was standoffish though still friendly—not so much hard-to-get, but insinuating the complexities of blood he knew Perry would appreciate.

"I thought it'd be a hell of an interesting experiment. Son adapting father." Dad was in murky waters but I didn't intervene. "I like the *idea* of it."

Thad walked closer to a framed watercolor.

"Recognize it?" my father asked. "One of Jack's."

"Yes," said Thad. "I do."

It was a woman with her legs spread, hands cupping a resplendent purple vulva.

"A recurring theme," he said, not without humor. "You know, Perry . . . what *really* interests me—at the *moment*—and I'm not saying I wouldn't want to take a stab at *Chrysanthemum* because that intrigues as well, it really does."

"OK." He exhaled, giving Thad his full attention—like a merchant ready to barter.

"What I've *really* been thinking about is your *book* series."

Dad wrinkled his brow as if downshifting to a lower mental gear. He politely nodded. "Miriam mentioned something about that. Now *I'm* intrigued. Tell me more!"

"Well, I guess I'm a little perverse! Since my father's death, there seems to be a lot of interest in Michelet properties in general. Someone even wants to do my first book, *The Soft Sea Horse*."

Miriam appeared in the door. "Mikkel Skarsgaard," she said.

"The marvelous DP," said Dad authoritatively. He had a staff of people paid exclusively to keep him abreast of rising (and falling) hipsters in the art and film worlds.

"I'm really interested in doing a *Starwatch* book . . ."

" 'Prodigal Son,' " said Miriam, offering what my father already knew.

"It's *transgressive*," said Thad.

"He wants to do something . . . subversive," said Miriam. "Counterintuitive."

They were wisely appealing to the "collector" side of dad, the Perry Krohn who'd been known to chicly underwrite tedious performance pieces. He laughed amiably.

"It *does* seem a bit of a waste of your talents."

"I—I can't explain!" said Thad, grinning ear to ear.

"It's his Matthew Barney moment," said Miriam.

"I love Matthew Barney," said Perry.

He seemed to brighten and grow vacant all at once because though the analogy made no sense whatsoever my father was afraid that it did and he'd missed something. He indulged them because he didn't remotely want to be the butt of a joke, no matter how obscure.

"It'd be *great*," said Miriam, jauntily bringing things back down to Earth. "I mean, Thad's such a wonderful prose writer as is."

"We're talking about you novelizing 'Prodigal Son'?" said Dad, to clarify.

"*Yes*. I'd actually love to do it as *two* books," said Thad, overenthused (and with Black Jack's will in mind; two books would increase the odds). Perry all but scratched his head—at least he was still smiling. "I'm serious!"

"All right, then let's make it happen!" said Perry, leading us from the library.

Thad gushed his thanks (as if that were all that was legally required to seal the deal), while Miriam obsequiously trumpeted the Dadaist brilliance of it all. My guess was that Father thought it more socially expedient to acquiesce than debate the point. It was some kind of silliness.

I decided to talk with him about the whole business later on and promised as much to Miriam. I was a little concerned Thad hadn't given enough lip service to *Chrysanthemum*, which after all was my father's baby, or should I say, orphan. I could illuminate the testamentary backstory, without which Thad's zeal must have seemed bizarre—here was an opportunity to score a classy screenwriting credit for a significant chunk of change yet for some reason young Michelet was hell-bent on churning out one of the cookie-cutter volumes of an obscenely banal book series instead, a series already vaguely embarrassing to his employer, a man who prided himself on being a bibliophile (and author) yet whose only aggressive contribution to world literature thus far was this commercial *offal*, this worthless waste of tree and ink, this dumb and dumber encyclopedia of embroidered teleplays. On the other hand, Perry had always shown a sense of humor when one least expected, a levity about his life and the grotesquely lucrative permutations it had taken: that was his saving grace. Emphatically, the only way any of this might go down would be if yours truly laid out the cold, hard facts of the situation, IRS and all. Best not to be underhanded with Dad—it would only backfire. I'd clear it with Meerkat first, but knew she'd be game.

As we rejoined the others, I overheard Miriam "spinning" my father while they walked, arm-in-arm. "It's gonna be *great*," she said. "And I know he'll want to do *Chrysanthemum* too. The novelization will be a warm up."

Now Dad was having *his* fun. "If he agrees to costar in the next *Starwatch* feature, I'll think about it. And I mean for scale!"

— • —

We settled onto the patio to watch the beachscape.

"The sea is high today, with a thrilling flush of wind," Thad declaimed. The first line, he said, of *The Alexandria Quartet*.

Nick moved his chair closer as if for a tête-à-tête, which didn't make the budding Morloch happy (as the sun dipped, his warm-demeanored ensignhood began to chill). Clea smartly created a diversion, tearing off to frolic with a golden retriever. Miriam followed in Frisbee'd pursuit and the captain's partner joined them, demonstrating an exemplary wrist-flicking technique. Gita, who'd vanished upstairs awhile, reappeared at the outside elevator. Seeing her, Thad affectionately made the starship *whoosh* as Carmen pushed Mom toward our remaining little group.

"The technology of the palace is quite impressive, Captain, don't you agree?"

Laughton looked over with a vacant smile; he may not have heard through the crashing of waves.

"I mean," said Thad, "you must be aware there are no oceans—not as you know them—in the Vorbalidian sector. I hasten to add what you're now seeing isn't a holograph: it's an aggregation of supercells, a benignly metastatic *reconstruction*, not a replica, of the immense body of water known as the Pacific that is native to your planet. Scratch the surface and you'll even find fish and flora. *Some* genetic differences but fish and flora nonetheless—actually quite edible!"

"Aye-aye, Ensign Rattweil, or shall I call you Prince?" said Laughton, getting into the spirit.

"You may call me Morloch."

"The Artist Formerly Known as Ensign," I said, going retro for the sake of the gagline.

Gita wheeled to the terrace on her own power.

Thad acknowledged her with a wink. "Hello, Mother. Glad you could join us."

"That's *Queen* Mother, to you," interjected the drunken captain, announcing himself as a formerly closeted traveler, now from "outed space."

Gita drank from a flute of Champagne before saying, "Otherwise known as Her Royal Pain—to my husband anyway."

Nick tried to play but was frozen out.

His wife wisely retreated in the direction of the Frisbeeites.

"Commander Karp," said Laughton. "Have you been introduced to the concubines?"

"*Incredibly* authentic," I said, snapping sordidly into character. "I believe X-Ray is making the formal request we be allowed to bring them aboard—scientific study, of course."

Clea and Miriam laughingly returned to the deck. They were wet to their hips.

"Oh my God!" said Clea, breathlessly. "It is *so beautiful*."

"The water is *amazing*," said Miriam.

In the distance, the captain's partner still frolicked, joined by flat-stomached stringy-haired teens and a few more cash-rich dogs.

"Aye, Ambassador Trothex! We were just talking about the astonishing Vorbalidian science. The water, not being water, feels more like water than water itself!"

"It's a rare thing when we Vorbalids are allowed to enjoy the fruits of our own technology," said Clea. "It is only because of your diplomatic visit that we've been sanctioned to experience 'the Malibu.' Do you have a name for this sort of activity, Commander? Other than the subgenre 'R and R'?"

"Yes," I said, eyebrow raised. (My Cabott impression.) "I believe the Earthling slang is an obscure, three-letter word. The pronunciation is 'fun.' "

"*Fun*," echoed Clea, morosely contemplative.

Miriam giggled as the game devolved and everyone made a dash for fresh rounds of food and drink. Only Thad remained engrossed, albeit in a softer, minor key.

"I will have to fight my brother Morloch," he said to himself, resigned. "It's the only way the others can be saved."

I didn't think anyone else heard but then I saw a perturbed look on Gita's face. Sensing something wasn't right, she engaged "instruments" in an effort to stabilize. Mother delicately brought up the canceled Beckett play (I told her about it a few days ago), and how much she admired anyone with the fortitude to tackle "the craggy Irishman"—like a famously genial professor, she added a subtler intellect to the grosser Perry Krohn equation, for balance. Under the pull of her gentle conversational prodding, Thad eventually broke free of the tractor beam of Vorbalidian constructs. He spoke for a while like a charmingly distracted, slightly defeated person.

She even asked after Morgana. He said that when his mother heard he was doing *Starwatch*, flowers had been sent (chrysanthemums, actually) along with a note: "Beaming down lots of love." Gita laughed. She told him she knew Mrs. Michelet's work though admitted confusing it with "that Ettlinger woman," which he got a kick out of. For a moment, I panicked Mom was going to ask if he'd ever sat for an official portrait but my worry was needless.

Thad espied a small, wet neighborhood boy, a shivery partycrasher of about nine, standing at the cornucopia of the buffet table cogitating over what he might help himself to. Mars handed the towhead a towel; without taking his eyes off the food, the visitor draped it over his blonde-downed, sparrow's shoulders.

"There's something so . . . perfect and monstrous about the drowning of a child," said Thad, taking the child's measure.

The comment jarred Gita anew. I moved closer, as if to shield Thad's words from the guests and muffle him from the world as well.

"Jeremy was like that when they found him—down in the flooded library of the Aegean, the *tiniest* Leopardi. I made my way through schools of Father's iridescent books. Heartbreaking it was, to see him broken on the reef with his funny glasses."

Gita glanced at me then put her hand on Thad's.

Clea joined us with a plate of pasta and eggs, and an unsuspecting smile.

"He already had little scales. The eyes were hooded and when the lids opened . . . cobalt blue! Like the most fantastic marbles. Beautiful—*beautiful*. He hung there in the water, twisting ever so slowly . . . the softest of sea horses. Oh, it was him all right! The picture pride of Hollywood. I *knew* it was him. 'Too many fall from great and good for you to doubt the likelihood. *Die early and avoid the fate'*—"

The captain bounded over unawares, Miriam at his heels. Observing Clea's darkened face, and mine and Gita's as well, the book agent knew something was up.

"Well, well," said Laughton, still oblivious. "I see our beloved ensign is in sequestration with his mum, the Vorbalid queen!"

"That would be *you*," his boyfriend shouted, approaching the bridge.

"Thad," said Gita. "Are you all right? Would you like to go in and lie down?"

Everyone instantly grew solemn-faced. Father came out. Thad was still fixated on the towel-shrouded boy, who, plate filled, shuffled back to sea and sand.

"Headache," said Thad, without much conviction.

Clea knelt by his side and quietly asked if he'd brought his "medicine," whatever that was code for—in moments like this, I'd gladly have forked over heroin. I just wanted him "fixed."

He'd be fine, said Thad, if only he could "catnap." Clea and Miriam helped him to his feet. Carmen met them at the elevator and up they *whooshed,* as if to sickbay. Nick made a few predictable comments about how his mother, who lived in a place with the wretched name of Slough, also suffered migraines—remarks calculated to communally minimalize Thad's short-term miseries while self-servingly allowing the director to keep his eyes on the prize of any long-term Thad-related goals. The tomb-raiding wife nodded along, in mercenary cahoots to rescue and coddle future deals at any cost. Thankfully, the couple soon announced they were going home (a Point Dume rental). The captain and his partner discreetly ambled down the coast to let things settle before taking leave. Dad wondered aloud if we should call Thad's personal physician, then excused himself to retrieve a bottle of wine from the cellar.

I sat with Mother and she looked so sad.

Her gaze fell over the water, blinking at gulls and whitecaps.

"What an awful time of it some people have, Bertie. What an awful time."

THAD SLEPT NEARLY TWO HOURS with Clea beside him.

Meerkat and I spooned on the couch, dozing off between cigarettes, kisses, and long vacant stares at the broiling, turquoise-veined ocean. We didn't hide our affections from Mom, who was perfectly content to sit and read her Sunday *Book Review*. With a rare full house, she was comforted by the resurrection of family.

Upon awakening, Thad took a shower (we all did, in various venues) and drew a serious second wind. It was dusk when he resurfaced, fully dressed and headache-free. Mom invited us to stay for supper but Thad sang "Hello, I must be going," explaining he had an early call. He suggested that Clea, Miriam, and I remain; he'd send his driver for us later, which of course was completely absurd.

— • —

On the way back to Shutters, Thad suggested we dine at Chez Jay, a favorite beach haunt. (He was often ravenous after a migraine.) I wasn't up for it, and neither was Miriam—the protracted outing was beginning to acquire a manic, marathon flavor—but we acquiesced, mostly out of caution due to the weirdness of what we had earlier witnessed. Thad still didn't seem himself.[16]

By the time we were seated, the mood had soured; congealed might be a better word. Miriam became the codependent poster child, overly solicitous of the group gestalt, her words and gestures abrasively convivial. Clea, obviously intoxicated, sniped at my "addiction" to Diet Coke—clearly, my sobriety made it impossible for her to fully enjoy her loadedness. I wanted to flee but reminded myself that apart from possessing a psychotic component which, without warning, blossomed into hallucination, our troubled friend was at this point somewhat of a wild card, and volatile enough that I worried for the girls' safety.

For sport, we began trashing Nick Sultan and his wife. The tiny grenades, lobbed at an easy, faraway target, provided comic relief. This went on for a while. More drinks were served, more plates of calamari consumed. Clea went to the head for a *long-ass* time. Just when Miriam got up to check, she returned—the wily Meerkat kept right on going, cool as could be. Thad sat there, drinking and covertly eating pills; the man had a whale's bladder. Steak and lobster arrived. I thought we were over the rough part (something having to do with a private, fanciful theory that food would absorb the chemicals) when a man with longish hair appeared.

I braced myself, hoping it wasn't a *Jetsons* fan.

"Excuse me," he said with an accent I couldn't identify. "You are Mr. Michelet?" Thad looked up with a cold smile, readying himself for whichever assault. "I am Mikkel Skarsgaard. I am planning to make a film from your book, *The Soft Sea Horse.*"

[16] Please forgive the small, broken promise of this final annotation. But in the rereading, "Thad still didn't seem himself" now strikes me as presumptuous and a little arrogant. I don't think any of us know who we are—let alone what defines others. Maybe that's just the Culver City guru in me talking.

"Ah!" said Thad, welcoming. "The cinematographer! Hello! Hello!"

Miriam and Clea chirped eager greetings. Thad asked him to join us.

"But I don't wish to disturb you!" said the respectful Dane.

"No no! We insist! We're so bored with each other's company!"

"Yes?" he said, diffidently. "But there are three of us, no?" He nodded toward a back booth. "It is OK?"

"It is OK!"

Mikkel gathered his friends while an animated Thad requested more chairs. I was grateful for the change in mood a new cast of characters would bring. Besides, it was a nice omen. Mikkel seemed the kind, unpretentious director type, his civil, unassuming demeanor in pleasant opposition to Nick Sultan's tritely raw ambition.

He returned to the table accompanied by a pale, towering, beetle-browed man—and Sharon Stone. I'd never seen her in person (I wasn't a huge fan) but had to admit she was gorgeous. She wore blue jeans and a cowl-necked sweater that coddled her American thoroughbred bones—the kind of beauty you'd find in a *Town & Country* spread, loading up a vintage Wagoneer with groceries in Montecito in one photo, attending a cancer gala in La Jolla with Watson and Crick in another. Mikkel said they were old friends; I assumed he'd shot one of her early films. (As if in deference to the skittishness of their reedy, frozen-smiled companion, the DP's relationship to the latter was left unexplained.) Running into them was truly auspicious because Mikkel revealed that Sharon had been considering the "movie star" role in *Sea Horse*—the fictionalized woman with whom the fictionalized Jack had an affair, in fictionalized Capri. Ms. Stone was a bit of a culture vulture, sharing that she'd actually seen one of Thad's avant garde theater productions in Vienna, which excited him enormously.

When Clea reminded her they'd met some years ago at the Venice Film Festival, Sharon said "Yes!" though it was obvious she didn't remember. I could see that she recognized Clea from the movies but wasn't able to place her. Then Miriam announced who her mother was and everything changed—Sharon was suddenly thrilled. She was "hugely into Roosevelt Chandler" and mentioned having developed a biopic with Milos Forman that never got off the ground. Clea said she'd heard about that and was sorry it didn't happen. In the spirit of genetic brushes with the high and mighty, Meerkat impulsively introduced me as Son of Perry Krohn. The gracious celeb claimed to be a fan of *Starwatch* as well, and knew (through Mikkel, who'd been told by Klotcher) Thad was doing a guest spot; Miriam efficiently informed that Clea and I were "costarring." The actress then turned to our host, and considerately acknowledged his father's passing. She spoke of her own near-death experience a few years back, when she hemorrhaged into her skull—a natural cue for Michelet to talk Migraine. I asked Mikkel a question or two about *Sea Horse,* availing Thad and Sharon their medical bonding moment.

Sharon was flying to New York early in the morning. She stood to leave, shaking hands all around with that special brio and fanatical eye contact movie stars seem to conjure at will. She saved Thad for the end, accurately assessing his dominance in the present pecking order—another hardwired, faultless celebrity instinct.

I was a little surprised when the two men remained.

"She's so lovely," said Clea.

"A very special lady," said Mikkel.

"Did she actually have a stroke?" asked Miriam.

"It was . . . a bleeding in the brain," said Mikkel.

"Everybody should have a stroke and look so good," said Clea.

"She tells the story—one day you'll hear. They were wheeling her for the surgery and the doctor was holding a paper in his hand. 'Look! We just got a fax from *People* magazine!' Can you imagine? He was *happy.* She fired him, right from the table. She is like a general, a warrior! Sharon wants to make a one-woman show. Would be amazing, no? Everyone would see it. Now she doesn't give a fuck about people and how they perceive of her. Since it has happened, she is only filled with terrific joy and happiness for all the people. Not cynical Hollywood bullshit. And ten times more amazing looking than before surgery, no? You can see! The skin glows, like an angel. Something I think really *spiritual* happened. Maybe you can help her write a play," he said to Thad.

"She's incredibly beautiful," he answered, affectlessly.

Her sudden exit had left him strangely deflated.

To be social, Mikkel asked how I made my living. (I guess he'd zoned during Miriam's presentation of my curriculum vitae.) I told him I was an actor. This time, it was Clea who felt compelled to add that my father was the creator of *Starwatch*. The DP's eyes lit up—as if by the stitch of a master tailor I had been transformed from klutz to *fashionista*.

"I can't wait to begin the script," said Thad, trying to jump-start himself.

"Mordecai is hoping to make a deal very fast," said Mikkel.

"Mordy's a character, isn't he?" said Thad.

"Did you know Christopher Nolan is to exec produce?"

"No," said Thad, with the open smile of a naïf. "He is—"

"*Memento.*"

"And *Insomnia*," added Clea, authoritatively enthused.

"Wow," said Thad. "Do you live here?"

"I am in New York, mostly. But when I come, I stay at Silver Lake."

"Are you in Denmark much?" asked Miriam.

"Two times a year, but not really for film. Lately, because my mother has been ill."

"Sorry to hear it," said Thad.

"Ironically, I am there quite soon to shoot the Spielberg, which locates in Copenhagen for eight weeks' time. So it seems I cannot get away."

"But you'll be able to see your mom," said Miriam.

"Yes. A big side benefit," he said, with an empty smile meant to charm.

"We didn't meet your friend," said Thad, gesturing at the tall, silent one.

"This is Henrik," said Mikkel, in that smug way people have when introducing strangers to a legendary vintage from their private reserve.

The rangy eccentric dutifully echoed his own name, inducing Clea to remark to Miriam, sotto, "He's like something out of Hans Christian Anderson!"

Thad focused on the DP. "I haven't written a script in a while—how do you like to work?" Then, without waiting for a reply: "I'll probably bang something out then come see you for an 'intensive.'"

"Well, it is something we would have to discuss," said Mikkel, stiffening. "I am usually making an adaptation myself. This I try and do first." He caught Thad's look and awkwardly amended. "But who knows? Maybe we do *both* ways. We both together on parallel track: then compare notes!"

The nascent director's hedge had failed. Clea and I squirmed.

"You can make a very much lot of money," said Henrik, precipitately.

"This giant fellow is a money man!" said Mikkel, patting his friend's shoulder.

"We *furnish* you with money," said Henrik, oddly emphasizing the word.

Gauging Thad's mood, Mikkel said, "Oh please, not now!"

"You are his agent?" asked Henrik of Miriam, somewhat aggressively.

"His book agent, yes."

"You are not theatrical?"

"No," said Miriam. "But any option of material would go through me."

She wasn't sure why he was asking, and felt silly having replied with such formality.

"Ah! Do you drive a hard bargain?" Henrik lit up. The fairy-tale wraith had found his métier.

"She's been known to," said Clea, in biker chickese.

"But I wished to speak about something else," said Henrik. "May I? Candidly?" Mikkel put a hand on Henrik's arm, as if to demonstrate that his friend was an unruly, amusing child who it was best to indulge without taking seriously. "I am a designer from Oslo. Your father's books are *very* big in Norway! I design *furnishings,* for the home. We would like to do a Jack Michelet line, like the Ernest Hemingway Collection—Thomasville. You heard of the company Thomasville, no? They do Hemingway, Bogart—I think soon they do Fitzgerald. All our research has adjudicated a Jack Michelet line would performance *very* well. I have seen photographic archives of the Vineyard compound and the homes your daddy, Black Jack— what *fantastic* nickname, no?—lived in through the many years. You lived there too, yes? No? You can be wonderful to consult! But this thing I am saying is that you would be *perfect* to announce it on television."

"What?" said Thad, beyond flustered.

"The line," said Henrik.

"Your movies have done well in Norway too, yes? No?" said Mikkel.

I thought it ill timed that the semifamous DP, close to optioning one of Thad's books for his directorial debut, would allow the lobbying of his friend's outrageous endorsement gambit. On second thought, maybe it was part of an overall deal the peculiar twosome had struck, and that in exchange for funding *Sea Horse,* Mikkel was beholden to "access Hollywood" for Henrik's ludicrous hustles.

"Everyone in Denmark loves *The Jetsons* and *Don Quixote,*" said Mikkel. "You are—what is the phrase?—instantly recognizable."

"We would fly you first class—maybe business," said Henrik, elbowing Miriam as he chuckled. "No, I am kidding. It is private plane, the same we rode Jim Carrey. The taping of our fantastic commercial would take only two days, *max*, for a *very* nice amount of cash—or gold bullion!" He winked at Clea. "I kid again."

He began a travel agent's monologue about the splendors of Copenhagen and how everyone (we were all invited) would be shown its wonders.

Mikkel presciently changed tack. "Does Mordecai make the deal for underlying material?" he asked Miriam. "To effect the option?"

"I'll give him a call," she said, coolly.

"Mordy said it could be five thousand—which, frankly, Miriam, is too much!" She flinched at the DP's familiarity. "It is an independent production, yes? No? And no one has shown interest! The book is out of print many years, yes? No? So I am asking for a little break. The room to *wiggle*. You can help affect that, yes? OK? It will be a showcase for the novel, of *course*, but I am thinking to do not so much an *Adaptation* like Charlie Kaufman but as a screenwriter to of course take certain liberties. I will keep the twins, yes, the drowned boy he is *amazing*, and Black Jack who is like Jack Palance in *Contempt*, no?—another Jack!—but also I wish to make myself a bit of a character in the movie. (This, the one thing I like very much about *Adaptation*. The rest, I was not so thrilled as everyone. But still it is a good movie, *very* good. I like Sofia better.) I wish to make a bit of experiment, for myself to act. I have spoken with Christopher Nolan and he excites. We potentially shoot in Denmark, for the light. You cannot find that light here, yes? The light here is *amazing*. I talk with Wim about this just last night. The light *there* is from my soul! I wish to make a 'film blanc,' not film noir!—this is what they called *Insomnia* too, did you see it? You saw it, no? We may ask Al to do a little something for *Sea Horse*. If his life and schedule allow. Pacino has busy, busy life! But he is amazing. He would do this for Christopher. I wish to explore what it means the tradition of a DP directing a first film. A *Danish* DP—like me, yes? No?—who makes film in the middle of divorce."

"Like yourself!" said Henrik, gleefully.

"Yes, myself!"

"A *Sea Horse* marriage—also 'out of print'!" said Henrik, wickedly. "A marriage that is now *unfurnished*."

Mikkel laughed, ruefully. "So I was thinking more in the 'ballpark' of a few thousand for the option, the rest deferred. Back end. We *all* defer on this project."

"We have back ends like Jennifer Lopez!"

"It is a project of love, OK? No? Just so when you talk to Mordecai."

Miriam nodded in exasperation. We wondered how much longer the onslaught would last. Clea had literally wedged herself into Thad, to brace him.

"We can pay you with a Jack Michelet sofa!" said Henrik, nudging Thad while clapping enormous, skeletal hands. "I can tell you are a couch potato so you'll love the design! Your daddy had eyes for things inventive but solidly built—like his women! He liked the women, yes? You are like that, no? We are all like that, even the women like the women! But in his fiction he could create a mood, an *ambience*. Is what he did with novels, yes? You try to do that, *almost*. I only read your one book, the *Sea Horse*. But one day you succeed across the boards! One day we have the Thad Michelet sofa, father and son furnishings!" His voice lowered and he grew serious. "The architectural look of Mr. Black Jack was colonial elegance—very much closer to Papa in Cuba. Or the Bogart Romanoff party table, have you seen? I send the Thomasville catalogue, you will *love* their Chesterfield table. A leather sleigh bed and *amazing* Bogart 'El Morocco' bar and stool. In our collection we have the Michelet 'Vineyard' divan.

"I am calling the fabric *Chrysanthemum*—all named after books and residences—already I am visited the best mills in China."

LATE MONDAY MORNING I LEARNED Thad awakened around
2:00 A.M. with another migraine. Clea took him to Cedars. Again,
production boards were juggled so that his services weren't needed
until the following day, when the duel between Morloch and the
ensign was to be staged.

At this point in 'Prodigal's' scenario, the starship ensemble
felt the full, bipolarizing tug of the Dome, causing that debilitating
condition known as Stanislavski syndrome. Nick Sultan spread his
auteur wings—he thought of himself as a kind of boob-tube
Sam Mendes—but sadly, such happiness would not be sustained
through production's end. Vorbalidian prosecutors wore absurdly
powdered wigs as the *Demeter* crew, in stylish captives' robes and
chains, stood trial for their very sanity. Emissaries of the king,
high-minded twits, malevolent magistrates, and venomous palace
prosecutors skedaddled like extras in Mr. Sultan's long-forgotten
RSC production of *Marat/Sade*. The normally laconic android
grew hysterically loquacious; the captain whined, whinnied, and
brooded in aforementioned junior college *Hamlet* mode; X-Ray was
placed on suicide watch after pronouncing he was "more fit to work
in a slaughterhouse than a temple of healing"; whilst I, ruggedly reliable, peripatetically priapic Karp, found myself literally and metaphor-
ically impotent, a pilot whose pilot light had gone out, a flyboy
castrati whistling in the Domed dark.

Such was the cheap stuff Emmy dreams were made of.

—•—

The next morning, I drove to the Margaret Herrick Library over on
La Cienega.

I'd been there before to poke around, chasing story ideas that
never panned out. It was a clean, well-funded place, somehow connected to the Academy. The cool, classical hush of its interiors
reminded me of the Huntington in Pasadena. I filled out the form

and a few minutes later an officious clerk returned with a folder of clippings, production notes, stills, and related ephemera.

Son of Author Michelet Drowns

(Italy) The 12-year-old son of Pulitzer Prize–winning novelist Jack Michelet drowned Monday during the shoot-ing of a film off the coast of Capri. Jeremy Michelet was missing for several hours from his father's yacht, *The Soft Sea Horse*, which was being used as a location for a movie based on one of his books. The body was found later that day by a fisherman. The production of *The Death of a Translator*, starring Alain Delon and Sophia Loren, has been suspended for a week. Mr. Michelet wrote the screenplay.

There were photos from the press kit—Jack with the director, Jack with Sophia, Jack with Alain—but nothing of the boys.

I closed my eyes and set the stage, remembering what Thad once told me: reflexively supplanting Jeremy's face with that of Leif Farragon's, I imagined the twins in the water . . . saw the boy sinking, and Thad saying nothing for the longest time. It must have been dreamlike, as if nothing had happened . . . yet *everything* had, everything and nothing all at once! Life and death, past and future, each canceling out the other—precisely how *I'd* felt (in far lesser degrees) upon learning Roosevelt Chandler was no longer of this world. Suddenly, lugubrious manila file in hand, I felt like a cow-ard for being able to walk away from the scene of the crime (his monologue about the killer from *Chrysanthemum* came back to mind) and *stay* away so many years. But Thad was left to simmer and boil, forever connected by tissue and bone to his overthrown, ambivalent beloved. And the worst was yet to come: soon to be ruled against by that monstrous Neptune, and sentenced by Mom, in absentia, before eternal banishment to the suppurative Hades of Migraine . . .

"SO, WHAT DO YOU THINK about hiring Thad?"

"For what?"

"To write one of the books. You know—'Prodigal Son.' "

"What are you, his agent?" said Perry, sardonically. "He needs one, by the way. Miriam's a nice person, but a little quaint. What the fuck do *you* care, anyway? We get *drones* for that—it's practically a software program. Why is he even interested? I mean, are they serious? Is it supposed to be 'camp'? Because I'm *tellin'* you, it *ain't*. *Much* rather see him do the movie. Anyway, we can't *pay* anything to write that crap. It's fifteen grand. *Maybe.* He'd get more spending a day at a *Starwatch* convention."

"Dad, can I tell you a secret?" His ears pricked up. "But this is . . . something you *cannot* talk about. With *anyone*."

"What is it?"

I told him about the IRS trouble and the $10 million proviso of Jack's will.

"Jesus," said Perry, taking a deep breath. "That's astonishing! My God. All right—let me think about this." He nodded, stroking his chin. I was really glad that he "got" it; I knew I had him. "OK. I'm inclined to do it. Jesus—that's like something out of one of his father's books! Boy oh boy. *Nasty.*" He laughed but not in a way that was cruel. "Nasty, nasty, nasty! All right, let me mull this over, Bertram. But I'm predisposed. And don't discuss it—not yet. You know, you should get a fucking commission if he pulls this off! Which, by the way, I very much doubt is possible. Because I have to tell you: only one or two of those titles ever made the list that I *know* of, maybe only one." I told him he was wrong about that. "The *Times?* The *New York Times?* And that's the stipulation? Holy shit. Well, that must have been a while back, when the show was at its peak. We're talking *paperback* list—hardcover, forget. The series isn't so popular anymore. In fact, we might phase it out entirely."

Watching him, I knew he already saw himself in the index of some future Michelet biography: Krohn, Perry Needham, *generosity of*.

"You know, I'm worried about your friend."

"What do you mean?"

"If you're going to be his patron, maybe you should look after him a bit."

"In what way?"

"I got a call. From Sherry Evans. Clea has a nasty bruise on her jaw. Did you know about this?"

"No."

"She said she fell in the bathroom."

The comment had big quotes around it.

"When?"

"She called about an hour ago."

"Who's Sherry Evans?"

"A makeup gal. She was concerned and didn't know who to tell." (He'd inadvertently exposed a lover.)

"I'll talk to Clea," I said.

My heart was racing.

"Maybe you should talk to *him*."

He walked to his desk and retrieved a book.

"Did I show you this?"

It was a copy of *The Soft Sea Horse*.

He held open the title page to display Thad's dedication.

> *a Perry Menopausal, con mucho cariño . . .*
> *"E le morte stagioni"*
> *Ever Thine,*
> ♥
> *Thaddeus (Leapin') Leopardi*

"Do you know what it means?" I felt like an ass but nothing else came to mind.

"Not a clue. But you'll handle him—I mean, you're gonna be his *padrone*, right?"

— • —

A sense of panic and betrayal gripped me as soon as I left my father's house.

I frantically called the studio but Clea was in the middle of a scene. The A.D. intuited my concerns and assured she was "totally OK." I asked about Thad and he said, "Seems completely fine." (Like a candy striper reassuring a distraught relative.) I would have driven directly over if not for the big meeting at HBO, though it probably was better I didn't. If Perry's allegations were true—that Thad struck Clea, stoned *or* stone-cold sober—I wasn't sure I'd be able to control my temper. I didn't enjoy the feeling. I never liked the out-of-control thing.

I went to Century City with some agents from CAA and my dad's old friend, Dan Fauci. When Dan was head of Paramount Television he made something like ninety pilots. Now he had a development deal, with an office on the lot. He had graciously played "rabbi" on *Holmby Hills*, overseeing my work on the outline; although by now I'd written an extensive précis, Dan said it was important "not to leave anything behind" after the pitch. *No written material*. But it was key to have done your homework so that any questions from the network could be finessed.

The meeting went well, or well enough—hard to gauge because it was the first I'd taken in my spanking-new role of all-seeing all-knowing writer-creator. I felt a little heady: you could see how guys like David Kelley or David Chase or David Milch (pick a David, any David) got hooked. No one brought up my father and that showed some class. But Perry was no David—he was demographically over-the-hill.

On the way out, a young exec sidled up to say he was a big fan of *Starwatch*.

"Clea Fremantle came in last week to pitch a show," he said.

"Really?"

There was something about the way he asked if I knew her that made me instinctively play down our relationship. Later, I felt sleazy about it. Anyhow, she'd never said anything about pitching HBO.

"It was so crazy! She came in with Thad Michelet—in fact, he's out here doing a *Starwatch*. But you already know that."

I could tell he wanted to gossip but was being politic.

"Yeah, he's great!" I enthused, vacantly. I know it was seedy but I was distancing myself so the guy would feel comfortable about telling all.

"They had this *insane* sitcom idea, kind of like a *Curb Your Enthusiasm*? About the almost-famous kids of famous parents. I mean *grown-up* kids—like Thad and Clea! They sort of typecast themselves." He played it close to the vest, subtly scanning my allegiances to measure just how far he could go. "It's a *really* funny idea, but—well, the meeting was *strange*."

"In what way?"

I smiled, indicating that I was up for a little slander.

"He's a character!" said the exec.

I could tell he was getting ready to spill.

"Pretty interesting guy," I said, cagily noncommittal.

"*Wild*. And *she's* wild *too*. Looks a *lot* like her mom." We were halfway down the hall, ahead of the others. "And I'm a *serious* Roos Chandlerphile. A Roos*aholic*."

Morbidly, I steered him back. "So, what happened?"

"Do you promise not to mention this? I mean, to either of them?"

I nodded eagerly. The exec knew he could be reasonably sure I wouldn't pass on anything that was said in confidence, for fear it might endanger my *own* project. He was smart and brash, and enjoyed the spice of telling tales out of school.

"I thought you would have *heard* this already," he said, lowering his voice. "I think they were loaded. I don't know"—the slight backpedal. "Does she have any problems like that? I hear she's been in a bunch of rehabs. But she was *really nervous*. She *looked great*—it wasn't like she was 'out of it' or anything. And he was . . . *he* was—I don't know *what* he was!" The exec laughed. "He's kind of from another planet? Right? That's why he's perfect for your show! Not *Holmby* but *Starwatch*," he said, wryly. "So they pitched us and we *liked* it, it's kind of a hoot, kind of a cool idea, needs a tweak, and then we ask them about the characters. And Clea says *her* character is the daughter of someone like her mom, like *Roos,* only in the *show* her mom's still *alive*—that was actually kind of touching—and *Thad*'s character is like the son of—instead of a famous novelist— the son of a *famous film director*. And then Terry or someone in the room said that the film director thing might be a little showbizzy and since Clea's mom was already going to be this big *movie* star, why not just make his dad a *novelist*—you know, a literary thing, you know, just *do* it, right? And I think the comment was a good one because it's not like anyone—I mean, Clea—was tiptoeing around because everyone *knows* who Thad's father is, or *was*—we ain't dummies! Right? And you're here at HBO pitching a show where you're basically *playing yourselves* so why not just drink from that well? Just, like, *do* that. Anyway, he got *so pissed off*—Thad—it was like suddenly he woke up and realized he was in this room *hondling* a series about the loser son of a superfamous man—*hello*. I mean, that's part of the premise! It wasn't *our* idea." He laughed. "And Clea tried to calm him down, and then—I can't believe you didn't hear this! He, like, *pulled out his dick.*"

"He what?"

I wasn't sure if he was joking.

"We asked what one of the shows would be like—you know, we always try to get some idea of a typical show—with you, it's different, you gave us an entire season!—anyway, it's not something that needs to be carved in stone. So I said, Tell us about the pilot. Walk us through. Which is something I don't always do, depending on the talent in the room. Right? And Thad, like, turns around—does a one eighty . . . we all thought he was turning around to like get into character! And when he turns back, his *dick* is out, and he says, 'I'll walk you through!' And then he like starts to *whack.*"

"Are you serious? What did everyone do?"

"Jane *totally* walked out—and she's *completely hardcore.* I mean, *Jane's* the one who's always pushing David to go further with *Deadwood.* Clea told him to put it away—'Put it away!'—it was so surreal! She sounded like Joan Rivers! And then they got into this *slapping* thing—"

"Jane?—"

"No!" he said, laughing again. "But that wasn't so far off! *Clea and Thad.* They start to like *slap* each other, it was *so* David Sedaris! Then he runs out and Clea stays behind and someone calls security and we all felt really terrible. I mean, for *her.* And one of us— Patrick, I think—rushes into the hall to make sure Thad wasn't like *going after Jane.* I'm not even kidding. I think Jane locked herself in her office. I mean, there was never anything 'threatening'—it was more like burlesque, whatever. But it was off-the-wall enough that people were *really disturbed.* And Clea . . . I didn't know what to say to her other than I was such a fan of her mom's—and of *her,* too, and that I really liked her movies—and it's true, I think Clea did some really good work. And she just seemed so *grateful* that we weren't like telling her to *leave.* Get the fuck away! Because she's kinda great, right? And she like tried to turn it around and said, 'Well . . . could we at least maybe do a movie about my mom like that Judy Garland thing you guys did?' (That wasn't even ours.) Something she could produce. 'I love you guys so much'—that kind of thing. Half crying. *So* sad. Because she *does* have access to all this stuff about her mom no one knows about. That's what she was saying, she was like *pimping* at this point. Vamping. We couldn't really respond to the biopic thing so I just kind of put my hand on her shoulder and she started full-out bawling and talking this—stream-of-*consciousness*—about this *other* idea, how we could maybe do a *game show*—this Hollywood Squares thing with the children of famous people . . ."

Elevators *whooshed* open just like on the *Demeter*. The agents and HBO execs, who'd been having their own cliquish postpitch huddles, converged for friendly good-byes. As the metal box whisked us to valet level, the ground beneath our feet moving softly, ever downward, Dan said he was almost certain we had a deal.

THAT NIGHT, I WENT OVER to Clea's.

She answered the door in darkness then retreated to the bathroom. When she emerged, I could see the freshly applied foundation covering a darkish bruise on the delicate line of her jaw. I asked about it and she said she got loaded and fell in the bathroom. Before I probed further, Clea assiduously volunteered that her boyfriend hadn't struck her. I wanted to believe it. Then she disarmed me by tearfully asking for help—would I take her to the Pacific Group on Wednesday?—a brilliant strategy that worked like a charm. Not only was it impossible to turn her down but Clea's helplessness made me begin to think she was telling the truth about her injury. After things settled, I brought up the weenie-wagging incident—we both began to laugh. Without elaborating, she said HBO could go fuck themselves because Fox and Showtime were practically in a bidding war over her idea.

She poured herself a glass of wine and slunk into my arms. *Ah— so this is how it's going to be until one of us goes quietly or unquietly to our grave . . . that warm, fuzzy, incestuous, tortured family feeling, the blurring of lines, the love and sex jumble, the caretaker thing, the quick-fix embrace, the sacred Denial.* We were like bystanders you see on television after suicide bomb attacks, numbly clutching each other in front of splintered buses and orphaned cell phones. *I get it. This is how it's always been and always would be between us—*

She lay like that in the crook of my soul and I smelled her treacly breath, and the scent of her tears too. I *did* decide to go see Thad, though; I couldn't have lived with myself without investigating. I knew that Clea was a big girl and there were things I couldn't protect her from, but now was the time to show my colors—as her oldest friend, former lover, brother-protector. Thad needed to know I was her ally, a force to be reckoned with who would stand up for her in this world and the next. What Clea told me a few minutes later only strengthened my resolve.

She was going to have his child.

THE FIRST THING I SAW upon sitting down (Thad skittered to the bathroom after letting me in, just as Clea had the night before) was a "personalized" form letter on the coffee table:

HOW TO PREEMPT THE IRS "9/11"—AND WIN!

Hi Thad,

I'm Leonard Mednick. Even with their **$3,856,978** tax lien, **Thad**, the IRS still remains equipped to *vilify . . . shame . . .* and *crash planes into your income and hard-earned nest egg*— but they won't succeed when you learn how to PREEMPT THE IRS' LEGAL "9/11"!

I'll wager if you're like thousands of other taxpayers I've helped "liberate" in my *28-year taxpayer advocacy career,* you will be more than curious to know the impact that lien will have on you. I'd also bet your bottom dollar (*the IRS will want that too!*) you'd like to learn the location of whatever "sleeper cells" the IRS has in your city limits and how to respond effectively. Let's start with a little analysis. Ready, **Thad**? Then get on the couch!

THE IRS LIEN OPERATIVE

Your tax lien is a key IRS "Sleeper Operative." While I consider the lien the mildest of these terrorists, it's still a major PAIN IN THE BUTT! It ruins your credit rating and the IRS winds up with a security interest in what you currently own, as well as in any future assets you may come by. *It is as if you and your loved ones have been annexed by a country that does not share your beliefs.*

Worst of all, this lien applies to your home, car, collectibles and any other asset where you've built up equity. Eventually, when you sell or transfer assets, the IRS "sleepers" grab the proceeds or the property! In most cases, *even despite bankruptcy,* the IRS can *and will* keep your lien on the books indefinitely! You may as well be told to wear a "burka," **Thad**! Worse, your tax woe's become public. It is as if "bearded" IRS "Qaeda operatives" spray-paint your home, telling the world they know who you are—*and they don't like your "beliefs" or your "freedom"*! "*Thad Hasn't Paid the Tax—Let's Give Him a Dose of Fiscal Anthrax!!*" . . .

OTHER LEGAL TERRORIST TOOLS

If the lien isn't enough to make you "pull out your troops," the IRS then resorts to BEHEADING you through intimidation and confiscation. They achieve these goals with the *Administrative Summons* and either the *Levy,* the *Seizure* or both.

The *Administrative Summons* is a "fatwa" signed by an officer of the IRS "sleeper cell" forcing you to turn over embarrassing information exposing income and asset details. Defy the Administrative Summons and you can go to jail! Leonard Mednick is here to tell you, **THAD**, you will find yourself in your *very own personal* Abu Ghraib Prison, with close to all the "hoods," "unmuzzled dogs," and "genital humiliation" of the real thing. . . .

He entered the hallway impeccably groomed, but as he came closer I noticed the familiar residue of makeup at his collar. He had only one major scene left: the showdown at the Fellcrum Outback in which the ensign mortally wounds his evil twin. The choreography was complex but Thad said he was looking forward to fighting—and defeating—his own princely self.

"Everyone's fantasy, isn't it?" he said jauntily.

I told him I wasn't sure.

I had the feeling Thad knew why I'd come. There was a formality about him, not only in dress but in manner. He seemed completely sober and suggested we take a drive. I thought it a good idea, as long as I was behind the wheel. The airless suite felt messy and close—like an impoverished theater hosting a mediocre drama at the end of its run.

He asked after Clea as we pulled out of the garage. I told him I saw her the night before and she hadn't been well. He said, with indifference, that he knew she'd "taken a tumble"—meaning figuratively and literally. We small-talked while he stared at traffic. I asked how the "pitch" was going, devilishly suppressing a laugh at the image of him masturbating in the sanctum sanctorum of HBO. Apathetically, he said there seemed to be "interest." The man's hauteur was beginning to grate. Then, for the first time, he spoke of Miriam. She was "quite fond" of me and he wondered if those feelings were "reciprocated." I felt like we were in an old movie—his prim, folksy inquiry begged serious response. It was funny how he'd turned the tables; suddenly, he was Robert Young. Adopting his own aloofness, I said I wasn't sure where the relationship was going. He sagely replied that sometimes it was best not to have a destination. He knew she wanted to have kids and asked if I too had those "aspirations." I told him I *might* though not at this time. In life and career. And what have you. He said he understood—that he *more* than understood. I kept my mouth shut. Rightly or wrongly, I assumed Clea had refrained from telling him she was in the family way. But maybe she'd lied to me—or maybe it *was* true and Thad already knew, and was putting me on as well. He said that having children for the wrong reason was the worst thing people could do. He said he knew that from "experience." Miriam and I had a wonderful time together. Wasn't that all that really mattered? Now he was James Mason.

We went to Musso's for a drink. At the end of the hour, he got the idea to go up to the Observatory. I told him the place was closed for renovations but Thad insisted. (He'd never been.) It was a while since I'd visited and it took a moment to retrace the familiar route in my head: Franklin to Los Feliz, Los Feliz to Griffith Park. There was just no way I was going to consult the car's GPS.

On the way, I told him I'd finished reading *The Soft Sea Horse*.

"I was talking to Miriam—about how much I enjoyed it. And one of the things that interested me . . . do you mind talking about this?"

"Not at all."

"I was intrigued when she said that you were actually *there*—in Capri—when your brother passed on. And I—I wondered why you wrote about it . . . 'differently.' Because the book seemed so fearlessly *honest*. Fearsome. I just wondered why you chose to distance yourself. Why you left the character of that boy behind, in the States."

The question came from nowhere—instead of confronting him about having struck Clea, my subconscious played out its hand.

"*They thought I killed my brother.* Did Miriam tell you that? Strange! He *loved* to swim—to hold his breath. Years later I heard something that put me at ease, in a funny kind of way. A kid drowned in Hawaii, the son of a friend. He was sixteen years old, a surfer. Wanted to be a free diver—that's what they call it. Guys who take a big breath then go deep as they can. In the ocean. Ride down on a cable, four or five hundred feet. There was a film someone made about it—*Le grand bleu*—'The Big Blue.' French. Never saw it. The way you train is by holding your breath in a swimming pool. They compete by using eighty-pound weights. They take a breath and these weights pull them down; a balloon brings 'em up. You're never supposed to train alone cause apparently it's very seductive to hold your breath for such a long time. You can black out, even in shallow water. They say you just want to let go. And this kid, the six-teen-year-old, he'd sent an e-mail or something to a friend only a week before saying how euphoric it was to be under, feeling himself drift away. That's why you're supposed to train in pairs. The ol' Buddy System. And I think maybe that's what happened to Jeremy. He was always so proud of how long he could hold his breath—shit, I could go maybe thirty seconds but Jeremy was an athlete! That day . . . I saw him go down . . . then disappear under the boat. They were in the middle of shooting: I remember hearing the director, the voices of the actors during the scene. They were very strict about noise during whatever shot they were getting. I didn't want to call out. I didn't want to interrupt because I thought they'd get mad— Jack would get mad. It was the big scene between Alain Delon and Sophia Loren. *Le grand bleu*-job! I wasn't sure anything *bad* was hap-pening down there, anyway. With Jeremy. So I swam to the other side of the boat. Didn't see him, couldn't find him. The engine was off (they were shooting) so I wasn't worried about him getting caught in the rudder. I thought he'd gone back around but it turned out he got stuck beneath the hull. His suit got caught on something, whatever, he took in water. That's what the geniuses later said. The

CSI aquatic unit—hey, that's not a bad idea! *CSI: Marine. Le grand autopsy.* I couldn't see too well, I was looking under there, completely myopic. The water stung my eyes if I opened them. Jeremy used to tease me because I needed goggles even when we were in the hotel pool. Anyway, they found bruises and thought—good old Dad *suggested, that's* why they thought!—that I *hit* him. Do you know what that was like? To be accused? The police talked to me, *les gendarmes,* it wasn't exactly an interrogation. I can't even *remember* what the fuck it was. You know, I still can't watch *The Bad Seed.* When she drowns the kid who won the spelling bee? So she can have his medal?"

We drove in silence. A few minutes from our destination, he announced that Miriam had nearly closed the "Prodigal" novelization deal. The money wasn't much but the psychological boost came just in time: he wound up at L'Orangerie with Morgana who, adding perennial insult to injury, had extended her stay to take photos of Paul Auster while he passed through on a paperback tour. Auster was one of her son's pet peeves and she knew it. In retaliation, Thad said he was working on a "sweet little play" that would filet the Michelet dynasty in all its pornographic sound and fury. He acted out a barbaric monologue at the table, loud enough that surrounding patrons were captivated. Morgana, predictably appalled, stormed out. Thad received a letter the next day by messenger, warning that if he dared embark on such a venture, he would be excised from the estate—which he took as an idle threat, knowing in his heart of hearts this had already been done. As perverse parenthetical, he said he'd come to dinner with the sole purpose of soliciting her financial help in the matter of the lien. His hunch being, she might have agreed to help if he finally conceded to burial alongside Jeremy in the family plot, a desire which seemed to grow stronger in the old woman each year for reasons destined to remain cryptic, though the irony (happy family in death, if not in life) was not lost. As usual, things had conspired to undo him—so there he stood in the middle of that august *salle à manger* in crapulous soliloquy, shirt spattered in red wine–shallot reduction.

When he proclaimed that the estrangement, now official and irrevocable, was probably for the best, I half believed him. He had the natural-born talent to make one embrace hard endings, and fresh starts as well. Thad was positively giddy about the prospect of entering the *Times* bestseller list, thus foiling a grim practical joke orchestrated from the underworld. Besides, he still felt he could deliver something keenly poetic tucked within a Trojan horse. He said that "quality lit" and sci-fi had tango'd before: Margaret Atwood had done it—or was it Margaret Drabble? Doris Lessing too . . . He *did* have one small fear: that, of legal necessity, he'd be forced to share story credit with *Starwatch* staffers, i.e., while the novelization itself would have sole "written by" credit (Thad Michelet), it would include a "based on a teleplay by" credit (the geeks who wrote "Prodigal Son [Episode 21-417A]") as well. He wasn't sure if this was something that might potentially interfere with the parameters of the codicil; Miriam's lawyer was looking into it. Thad strategized he'd tell the writers what he was up to—in the worst case (in exchange for an agreement to remove "the teleplay possessory"), he'd cut deals paying out a small share of the $10 million, far more than the "schmucks with PowerBooks" were due for their standard share of novelization rights. Miriam said she wasn't sure how the guild would feel about it; bit of a gray area. (I could see Thad's paranoid Time Machine/Small Claims wheel whirring.) All, he added, would naturally be moot if the book didn't sell.

We reached the top of the hill and parked beside the ragged cyclone fence that surrounded ongoing construction. We wandered awhile, navigating an obstacle course of building debris and rubbish left behind by tourists, until we came into a depopulated zone with a grand view of the sky. It was jet black and remarkably clear. I watched Thad crane his neck to look at the stars, feeling a rush of sympathy and affection for the man. He had shown me a tender, stunt-free side of his soul; I was surprised and grateful, apart from feeling insecure that I had nothing comparable to give in return. I actually felt bad for having planned to corner him about Clea. I was suddenly certain of his innocence, and grateful the two had found each other.

"You know, when I first heard that human bodies were made from stardust, I thought it was a shuck. A Hallmark greeting card thing. But it's *true*—we're all dead stars." He had that wonderful, gnomish smile on his face. Black Jack *was* his Goliath; he'd slain him and lived to tell the tale. I felt proud. He took off his jacket, laid it on the ground, then sat. "They say that when our sun dies, it won't be anything spectacular. It's a middling star. That's the word astronomists use, 'middling'—tough crowd, those astronomists! And when an *ordinary* star dies—they call them ordinary! That's the official designation! I'm telling you, they're *tough* sons of bitches—well, they say ordinary stars end up as *inconspicuous white dwarves*. But the *killers*, the real shock-and-awe five-alarm cocksuckers, when *they* die, they leave black holes . . . take *everything* with 'em, even the light. *Even the light.*" He paused, marveling at the unfathomable implication of his own words. "Jesus. I'm in high Observatory mode, huh. I should work here—someone give me a job!"

As if softly unspooling more secrets, he began to quote his beloved Leopardi, but the words seemed such his own, so exclusive to the timeless moment on that slope beneath celestial seas, syllables engrained as stardust into his bones, that he became the prodigal son, exiled Vorbalidian prince come home to roost in phantom pain and stellar tomb, middling and majestic, murderous and mundane, in blinding darkness and vacuumed, vanished light—boyish, transgressive and humble, so that I felt the vibratory strands of existence cocoon around us, in the great transparent cathedral of our shabbily awesome, gloriously stillborn life.

"I have always loved this lonesome hill," he said. "And this hedge that hides the entire horizon, almost, from sight. But sitting here in a daydream, I picture the boundless spaces away out there, silences deeper than human silence, an unfathomable hush in which my heart is hardly a beat from fear. And hearing the wind rush rustling through these bushes, I pit its speech against infinite silence—and a notion of eternity floats to mind, and the dead seasons—*e le morte stagioni*—and the season beating here and now, and the sound of it. So, in this immensity my thoughts all drown. And it's soothing to be wrecked in seas like these."

IT WAS FRIDAY—THE LAST day of shooting.

Thad never arrived.

Clea began to unravel. I stood by watching Nick Sultan put extras through fruitless, unfilmed paces: palace guardians in Greek chorus groupings on the painted plaster desert of the Outback. They were to pound their tom-toms during the twins' battle royale which was set to unfold before a giant blue screen already in place. The old-school prop master stood in the wings holding ritual daggers in a customized teak box, ready to hand them to Morloch and the ensign if one (or the other) were ever to show. The harmless weapons were his responsibility but now that there were no warriors, he felt the chill of an unvoiced rebuke.

Hours passed. A pall descended. Lawyers, agents, and executives assembled. Stunt and camera doubles were ladled with the heavy cubist makeup of Vorbalids; it was decided Morloch's side of the battle would be shot first, buying time in case Thad suddenly showed. Nick got a second wind and the crew went to work with the careful haste required of a production crisis. The pressure was on but at the same time things seemed so hopeless that it was off, too—a chance for stalwart below-the-liners to pragmatically strut their stuff in per-spirey triple-time and ingratiate themselves to the studio. They'd be the real heroes of the day.

Clea sat in her canvas chair on the soundstage. The rest of us, temporarily liberated from our cages by Morloch to bear witness to his expected triumph (a few reaction shots were needed, nothing more), loitered in readiness. With the UPM's sober, nodding sub-mission, Nick Sultan reasserted to the studio brass there was no rea-son to worry because everything would soon be "in the can"—except for the ensign's half of the blue-screened tussle. Word filtered back: the CGI gurus had determined that an ensign look-alike could be hired for a half day of second unit inserts to be shot on the following weekend. (It was unprecedented to allow anything to interfere with production stream; the next episode, well into prepro-duction, was scheduled to begin filming on Monday.) The footage of the Rattweil look-alike would be framed in judicious mediums rather than close-ups, digitally doctored to enhance the more than serviceable resemblance between Thad and his double, then spliced into the fight scene. The experts' consensus was optimistic; failing success, redoubtable staff-geeks, fueled by Jerry's Deli triple-deckers and twelve-packs of Red Bull, were already drafting radical story structure alternatives. When it was time to go home (we broke an hour early), spirits were running relatively high under the circum-stances. The bullet, if not dodged, seemed to have passed through tissue without hitting any major organs.

In an attempt to throw a net over the missing actor, the studio had sent a P.A. to the Chateau earlier that morning. With the help of the conscientious hotel manager, the room was entered to ascer-tain if the guest had overslept or was in distress. Needless to say, Mr. Michelet was not to be found. The P.A. lay in wait all day long, to no avail. At 5:00 P.M., Clea and I relieved him of duty.

Throughout, I'd kept Miriam in the loop. She was awfully dis-tressed but we agreed there was no reason as yet for her to hop on a plane. There was general apprehension about Thad's physical and mental health, with even the occasional hint at foul play—ludicrous, but in our agitated exhaustion, we inevitably came to resemble newscasters during a disaster, vamping after losing live feed. Another sentiment, lighter in weight and leavened by anger, was the plain fact he had done enormous harm to his career, not to mention scotching any hopes of authoring a *Starwatch* volume, the scamminess of which now seemed abjectly pathetic. Miriam and I suddenly felt besmirched by the inanely precocious bestsellerdom strategy, mortified by our coconspiracy with this overtly unstable man.

Thus, Clea and I began our night watch.

Slowly, like the favorite Brahms intermezzo of her mom's that she had touchingly learned by heart in the last few years, Clea began to tap at the confessional keys. She told me she'd come over to the Chateau to be with him after our trip to the Observatory, and they had argued about "stupid things."

Something in her tone betrayed. I pressed for more.

"One summer, on the Vineyard—his father—" She closed her eyes and took a deep, actressy yoga breath. "We didn't fool around . . . but something happened."

"With Jack?"

She nodded, eyes shut. I was surprised, but only at my refusal all this time to see the obvious. "I was still getting loaded. Thad was being *horrid*. I'm not excusing it, Bertie—what I did—though nothing really *happened*—but it was enough, I guess. Thad was having an affair, under my nose. God, we were already *living* together! In Brooklyn Heights . . . and he was sleeping with this woman—*two* women. I found out about the second one by 'mistake.' He told me about the first. And then this thing happened with Jack, who was *always* inappropriate. He was just kind of out to get Thad. That's what he was into. And flirting—he always flirted with me, he flirted with *all* Thad's girlfriends. The reverse Oedipal, whatever. Is that what it is? And I was—I *wanted* to be punitive because I guess I knew it was over. He had *so hurt* me, Bertie. Why else would he have done what he did? I needed . . . I guess I just wanted to *end* it, in a definitive way. And that was pretty definitive! We didn't fuck or anything. *I didn't fuck Jack, OK?* I wasn't even going to *tell* him about it—that's what's so funny! *Jack* did. Jack got drunk and told *Morgana* and she was so freaked out that *she* told Thad. It was horrible. Horrible! Oh my God, that *night*—fucking O'Neill couldn't have written that night. And he *never* forgave me. Not that I expected him to. But when we got back together this last time—which was *totally* unplanned, I think it took us both by surprise . . . and—it seemed he'd gotten over . . . lots of *things*. He was different. I thought maybe the whole IRS stuff had . . . I don't even know what I mean by that. Sorry." She paused, to gather herself. "He never talked about—what happened. But right after Jack died, he began *alluding*. Especially when he got loaded. And it seemed like—well anyway, *that's* what we were fighting about. Last night. I mean, this is something he brought up on the *Vineyard*, at the *funeral*. All those insinuations—you didn't know what he was talking about, did you. On the Vineyard? I mean, did you even *hear*? I don't think you were even *aware*. *Miriam* was! She heard—Miriam knew. But she also knew how *crazy* everyone was back then—now, too, but *especially* then! It was a bad time. Bad, bad, bad, bad time. And Morgana was *totally* freezing me out at the funeral—and it's *still* about that. *All* about that—for her. But nothing really *happened*, I was a *scapegoat* because Jack Michelet fucked *anything that moved*—tuh-duh!—and Morgana *knew* it. It was part of their thing. She totally joined the Jack Michelet Corporation knowing what he was. That he—" She abruptly returned to the present. "But it *still* doesn't make any *sense*, Bertie . . . where would he *go*, why would he not show *up*? The last fucking day of the shoot! Bertie, I'm worried—*I'm really, really worried*. I'm worried he might actually have *killed* himself." She clapped a hand to her mouth, sorry to have said such a thing aloud to beckon supernatural forces. "Where would he have gone? Maybe he checked into a hotel somewhere and overdosed . . . should we start calling, Bertie? Should we try all the hotels? Do you think he could have done that?" She began to shiver and weep again, clutching onto me. "Bertie, could he actually have done that? Do you think? Maybe we should start calling the hospitals—"

"They've been doing that, Clea. Nothing's turned up."

"It doesn't make sense *he would just disappear.*"

She got the unshakable idea that he'd returned to Griffith Park to dramatically do himself in. It was close to midnight and I was worn down enough to think the notion plausible. She begged me to drive us. After much stumbling in the dark, I reached the site of our previous trespass—but all we found was emptiness.

ON SUNDAY, WE HAD PLANS for brunch.

Hugo's.

She stood me up.

I checked my voice mail. There was a message from the night before. It was Clea, saying he had called and "was fine." She was going to see him, but didn't say where.

THE NEXT FEW WEEKS WERE a blur of work, and I was glad.

HBO wanted to move forward with *Holmby Hills.* They had notes; Dan and I took the requisite conference calls. I did my bible thumping (and tweaking) at night, days occupied by the new *Star-watch* shoot. No one heard boo from our wayward couple. With an increasing sense of dread, I resorted to Al-Anon meetings, reminding myself I was powerless over Clea—powerless over her drug intake and her romantic life, if there was any difference between the two.

I spoke to Miriam constantly. I missed her but admittedly was confused. It'd been months since I'd slept with anyone else so I longed for her, physically. Besides, the whole Thad/Clea shitstorm had left me stressed out and lonelier than hell. I guess I still wanted her to come to L.A. on my own terms. I was a walking male cliché—obsessed with getting Meerkat into bed but still ambivalent about the relationship thing. I hadn't discussed my feelings (another male cliché) and psychotic as it might sound it just may be I was operating off the echo and reverb of my last conversation with Thad—the one where he casually implied Miriam wanted to begin some major nest building.

My inner life was crazed. I hung around newsstands, poring over health magazine articles about male hormones, male menopause, male ticking clocks. (Not to mention cutting-edge cancer-screening tests.) When Miriam finally said she was flying out, I felt instantly better. We could have the baby-thing talk—*after* we fucked. Might even pop the question. When I shared as much at an AA meeting, some smart-ass said, "The *question* is: 'Can we have an open marriage?' "

A week and a half after Clea split, I got a second message on my machine. (If she really wanted to talk, she'd have called my cell.) She sounded stoned and vaguely distraught. They were all right but "in the middle of moving." She'd "be in touch." Around that time, someone on the crew said he saw them over the weekend, at the Palms in Vegas. The gaffer didn't approach but said they looked "seriously fucked up." When I called the hotel, no one was registered under either name.

— • —

Miriam arrived on Friday and stayed with me in Venice. It was comforting to play house, even under somewhat surreal circumstances. The sex was good. We used it as an anchor—and painkiller. The TV news played nonstop coverage of devastation wrought by a series of tornadoes in the Midwest. Somehow that was a comfort too: happy-to-be-alive faces smeared with dirt and tears, possessions and personal histories flung to the wind. Whenever we saw the foundations of vanished houses and the shattered vertebrae of modest Main Streets, we conjured Thad and Clea as flying Dutchmen unable to dock in whatever harbor they'd been pharmaceutically listing toward. Then came the usual stories of buried house pets found miraculously alive among the rubble. We wished as much for our friends but knew the odds were against them.

The odds were always against everything.

MONDAY CAME. I HAD a few days off.

Miriam went to a business lunch and I killed time at the studio visiting Dan. I'd completed the outline revisions and turned them in—HBO would probably take a week or so to give a thumbs-up. Hopefully they'd be cool with whatever work I did and would let me start writing the pilot; I was getting itchy. It was all a little easier if you tried not to have expectations. Anyway, I had other worries: Clea and Thad. Being on the lot brought me nearer to my oldest friend and the mystery of her absence. I felt like a dad waiting around during an Amber Alert—utterly helpless.

I strolled to the editing bay to see Nick Sultan. Normally, he'd have already finished; in TV, it wasn't typical for directors to stick around to supervise an edit. They were hired hands and they knew it. But in this case, Nick was committed and determined. Because of "complications," the producers had given him more leeway than usual. The room was dark. The first thing I saw on the Avid was Ensign Rattweil, engaged in final combat on the Fellcrum Outback. The action kept digitally rewinding and repeating itself, images broken into millions of shardy, dust mote–sized squares. The dual was incredibly well done—you'd never know a look-alike had been employed. When I asked the editor how they'd managed, he smiled and said, "Movie magic."

Just then, Nick appeared in the doorway holding a container of Chinese chicken salad from the commissary.

"Did you hear?" he said.

"What?"

"Oh Christ." He steered me to the hall and whispered, "They just found the bodies."

HE WAS BURIED IN THE Vineyard with Jack and Jeremy, as his mother had wished.

Sudden death expunged her rancor; at last, Thad was brought into protective arms. It came to mind this was the closest he'd been to his brother in the forty-odd years since that time beside the gently rocking *Sea Horse* where they parted. Miriam said the configuration of monuments in the family plot put him farthest from Jack, which gave a small measure of comfort. She said there was a wake, with far less turnout than the one I'd attended, and Morgana had behaved much the same as at her husband's—brave and wittily stoic, boisterously bereft.

We scattered Clea's ashes at sea. There was to be no headstone or grave marking, by her request. TV tabloids and magazines made much of the lurid deaths, mostly on account of the illustrious parents. In the end, the light ("Even the light")—the white dwarves that were their children—could not escape the gravity of those legendary black holes.

——•——

My own mother took great care of me in the days that followed.

She got some of her old energy back and threw a lovely memorial. It was as if Gita knew that with this death—Clea's—I had finally graduated, and we now shared consecrated alma maters. (Heartbroken wolves cloaked in sheepskin.) The celebration took place on the beach, where I once fantasized they would exchange vows. Everyone linked hands and cried—friends from AA, the gang from *Starwatch*. Dad walked me to the wet sand and said that my eulogy was "the finest thing" he'd ever heard. With tears in his eyes, he begged forgiveness for all fatherly transgressions. He was a little drunk but his sentiments were in earnest. I *did* forgive him, from the bottommost bottom of my heart. I forgave just about everyone for everything, including myself.

Gita was right. School was out—forever.

I DECIDED TO GO TO Vegas to retrace their steps. (Later, I wondered if my motivation was born less from a sense of "closure" than the subconscious decision to tell this story.) No matter, I still needed to say good-bye; it felt just too miserable to let the memory of her last, plaintive phone message stand. Like some action hero, I craved pursuit—to chase the dispersed stardust of my first love.

To my surprise, when I told Miriam of the plan she actually

wanted to come along. We'd always joked about going to see Celine Dion. Now, she said, was our chance.

I rented an obnoxious silver Porsche, and we headed out on the highway, looking for adventure (and whatever came our way). It wasn't quite summer—the weather was tolerably warm. We used the Mirage as our headquarters; while Meerkat lay by the pool I got in touch with a detective who'd worked the case, and was naturally a mega-*Starwatch* buff. He provided me with a rough itinerary of Thad and Clea's meanderings in the days before their deaths.

We didn't get around to seeing Celine, though I *did* wind up at sundry downtown casinos offering $3.89 all-you-can-eat breakfast buffets. The detective said that once Mr. Michelet arrived, he managed to get his hands on a shitload of cash, wired from a bank in Fort Lauderdale. He blew through two hundred grand at blackjack (the irony of the name of the game wasn't lost on me) at the Palms. According to phone records, Thad and Clea were in constant touch before she left L.A. When she joined him, they pissed away another $75,000 (most of her savings, no doubt) at a divey gaming parlor off the Strip and by then were in for an additional fifty "large." I met with the owner, who was a fairly decent guy. His kids were huge fans of *The Jetsons* and when the hotelier saw the tough straits Thad was in, he offered to help. His son was being bar mitzvahed that weekend and the guy was ready to knock off $20,000 from the debt if the actor made an appearance at the party to sign autographs. They shook hands over it—but "Bonnie and Clyde," he smirked, were no-shows.

Miriam and I hit the Wheel of Fortune slots and took in a raggedy-ass rock-'n'-roll lounge revue. In the spirit of "What Happens Here, Stays Here," I sampled the Viagra I'd been carrying around in my wallet the last few months; it seemed the appropriate thing to do. The pill worked OK but I didn't get much sleep, and not for the reason you might think. When I finally passed out, I had recurrent dreams of snorting coke. In the morning, Meerkat and I had a stupid argument—it was definitely time to decamp.

Death Valley would be the next and last stop. Miriam didn't think she had it in her to go. I wasn't sure I did either.

I dropped her at the airport around 2:00 P.M. She tenderly kissed me, not envying the ordeal ahead. I hate to be noir about it, but somewhere inside that good-bye was the thought we might be done with each other for good. We embraced long and hard, the subtext being that we'd shared forbidden fruits. We knew our friendship would survive regardless of what the future held. It was kind of a cinematic moment, part *Casablanca,* part *Planet of the Apes* (just before Heston rounds the corner to howl at Lady Liberty)—because neither of us could shake the feeling that some awesome, half-buried truth was waiting for me in the desert.

THIS TIME, THE APPROACH WAS from the east—though all roads led to the Bun Boy Motel. Around the time I passed Pahrump, that first trip flashed back in all its carefree glory. It was like a teen memory: I heard the girls' voices and lusty giggles—I could practically smell them. Inseparable from Clea's image was Thad's, a grizzled, fine-witted contradiction, bellowing and gracious, born to be wild.

It grew hotter as I drove. Soon I was dipped in that serenely alien palette, the grotesque, infernal outcroppings and magnificent desolation of apocalyptic pastel. Déjà vu: that uncomfortable feeling the Furnace Creek Inn didn't exist, and somehow I'd taken a wrong turn, never again to reclaim my superheated Shangri-La. Then suddenly there it was, in all its Spanish Colonial glory, the parking lot oddly filled to capacity—just as before.

Upon arrival, the clerk did some registering too (of my face)—the same garrulous oddball who'd given us the lowdown on the

dicey denizens of that aridly majestic park. (My detective said he'd
been a helpful source.) He smiled broadly until his memory linked
me to the man whom everyone, postmortem, unfailingly called Mr.
Michelet. His amiable expression begged I explain my return. I told
him I was a friend of both Michelet and his companion—recent
acquaintance of the former, childhood friend of the latter. He
expressed discreet condolences. By now, other guests had gathered,
either to check in or have the registrar dispense a map to Scotty's
Castle along with a quickie historic spiel. I said I was going to
freshen up and asked how long he'd be at the desk. He got off at
5:00 P.M., he said—little more than an hour away. I told him I'd be
pleased if he would allow me to spring for a couple of date shakes. I
even dropped the name of the detective, respectfully adding that the
gumshoe told me to look him up.

—— • ——

We met on the terrace.

"He's a wonderful actor. *Was*. Always a favorite. They got here—
Mr. Michelet and your friend . . ."

"Clea Fremantle."

"I remembered them from when you came."

"They're hard to forget."

"Exactly!" he exclaimed. "But this time, I have to say they didn't
look so well." He lowered his voice, hesitant to desecrate the dead.
"A little 'worse for wear.' It wasn't so much *intoxication*,
per se. They just looked . . . exhausted. Like they'd 'been through it.'
We get people like that in the valley but not so much here at the inn.
I see 'newcomers' once or twice before they usually get—what's the
word?—*assimilated*. If you see 'em again, they've usually cleaned up
their act. Course most you *don't* see again. People on the run. Come
to the valley same way they go to Mexico these days only it's a little
tougher here. To get by. You don't have the sand and sea, the surfers
and beach life to lose yourself in. Harder to be invisible I guess. If

that's what you're after. You really kind of have to find a rock. To crawl under. Anyhow, they ate in the restaurant on Saturday night— I told Detective Raintree all this."

"I know that. And I appreciate you sharing it with me."

"Mr. Michelet didn't have a coat so I gave him one that we keep behind the desk for people who don't know about the code. It's unusual when a guest doesn't have a sport jacket but if it happens we're prepared. They looked a little better—I think they must have taken baths!"—again, the clerk seemed embarrassed—"and were pretty well behaved during dinner. I don't think anyone bothered him. No one asked for his autograph. But the girl—Ms. Fremantle—she's an actor too, isn't she?" He'd cordially slipped into present tense.

"Yes.

"Her mother was Roosevelt Chandler."

"That's right."

"After dinner, they went swimming. We have towels out there. We leave our guests alone. The caretaker said they sat by the fire quite a while. He left at 11:00 P.M. and they were still there. Not making a ruckus or anything but they may have had a bottle with them. That wouldn't be unusual. It's nice to have a little vino under the stars.

"I was working double shifts—I don't actually live here, I swear!" he added, cracking himself up. "Though sometimes it seems like I do. No one saw them in the morning, far as I recall. They break-fasted in their room; we have a record of that. They didn't have a suite like when you came before. A single, adjacent to the terrace. We call it the smokers' terrace. People can go out and get their nico-tine fix. It overlooks the valley—I think I saw you and your other friend up there. What was her name?"

"Miriam."

The guy didn't miss a thing. He was beginning to remind me of Norman Bates.

"They left around 4:00 P.M. on Sunday. I guess they found the car Monday morning, early. I think it hit a rock—it was only a rental sedan. Helps to have a four-wheeler if you're going up to the Race-track. Didn't y'all go up there?"

"Yeah," I said. "We did."

"Spooky place. They found your friend—Ms. Fremantle—on the periphery. Mr. Michelet was farther off. Did Detective Raintree tell you the position of the bodies?"

I stopped him short, done with the travelogue.

I thanked him for his time and set off.

"Drive safely," he said.

— • —

By the time I got there, it was nearly dusk. As I strolled the "periph-ery," a few hikers passed by and waved. Then I was alone with the rocks and the phantoms.

Raintree had reconstructed things thus: Thad and Clea were observed at the 49er Café, in late afternoon. They were drinking. It was noted by patrons that he wore a strange costume—one witness likened it to a toga—but all were in agreement the peculiar getup "wasn't the cleanest looking." The barkeep recognized Thad right away, and engaged the pair in friendly conversation. The actor said they were filming nearby. The barkeep didn't know who Clea was and later told the detective that it seemed "the female companion" was in some kind of distress. I was certain my poor, beleaguered darling had by then become captive (years of news reports about Stockholm syn-drome and the psychology of battered women sorrowfully told me so). They left just after sundown, driving about an hour before going off road, where the Taurus had indeed broken its axle.

As I walked, I saw them in my mind's eye—Thad, with the unerring instincts of a drunk, uncannily finding the Racetrack, almost 9:00 P.M. now—veering off asphalt in querulousness or exag-gerated jest before smacking the stone that cracked the undercar-riage. Explosion of expletives and laughter. He'd have been the first to leave the car—Clea, cowed—for cursory damage report. Futzing with keys, rumbling in trunk. Retrieving . . . then reconnoitering.

Clea pulling herself together then wandering after him into stillness, stoned, though maybe not, maybe even already having run through her stash—tragic!—stumbling along in numb, detoxed, zombified despair. Saw them clumsily pick through sharp-stoned black-and-blue darkness toward that dry lake of ancient monoliths, Thad yodeling, guffawing, shrieking, that tritely maddening bay-at-the-moon routine he did when out here last but no longer in the realm of charming, wild or willful, of "entertainer," or the realm of anything anymore. Clea dazed, shaken, animal-knowing this was the end as they lurched toward Paleolithic infield of petrified mud, deaf-and-dumb klatches of rubble, following her keeper's bruising makeshift path through sleeping creosote bushes, rattlesnake weed and moonflowers, gravel ghosts and cream cups, conspirational windflowers and whispering beardtongues.

. . . Saw him reach the lake bed and breathe, finally berthed on the cleared, smooth surface, untrammeled, almost hygienic in contrast to chaotic, uneven roadway, syrupy quiet all around again, Zabriskie Point stillness, cooler now that they'd stopped the trudge, *his* trudge, sweating the dope out, free at last from the nettles and brambles of their rugged, improvised trek: not broken, bullheaded Taurus rentals but twin Geminis, now he was home, a prince returned to Fellcrum serenity. He had doubles of the fastidious propmaster's daggers stowed—dagger back-ups! Dagger stand-ins!—imagine carrying them two weeks on the lam then thoughtfully transferring from suitcase to car—and used them to bludgeon because they could not properly stab. I saw him after his exertions, that stillness again, nearly religious, Clea's breath truncated then finally stopped, his own growing less ragged, all actions now become the same, flatness and lack of consequence, expirations and inhalations all one, the assault as if in a dream, bad script, bad dream from which he'd awake to complain of migraine, retiring to trailer or Chateau hours later or in morning to begin again but when he saw he could not waken, still the flatness of response, not remorse, more the *discomfort* of it and the wishing away, the *whooshing*, but the acceptance too, and the knowing it would all soon end. The irrefutable knowing.

Saw it all as I walked toward larger rocks. Moon full enough to see tracks from which the Playa took its name, slid-boulders like tombstones in my father's old E.C.s.

The detective said the ranger found Thad propped up against one like he'd been pushing—again, I saw: laughing, thrusting, cut-rate costume warrior wrestling sisyphean sculptor's stone, expiring herniated breath and life force as he butted, in breathing concert with mysterious forces that moved the rocks, Atlas strained and shrugged, and that was when the blood came through the mouth—choking on its torrent (so the coroner said), an aneurysm was what killed him and I thought: what a rare, good thing, how merciful of that which governs, knowing he wouldn't have had the will to finish himself and certain that was his plan because it was learned he'd left a gun in the trunk, forgotten but maybe deliberate in the forgetting, I wasn't convinced he had the strength to retrieve it, the gall, the stamina, better a gory red fountain through ruptured aqueduct of worn-out tissue than to lose one's mind, already lost, in prison, use-less hell of that, better to fatally shoulder Outback rock than suffer sick frenzy of renown accompanying incarceration and trial.

I phoned the ranger who discovered them but he was on holiday. I wondered if he was the kind of person for whom images fade or retain their power: clump of woman in early fossilized pupfish pur-plish insect hummed dawn, beat and disfigured though from a dis-tance merely at rest on outside oval track—farther in, the curious half-standing figure rooted in a brackish pool of his own black blood, barefoot in the interplanetary park, cheaply woven garment hanging like a sequined burlap bag, dull-edged dumb-bass Super Kmart dag-ger on hardscrabble desert floor, laughable instrument of the settling of royal disputes.

That was not the place I wished to say good-bye.

— • —

In the morning, I headed for Badwater.

The narcotic silence was there, and tourists too. I walked out as far as I could till hardly anyone was in sight. Sponged up the quiet. Said a prayer for Clea. Told her I loved her and would always be there. I remembered kissing her a lifetime ago in her mother's house and when I thought of Leif doing the same, sweet dimple-chinned Leif long dead and gone, I felt that familiar jealous twinge and laughed out loud in the sacred stillness, sobbing at the invincible riddle of it (imagining Clea laughing her tattooed ass off as well). Just then it struck me she would never age, she would always be that girl, the shy, nervous one with the outsized movie-star mom—and I, the nervous boy, forever groping and adoring in that celestial second-story room, beloved Californian winds in holy chastisement, roughing up the voyeuristic trees outside our window. The thing of it is, she *was* with Leif now; the kid had the upper hand but I was happy for him. I smiled with the maudlin thought they were together, "on the other side." What comfort!

Grateful to have this phantasmagorical inkling that my Clea could travel between worlds and boy-lovers evermore, if that was her wish.

I left the valley.

A WEEK AFTER RETURNING TO L.A. I was in my trailer working on *Holmby Hills*. We still hadn't heard from HBO but Dan said I should just start writing, to calm my nerves.

So there I was, trying to pound out a first scene—one already delineated in the "bible"—yet hopelessly stuck.

I lit a cigarette, drifting back to Anaheim.

"Where would you most likely find a denouement?" asked the unctuous host of *Who Wants to Be a Millionaire?*

Idly, I typed:

1. **In the bathroom**
2. **In a story**
3. **Under the hood**
4. **In Death Valley**

It occurred to me to write a movie about our ménage à trois but nothing coalesced—not that I'd spent much time mulling it over. It was way too soon. How to begin? (There wasn't even a bible!) I couldn't, in all fairness, favor Clea over Thad, though of course that was my bias. Anyway, all was moot because the biggest part of me wouldn't dare defile her memory by commodifying it, or worse, memorializing by screenplay, then failing—I was an old hand in the Failed Script Department. I decided it was only a daydream. The time had come to refocus my energy and discipline on *Holmby Hills*. I set upon the opening scene with renewed fervor.

While pondering my destiny—and developing a serious urge for Mexican takeout—Dad called. Nick Sultan was no longer involved in the *Chrysanthemum* project. Perry said that while he liked the final version of "Prodigal Son (Episode 21-417A)," "Mr. Sultan" had scored a studio tent pole that would keep him busy for the next two and a half years. *Good for him.* "Recent events" had convinced my father "to get off the dime" and develop Black Jack's novel himself. He wanted me to begin work on the script ASAP. He'd spoken to Dan Fauci and while things looked optimistic re *Holmby Hills* he said it was always good to have a few irons in the fire. Dad's production company would negotiate a fee with the lawyer of my choice. "I can tell you right now it'll probably be something in the seventy-five-thousand-dollar range," he said firmly, as if expecting me to bitch. He couldn't have been more wrong. *As the studio gods said, Let there be nepotism.* I got that puffed-up, mini-mogul feeling again; that's how much I needed a shot of self-esteem.

This one, I'd truly earned.

— • —

I put Clea's things in storage.

Her landlord quickly leased the Venice house—I knew, because I'd become a bit of a Peeper. I watched a hip couple move in, barely in their thirties. I actually drove by for a few months, hoping to bump into Clea's unquiet ghost. Sometimes I'd pull up to the curb and sit there in darkness. I wondered if the new tenants were in the business.

For a while I dreamed about her. I guess Clea's last "visitation" came when I finished reading *Chrysanthemum*. I was startled by the power of Michelet's novel—and its vengefulness. How strange that until recently I hadn't known the scandal behind it, a cause célèbre at the time of publication. My father never spoke of it; he presumed I already knew.

The book's protagonist is "Jack Michelet" (this, prepostmodern). "Michelet" has been short-listed for every literary prize known to man—winning most. He's married to a dilettante who takes artsy photographs of animals in zoo-cages, worldwide. Their son ("Tad"!), an unsuccessful writer of advertisement copy, and his fiancée, a one-time hooker turned day-care center operator, arrive at the house in the Hamptons for a weekend visit. "Michelet" seduces the bride-to-be in the nursery, where he gardens during writing breaks.

Tad and Melanctha could be overheard arguing about something in the kitchen, a friendly dispute over a recipe his mother was preparing for dinner. (They knew Michelet was giving Cly [*short for Clytemnestra!—BK*] a tour of the greenhouse.) The minute he said, "Show me," the girl's neck blotched and her chest began to heave. He watched a vein pound the way fishermen read the swells of a coming storm. He squatted down as she held herself open. It was musty and he leaned in to take a draught as mother and son bantered—good as having her. The cunt looked like a chrysanthemum. He knew from folklore that the flower's boiled roots could be used as a headache remedy, its violet petals brewed as potion. He would make it his official crest and seal. Michelet knew the mum needed darkness as well as light and that Tad did not have a taste for its cultivation, nor for autumnal colors, unaware even that such a thing blooms in the fall, as the days grow shorter. No, his son would never tap the balmy unskirted elixir for the migraines that had always plagued him, nor have the patience to read up on basics, chapter-and-verse: "As with all gardening efforts, it is not luck or the so-called green thumb that achieves results, but rather hard work and dirty fingernails." It was then that Michelet resolved to make the thing his corsage, and a cortege for her husband-to-be—and her mother-in-law too—but for now this floral, florid arrangement would be their secretum. Mum was the word, indeed. He stared at the petals with great keenness while kitchen voices grew mock-contentious and Cly's carotid beat furiously until without being touched, she came.

GITA ASKED ME TO DINNER at the Benedict Canyon pied-à-terre—as she wryly referred to all 17,000 square feet of it—on the night "Prodigal Son" was televised. She had taped it off an East Coast feed so we could fast-forward through commercials. Because of the deaths, the network had publicly brooded over whether to postpone, but in this, the time of love and media, a decision was made that to air was humane. Besides, the morbid hoopla had already been diluted by endless radio and TV talk-show dissections, now harmlessly joining the piss-stream of global atrocities and local horrors-of-the-week.

As I watched, I resolved to contractually extricate myself from the *Demeter* and its far-flung frontiers—I didn't think heart or ego could survive another tour. It was easier to watch Clea than I thought it'd be, her features subsumed in the latex cubism that was the Vorbalidian hallmark. The comically ghoulish effect took the edge off my sorrow. Watching with Mom was a comfort too (Perry was in New York). She was spare and solicitous, speaking only when spoken to. Not once did she acknowledge the silly sacrilege of this showcase for the dead. We'd grown closer through the ordeal, and that was the greatest comfort of all.

Ensign Rattweil dutifully defeated his twin. (At the moment it happened, I suppressed an unexpectedly gruesome image born of my recent trip to the Playa.) At hour's end, his crew safely aboard the starship, Captain Laughton plotted a course for Darius 9.

Dr. Chaldorer informed that if anyone needed him, he'd be in his quarters.

"A little primping and preening, X-Ray?" asked the captain.

"I'd be remiss," said the medic, "if I didn't look my best for those Darian showgirls."

"You might just find yourself a pair of platform shoes. Remember, they're seven feet tall. You wouldn't want to be stuck at . . . chest level."

"You know," he said lecherously. "I *did* order a pair. But they never came in!"

He *whooshed* out. Laughton asked Cabott what activities he planned to indulge in upon shore leave. The android said he was anxious to visit the famous Darian library of antiquities, rumored to contain a billion paperbound volumes. I innuendoed at what he'd be missing and was about to be admonished when Shazuki grew serious, asking the captain what it had been like to walk among Vorbalids.

He grew pensive, adopting that patented pose of brooding, poetic self-reflection honed over the seasons (just now as I write, the haunting *"e le morte stagioni"* comes back to me), usually reserved as a summing-up of lessons learned during whichever episode's excellent adventure.

"What was it like? A world of contrasts and extremes . . . of great savagery and unexpected kindness . . . of Machiavellian intrigue and humble, deeply *human* gestures. You ask me what it was like, Shazuki? Majestic and impoverished, ennobling and depressing—in short, a little bit of heaven and a little bit of hell. Under the Great Dome resides a place where man is forced to face himself, and learn unpleasant—*vital*—truths. A universal experience, so it seems."

"Thank you, Captain," she said, in simple gratitude.

Laughton began dictating his log.

"Star Date 41-17-7. We are now back on course, heading toward Darian 9 after an unprecedented diversion to the Vorbalidian System. Unwitting players in a political power struggle, myself and my crew were held prisoner, ultimately becoming spectators at a gladiatorial battle between Prince Morloch and his twin: our own Ensign Rattweil. The despotic pretender suffered death at his brother's hands—this, the happiest of outcomes. As we returned to the city, its streets lined with the joyous populace, it became clear that—"

"Receiving images, Captain!" interjected Shazuki.

X-Ray made a timely reappearance to the bridge as the crew gathered before the staticky starscreen. After a few moments, Thad appeared, flanked by Clea and the revivified Queen Mother. He wore a bejeweled crown, clutching a tall scepter. The three waved at their subjects. Thad turned to look directly at the *Demeter*, mouthing something which couldn't be understood.

"What's he saying?" said the frustrated captain.

The lieutenant commander furiously worked her controls. "I don't have audio . . ."

Laughton relaxed, drinking in the starscreen triumvirate.

"It isn't important," he said.

"The king isn't there . . ." noted X-Ray curiously.

"The king is dead," said the captain, with resolute benevolence. "Long live the king! Having defeated Morloch, our humble ensign has assumed the throne."

"Without a doubt," said the droid. "The emblem on his tunic denotes rulership of their world."

"Which emblem?" said the captain, straining to look.

"Above his heart, sir," I offered. "The 'chrysanthemum,' if you will."

Shazuki did her best to read the royal lips.

"He's *thanking* us, sir—both in English and his native tongue."

"Looks like Rattweil and the ambassador finally hooked up," I karped, back to horny, flyboy form. "Soon she'll be queen."

"Send a message," said the captain, all business. "From the crew of the USS *Starship Demeter*. Tell him that . . . as his shipmates, we were most honored to have served with him. That we shall always think of him, and forever hold him in our hearts. Wish the monarch and his people well. And tell him . . ."

He paused, searching for the proper words. His eyes grew moist.

"Tell him he is every inch a king."

Lights on the bridge lowered as camera dollied toward starscreen. The frame tightened until only an ebullient Thad and Clea could be seen, arm in arm, as at the moment rice is thrown at a wedding. I threw grains with all my might, across light-years of time and constellatory space.

AS I WAS SAYING AT the beginning of these pages: I was at the bakery awaiting a latte when a young father came in, holding a babe in arms. But let me paraphrase, and even add some detail, so the reader needn't thumb backward.

It was on a Thursday afternoon when I found myself at the Sugar Plum confectionary (now defunct), hand poised on legal pad, dog-eared copy of Jack Michelet's *Chrysanthemum* spread—forgive the word—before me. Something wasn't sitting well. I had consented to adapt the book for a welter of reasons which I hope I've made clear. But I didn't like the novel; in fact, I'd grown to hate it. Worse, I didn't feel wonderful for having taken the job in the first place.

I was on a third latte, this one by necessity decaffeinated. I'd mentioned earlier, one may recall, how experience had shown that I was somewhat of a "magnet for babies' eyes"—the bundle now before me proving no exception. He fussed and squirmed in Daddy's arms while fixing me with the expected stare, just long enough to get my attention.

His view then shifted somewhere beyond. I glanced, as did his father, to see where he was focusing, but the end point was amorphous.

That was when the infant, gaze unwavering, giggled with ineffable ecstasies—he was communing with the infinite, and like a bodhisattva, tried showing us the way.

"What do you see?" said his father. "What do you see?"

I looked and suddenly *did* see: the design of baby-faced Thad, and Clea too—and of the twins the coroner said were in her belly waiting to be born—saw Castor and Pollux, Leif Farragon and little boy Me. I looked and looked until the gooey sumptuous Badwater stillness lifted up behind them, behind *all* machinations, no matter how luxurious, threadbare, desperate, or giving, saw the selfless scrim that rose and ceaselessly fell upon this earthly stage of triumph and trespass, saw it *there*, in the eyes of this melodious sweetshop angel, cooing and gurgling like a desert fount, the fancifully ridiculous, idiotic heartbreak of the whole damn thing—and knew I could never face myself without at least trying to set it down as best I could.

So that's what I've done.

And I couldn't be more grateful you've stayed to the end. Maybe—*maybe*—I should have followed the advice of Jack Michelet when he said in that vile interview how certain pages should be burned. But I'm throwing *my* pages, and caution, to the wind.

Because as Mother loves to say, life's too short.

Don't you think?

About the Author

BRUCE WAGNER is the author of *Force Majeure, I'm Losing You, I'll Let You Go*, which was nominated for a PEN USA fiction award, and *Still Holding*. Two movies (*I'm Losing You* and *Women in Film*) adapted from his books have been shown at the Telluride, Toronto, Venice, and Sundance film festivals.

The Chrysanthemum Palace

1. Describe Bertie's character. How has his past as the child of a renowned television show creator and producer affected him? What do you think of the relationship he has with his parents, in particular his father? How has this essential relationship shaped his relationships throughout the book? What is your overall opinion of Bertie?

2. "It's funny what draws us to people; funny we don't often see the design of it." What draws Bertie to Thad? What about Thad intrigues and confounds Bertie? Do the two men share anything in common? Do you think Bertie comes to understand Thad throughout the story and does he ultimately forgive Thad for his final offense against Clea? What was your initial reaction to Thad and did it change by the end of the novel?

3. Discuss Thad's story about the time machine model. What does this story in particular reveal about Thad? Aside from the memory of playing time machine with his deceased brother, what do the time machine and Thad's subsequent belief that he imagined the whole story symbolize?

4. Bertie says of his relationship with Clea:

"We were like bystanders you see on television after a suicide bomb attacks, numbly clutching each other in front of splintered buses and orphaned cell phones. I get it. This is how it's always been and always would be between us."

Discuss how this notion is illustrated throughout the book. Why do you think the bond between them was as strong as it was for as long as it was, despite the years of estrangement?

5. Throughout the novel, we are given glimpses into the story line of Thad and Clea's episode of "Starwatch: The Navigators." What are the parallels between what is happening on the show and what is actually happening in real life? What effect do you think these similarities ultimately have on Thad?

6. Why do you think Morgana and Jack Michelet emotionally and mentally abuse Thad? How much of their inappropriate behavior do you attribute to the loss of their young son? Bertie says of Morgana: "Sudden death expunged her rancor; at last, Thad was brought into protective arms." Do you think Morgana achieves any kind of salvation after Thad's death?

7. Discuss the relationship between Miriam and Bertie. What initially brings them together? Do you think his feelings for her are genuine and vice versa?

8. The final time Bertie sees Thad he says: "I watched Thad crane his neck to look at the stars, feeling a rush of sympathy and affection for the man. I was suddenly certain of his innocence." What does he mean by this? Do you agree with this perception? How does this last melancholy interaction between Bertie and Thad contradict what Bertie discovers about Thad's death?

9. The word "denouement" is mentioned twice in the story. What was your reaction to the denouement of Bertie, Thad, and Clea's story?

10. What do chrysanthemums symbolize in the novel? What does the title mean?